Behind The Walls

ELAINE ORR

Copyright ©2023 Elaine L. Orr

All rights reserved.

No part of this publication may be reproduced, distributed, or transmitted in any form or by any means, including photocopying, recording, or other electronic or mechanical methods except as permitted by U.S. copyright law.

ISBN-13: 978-1-948070-94-2
Library of Congress Control Number: 2018913595

Behind The Walls is a work of fiction.

Behind The Walls
ELAINE ORR

Behind The Walls is licensed for your
personal enjoyment and may not be duplicated in any form.

Discover all books in the Jolie Gentil Series

Appraisal for Murder
Rekindling Motives
When the Carny Comes to Town
Any Port in a Storm
Trouble on the Doorstep
Behind the Walls
Vague Images
Ground to a Halt
Holidays in Ocean Alley
The Unexpected Resolution
Underground in Ocean Alley
Sticky Fingered Books
New Lease on Death
The Twain Does Meet (novella)
Jolie and Scoobie High School Misadventures (prequel)

Look for the **Family History Mystery Series**,
set in the Maryland mountains.

elaineorr.com

elaineorr.blogspot.com

Dedication

To my sister Diane, who keeps more balls in the air than the Harlem Globetrotters.

Acknowledgements

Thanks to the Decatur critique group for asking good questions and pointing out some of the things that looked obvious to me, but might not to a reader. Lorena Shute again came through as a good cold reader and copy editor. As always, thanks to my husband, Jim, for putting up with the crazy schedule I keep when I write.

୧ᘏ৶

Chapter One

"AND WHAT DO I HEAR for this antique brass bed with its pink ruffled bedspread?"

"How about ten dollars to burn it?" Scoobie asked, quietly.

"You secretly want those ruffles," I said, eyes on the elderly auctioneer.

Scoobie snorted. "Not on a cold day in Hades." He winked at me and turned to walk toward an elaborate train set that had been set up on a piece of plywood.

The beautiful spring Sunday buoyed my mood. Nothing keeps a Jersey girl down long, not even Hurricane Sandy.

My eyes swept the crowd as well as the assorted furniture and remnants of lives. I wanted furniture for my bargain-priced bungalow a few blocks from the center of Ocean Alley, five blocks back from the ocean.

My house would have been a lot more expensive if all of the plumbing worked. Considering that not long ago my future seemed destined to be a room at Aunt Madge's Cozy Corner B&B, I relished having a house, no matter how small. Except for the rotten wood on part of the back porch and the bit of mold in the living room. Okay, there's no such thing as "a bit" of mold, but after a week of bleach and sponges, I think I got it all.

I put a lot of things in storage when I left my gambling husband eighteen months ago, but I hadn't kept much furniture other than what I took with me to Aunt Madge's. Robby and I had bought every piece together. I didn't need to look at it.

So here I was at the Sunday auction of Moira Peebles' possessions. I had already bought her home, but its contents had been in a storage locker a few miles inland since late last fall. According to the *Ocean Alley Press*, she had passed peacefully, so I didn't feel bad, the way I would if it was an auction because people got booted out of their home.

This auction had things from many people who had contracted with the auction company but didn't have enough to warrant a sale of their own. Like most local auctions, furniture covered a yard and tables held smaller items.

I looked again at the rows of tables with odds and ends that would be sold in a couple of minutes. Aunt Madge had warned me that auctioneers knew people want the furniture but not a lot of the miscellany, so they made buyers wait while the junk sold.

The elderly auctioneer's voice cut into my thoughts. "And look at this…thing. I'm not sure what the holes in this metal box are for. Humph. And there's this sliding mechanism." He leaned over to talk to a younger colleague, and then his face turned a deep shade of red. "You just don't see a genuine suppository mold anymore."

Laughter swept the crowd and I deliberately did not look at Scoobie.

The auctioneer went into his rapid-speak patter, which meant I didn't understand what he said except, occasionally, the amount of a bid. I planned to bid on a small sectional sofa and maybe a dinette set.

Auctioneer Norman Fitzgerald turned his attention to the tables of household goods, small tools, art supplies, and costume jewelry. *Really? Who would buy used crayons and paint brushes?*

"Jolie!" I followed my friend Ramona's voice and saw that she was looking at the art supplies. She does pen or charcoal drawings on the boardwalk all summer. *Maybe I do know someone who would buy used art supplies.*

"Hey, Ramona." I walked toward her.

She studied a large box of colored chalk. "I've never done anything with chalk because…"

"Too many colors for you?" Scoobie asked. He grinned and moved aside a few inches as she tugged on his dark blonde hair, which today hung over his shirt's collar. His sometimes cocky demeanor belies his struggle with depression, which he works hard to manage.

"You're as funny as sea nettles," she said. "I've been thinking of doing some chalk drawings on the part of the boardwalk that's concrete, you know, near the bandstand. It would be like free advertising for my caricatures. But I'm not sure I want to put in all that work and then have the rain wash it away."

"Maybe you could draw stuff on the sidewalk outside the Purple Cow. Roland would love that." I tried to hide a smirk. The owner of the office supply store where Ramona works is a nice guy, but he's a serious businessman, despite what he named his store.

"That'll be the day." She shifted through more of the art materials. "I'm going to bid on the easel over there."

I followed her gaze. I hadn't noticed some of the furniture and such that was on the other side of a large tree, so I walked over to look at it.

There were two recliners, one of them quite new with a handle that raised the seat, and a large rocking chair that I thought was maple. I felt as if I was looking at Moira Peebles' progress through old age. First a standard rocker, then a recliner, then one that helped her get out of the chair when she couldn't do it herself.

As if to affirm her (or someone's) physical decline, there was a port-a-potty next to the newest recliner, and one of those bedside tables you roll up and down. I pushed this depressing mental picture aside and checked out several pieces of oak bedroom furniture. Aunt Madge's affinity for antique oak had become mine.

I really liked a large chest of drawers. It would fit perfectly along one wall in my small bedroom. I tried the drawers. All but one were a little sluggish, but I knew Aunt Madge could tell me how to fix that. I couldn't get the top right drawer opened, and gave up.

I fished my customer number out of the pocket of my navy blue slacks. I would need to hold it up to bid.

TWENTY MINUTES LATER I had not gotten the sofa or dinette set, and I was determined to win the chest of drawers.

"Ladies and gents, this is a beautiful oak bedroom set, probably from the early 1900s or so, but you'll have to be the judge of that. Let's open the bidding on all four pieces at four hundred dollars."

I didn't want a bed, chest of drawers, dresser and mirror. Especially the mirror. It was so old the glass was sort of wavy.

No one said anything, and Fitzgerald brought the opening bid down to three hundred dollars. Finally, he said that as much as it pained him, he would break up the set. Lively ensued for the dresser and mirror, which went for a price well more than I would have paid.

Two women who looked to be sisters conferred about their purchase as the bed went up for auction. There were fewer takers there, probably because the mattress and old-fashioned springs would have to be replaced.

Finally, the chest of drawers came to the so-called auction block, which was actually a sturdy picnic table. I'm short, so I moved a bit to the right so the auctioneer would be able to see my bidding number.

"We'll start this beautiful oak-crafted chest of drawers at one hundred dollars," Fitzgerald said.

No takers. When he was down to fifty dollars for a starting bid I held up my number, which was fifty five.

"Who wants to go to sixty dollars for this handsome…?" One of the two women who had bought the dresser held up her number and he nodded at her. "Okay then, how about seventy?"

I held up my number and he nodded at me. I was not going to go more than one hundred dollars, and had about resigned myself that I would not get the chest when I saw the two auburn-haired women, who were not a lot older than my twenty-nine years, exchange a look. *Aha. They're running out of money.*

I bid one hundred dollars and was disappointed that they bid one hundred five, but I took a chance and raised my number when the auctioneer asked for a bid of one hundred ten dollars.

"Do I hear one-fifteen?" he called out.

I held my breath. When several seconds passed, he pointed a long finger at me and said, "Sold to number fifty-five for one hundred ten dollars."

I felt very pleased with myself. When I finally got all my stuff moved into the bungalow I'd have a place to put clothes. I walked toward the chest and met the eyes of the taller of the two women. "All's fair in love and war, I guess."

She smiled, but seemed to be covering irritation. "Yes. I should have taken a bit more out of the bank this morning," she said. "Fiona Henderson."

"And I'm Patricia Franklin," the other woman said.

"Jolie Gentil." I pronounced the J and G softly and letting both names end in the sound of a long e. It's French, and means *pretty nice*. I periodically grouse at my French-Canadian father for his choice, and am constantly telling people it's pronounced Zho-lee Zhan-tee.

"I think I know your aunt," Patricia said. The dark-haired man holding her hand retained his somber expression and said nothing.

I smiled. "Who doesn't?"

Behind Fiona, a man said, "The drawers are awfully shallow. You would have hated it."

He appeared to be about forty, with the sort of rugged good looks that I associate with a tennis coach at a private club.

"Men. What do they know?" Fiona asked.

We all laughed politely, and they moved away. The man continued to gently tease Fiona, and she swatted him on the fanny.

I tried to tackle the recalcitrant drawer again.

"Want some help?" Scoobie asked.

"Let me give it one," I tugged, "more" a bigger tug, "try." The drawer slid open abruptly and it forced me to step backward three paces.

"Stuff in it," Scoobie said as he peered in the drawer. "Oops, ladies' stuff."

I pulled out something that was a kind of filmy pink and quite large. I held it up and started to laugh. "I'm not sure I've ever seen underwear this…"

At the sound of clicking, I looked up to see the junior reporter from the *Ocean Alley Press*. "You print that and you're going to have to park your car indoors!" I yelled.

Several people turned to look at us.

"Oh, I won't!" She backed away, stumbling slightly over the bottom of her jeans, which were overly long with holes along the sides at artful intervals.

"Now, now," Scoobie said. "You know who gives Tiffany her assignments."

"Yeah, yeah, and I heard her emphasis on the word I." A picture of George Winters floated to the front of my brain. I had an achy feeling in my stomach and turned back to Scoobie. "Who do we know who has a pickup truck?"

"You came to an auction to buy furniture and didn't think about how to get it back to your place?"

"There're guys who hang out at these auctions with their pickups. I'm going over there to talk to a couple of them. It'll be cheap."

Half an hour passed quickly as the auction wound down. Eight or ten people either called over to me or stopped to talk for a couple of minutes.

Ocean Alley is only twelve blocks back from the ocean and about two miles long. I went to eleventh grade here. When I first moved back from Lakewood, I resented that the town was so small. It didn't take much time for half of the year-round residents to know I was the soon-to-be ex-wife of a man who had gambled away all of our money. And started on his bank's before they wised up to him.

Now that I've been here a while, I like the cozy atmosphere in the off-season. People always nod if they meet your eyes in a store, and I've rekindled friendships with people like Scoobie and Ramona. Well, Scoobie. Ramona is pretty much a new friend. The only thing I really remembered about Ramona was that I tripped over her art portfolio in geometry class.

I meandered back to the chest of drawers and stopped about five feet from it. The drawer I'd had so much trouble with was gone.

"YO, JOLIE." Scoobie gave his traditional greeting as he walked onto my front porch. Then I heard him swear, rare for him.

"What?" I called.

He poked his head around the door jamb. "There's so much old junk on your porch you're going to get somebody killed. Is it safe to come in?"

As I continued to scrape mottled wallpaper off the plaster wall in the living room I glanced toward him. I still seethed about buying a chest of drawers that was now minus the top right drawer. "I'm going to put the gardening stuff in that tiny shed out back. And it's as safe as it was yesterday."

"See you later, then." When I threw a small gob of soggy wallpaper and glue at him, he added, "Now you know why I asked. Want some help for a few minutes?"

Scoobie's getting a two-year degree to become a radiology technologist. This particular Monday he had just finished a test on radiation protection that he'd spent half the night studying for, so I shook my head. "Nope, it's almost four o'clock, I'm getting ready to quit for the day." I pulled off a rubber glove and lobbed it at him.

"A little hostility on the horizon?" He easily avoided the limp glove and stuck his head in the small refrigerator that sat on a card table and pulled out a bottle of water.

Scoobie and I didn't really see each other after eleventh grade until just before our tenth high school reunion, which was eighteen months ago. But if we hadn't been good buds before last October, protecting the Cozy Corner B&B the night Hurricane Sandy landed in New Jersey would have bonded us for life.

He sat in one of the two canvas chairs, the only furniture in the small living room beside the rickety card table, and looked down to where I was sitting cross legged on the floor. "How come I never knew you could do practical work like this?"

I tucked my shoulder-length hair behind one ear, and then studied the goop on my fingers. No doubt some was now in my hair. *Oh well. Maybe my brown hair will have some highlights.* "You know I didn't know. Aunt Madge and Harry have been teaching me the easy stuff."

Aunt Madge has always done her own maintenance at the Cozy Corner. Her new husband, and my boss in his appraisal business, Harry Steele, has spent almost two years refurbishing a Victorian style house that used to belong to his grandparents. They are patient teachers. That's good, because my living room reflected a hodgepodge of remodeling efforts, with the only original wall being the one with the cursed wallpaper. That wall was as solid as the concrete used for the post-hurricane boardwalk pilings in Ocean Alley.

"Hey, can you help me with one thing? There's some wallboard that's still attached, and I want to check behind it to make sure there's no more mold. I couldn't pull hard enough to get it off." The bare studs in other places along the wall were testament to at least some arm strength, despite my having had a broken wrist a few months ago.

"As long as I don't get too dirty. It's my night to work in the college library."

This is a perfect job for him, since he doesn't always like to have a lot to do with people.

I stood up and brushed off my tattered jeans. "You won't."

Scoobie followed my gaze to the other side of the room, picked up my heavy-duty work gloves from a window sill, and put them on. "This is worth two cups of coffee at Java Jolt."

"Three if we don't find any mold." The house had been thoroughly cleaned after its bout with the storm last October, but the heat had been off all winter and the humid beach air was perfect for mold growth.

The hole I'd made in the board was at the height of Scoobie's head, which was about eight inches higher than my five feet two. Scoobie got a grip and pulled hard. The wallboard made a sound like ripping heavy-duty cardboard, and generated big puffs of dust. We stood back to avoid it. "One more tug ought to finish it."

I nodded and sneezed.

Scoobie pulled hard and the wallboard split and broke. When we had brushed dust off our clothes I peered at the studs. "I don't see mold, do you?"

"Nope." He picked up a small draw-string canvas sack. "What's this?"

We looked at the contents as he spilled them into his hand. Scoobie held a bunch of shiny stones that looked like diamonds, three bracelets that appeared to be gold, and two that looked like heavy-duty, rust-colored plastic.

Our eyes met. "This is worth at least ten cups," he said.

Chapter Two

"WOW." I BENT TO retrieve a bracelet that had dropped on the floor.

Scoobie dumped the rest of the bounty on the card table. "Wonder how long it's been there?"

I glanced at the wall. "It's newer wall board than the rest of the house. That's why I had trouble pulling it down all the way. Still, it's probably been there two or three decades, at least."

He stared at the jewelry. "Who owned this place?"

"Same woman who had stuff in the auction, Moira Peebles. She hadn't paid taxes for the eighteen months before the hurricane. That's why the house was in the tax sale so soon after Sandy."

Aunt Madge told me that Mrs. Peebles had deemed herself fed up with tourists tromping through her yard and had moved in with her daughter in Newark. I also knew that the house's value would have declined when the real estate bubble burst, so the storm could have been simply one more reason to let go of the house.

"Yeah, I remember now," Scoobie said.

"I looked at the first few pages of the title search. She owned it for less than twenty years. Before that, the woman who owned it had it for maybe thirty-five years." As an appraiser, I'm used to looking at all kinds of documents related to real estate. But while I'd glanced through the paperwork at settlement a couple of weeks ago, my focus had been more on all the work to do before I could move in than on a pile of papers.

Scoobie's eyes went to the shell-shaped, battery-operated clock that hung crookedly on the wall that separated the living room from the kitchen. "I'd like to stay and play bob for baubles or something, but I have a couple of things to do before I go back to campus."

"You want a ride?"

"Nope. Bus as usual. You okay with having this stuff here?"

"Probably better if I take it to Aunt Madge's." I grinned at Scoobie before my eyes went back to the jewelry. "She'll probably know about somebody who had stuff like this stolen thirty years ago, and maybe she even knows the person who owned this house back then."

Aunt Madge is a walking local historian. On the other hand, she prides herself on not being a busy body, so she might not know any really good gossip about possibly stolen jewelry.

"It might not be something sinister." He smiled. "Could be an eccentric homeowner hid it and her descendants have been looking for it for decades. They'll be happy it never made it to the landfill. If you get another reward you can actually furnish this place."

As I waved goodbye to him from my front porch—my porch! —I reflected on the last few months. It wasn't just the hurricane and Aunt Madge and Harry's wedding that cluttered my thoughts.

My boyfriend George Winters, local reporter and a good friend to Scoobie, broke up with me, and it was pretty much my fault. Not that I'd tell him that. I'd also helped solve a murder that happened not long after Sandy, and the victim's parents had insisted I take the reward they had offered. That's why I had money for the down payment.

I could hardly wait to move in. Only the volume of dust and general look of a construction site were keeping me, and my cat Jazz, at the Cozy Corner a little longer.

I thought for a moment about the luxury condo Robby and I had owned in Lakewood. He hadn't been able to do a large refinance on it, but he'd gotten a small home equity loan with my forged signature. That money had made its way to casinos along with any other cash he could lay his hands on. *And some people wonder why I don't trust easily.*

I walked back into the living room and looked at the pile of jewelry. I appraise houses, not jewelry, but even with my limited knowledge I knew this could be some serious booty. I had no thought of keeping it. Even though I had bought the small bungalow at a tax sale, I did not think something seemingly this valuable should fall under the finders-keepers-losers-weepers code of conduct.

Any appraiser worthy of the job keeps a digital camera close at hand, so I dug mine out of my purse and separated the individual pieces to get better photos. When held as a group, the three gold bracelets were heavy. One was just a quarter of an inch wide and limp. Another was very wide and stiff. It reminded me of something Roman soldiers wore, except it had a kind of feathered pattern. The third looked like a bunch of tiny squares strung together and was not as shiny as the other two.

The two that weren't gold were a color between cinnamon and rust, and at first I thought they were hard plastic. The more I looked at them the less I thought they were typical plastic. I shrugged and photographed them separately.

After I photographed the bracelets I lined up the nine diamonds by size, smallest on the left. The one my ex-husband gave me for our engagement was half a carat. Robby later hocked it and convinced me I must have lost it, which had me apologizing and crying for weeks.

I judged two or three of these to be roughly the same size and a couple smaller. The others were larger, perhaps as much as a carat. I took several pictures of them, each one with a glare on some of the diamonds. I gave up trying to snap one without any glare.

The more I thought about it the odder it seemed that there were so many loose diamonds. They could have been removed from older pieces of family jewelry, but it seemed unlikely. The words *jewelry heist* came to mind and I almost giggled.

I took a closer look at the canvas bag. It was similar in size to a cosmetics pouch or the plastic case of drill bits that Aunt Madge has in her tool box. The bag wasn't ancient, but it wasn't new, either. I turned it over, wishing it would have the name of a jeweler on the other side, so I would know how to start looking for the former owner. Nada.

I was about to take a picture of the bag when my cell phone chirped.

"May I speak with Joe-Lee Gentle?" the man's voice asked.

When people mangle the pronunciation of my name it's a clue we don't know each other. "This is Jolie Gentil," I said, pronouncing it correctly.

"Gosh, I guess I said that wrong." He laughed.

No kidding.

When I didn't respond, he continued. "I'm thinking of buying some property in Ocean Alley, kind of a hurricane bargain thing."

I fumed inwardly. The vultures swarming the shore to take advantage of the despair some people feel are no different than carpet baggers after the Civil War. I still didn't say anything.

In my mind I saw a cigar-smoking, middle-aged guy with a ten-gallon hat, feet propped on a huge wooden desk.

He seemed to sense I did not like what he said, because his voice became less certain. "So, uh, I wondered if you could show me around town?"

I let his words hang there for about three seconds. "I think you may have me confused with a real estate agent. I'm an appraiser. After you sign a sales contract, the prospective mortgage company hires me to establish what the property is worth."

His tone became impatient. "I know the difference. I was told that you were a go-to person, someone who could help me know if a property's a steal, or if it's priced too high. Real estate agents collude on prices, you know."

"Somehow I missed that. Let me give you the name of someone who knows this market like barnacles know boat bottoms." The man sputtered a little while I recited Lester Argrow's name and number, but then I could hear the scratching of a pen and he was silent for a few seconds.

Lester Argrow is Ramona's uncle. He is the biggest pain in the backside in the Ocean Alley real estate cadre. Maybe in all of the Jersey shore. But he knows how to sniff out good deals and he sends a lot of appraisal work to Harry and me.

The man regained his bluster. "How about just a ride around town? I'll buy you a cuppa joe."

"Thanks, Mr…" He had not given me his name, so I let the words hang between us as I buried the canvas bag, with the jewelry in it again, in the bottom of my purse.

"Dorner. Clive Dorner. I'm not talking about formal showing, you see…"

"Mr. Dorner, I'm in the middle of tearing down walls at the house I just bought, and I'm late for an appointment. Lester knows me well. If you two find a property that suits you, he'll very likely come to Harry Steele and me for the appraisal."

"Who's…?"

"Thanks for calling." I hung up, shaking my head at the man's arrogance.

THE JEWELRY INTRIGUED AUNT MADGE, but she had no thoughts about anyone who had had it, or pieces like these, stolen.

Harry nudged her elbow with his. "Sounds as if they placed them there deliberately."

Puh-leeze. They're pretty good about not doing constant mushy stuff, but it still seems weird to see them practically sitting in each other's laps. They have only been married about six months, but other than the cooing they act like a couple who have been together for decades.

Aunt Madge is only a few inches shorter than Harry's five-ten, and she looks his age of almost seventy rather than her own of early eighties. They are both very fit, Aunt Madge from climbing stairs many times a day and Harry from almost two years of hammering, sawing, and painting at his house. It used to belong to his grandparents and is his retirement hobby.

Aunt Madge and Harry were next to each other on the loveseat in her great room, or sitting room, as she calls the L-shaped area that has her living room at one end and kitchen/dining room at the other. I sat in a high-backed chair across from them, the jewelry on the coffee table between us.

"I want to tell the police about this, but I don't want it in my house overnight. You don't care if we put it in your fire safe, do you?" Aunt Madge has one of those small metal boxes that's not much bigger than a shoe box. It wouldn't keep much protected in a fire, but she reasons that it's better than putting B&B guests' checks under the mattress before she gets to the bank.

"Of course not." Aunt Madge began to pick up the diamonds to put them into the bag.

I begged off having dinner with her and Harry by saying I was going to meet Ramona, and then high-tailed it to the office supply store where she works. The Purple Cow is open until six, and I knew she worked until then today.

I like spending time with Aunt Madge and Harry, but a threesome dinner requires a lot of conversation. I was tired and achy after a day of scrubbing and sanding.

As I drew close to the store, I saw the white board on its easel on the sidewalk just outside. Ramona writes sayings on the board every day that she's working, and she has begun to suspect that Scoobie is the one who rewrites them now and then. She isn't sure, though, and I'm not about to play tattle tale.

Today the sign said, "Learn to be patient in the presence of your own thoughts," and was attributed to Verlyn Klinkenborg. Under the name someone had written, "Klingons live!" That was x'd out and under it was, "Resistance is futile."

I chuckled as I walked in, and tried to hide it when I saw Ramona.

Her usual dreamy voice came across the store. "Don't bother, Jolie."

"Don't bother?"

"I have a new policy. I'm going to leave up whatever they write." She placed a couple of boxes of pens on a shelf, rather harder than necessary.

"Not going to let it bother you?"

"Not going to let anyone know it bothers me. I still think it's Scoobie, but he's usually working now."

I wouldn't touch that if someone offered me two bushels of crabs. "You haven't talked to him, have you?"

"He called a few minutes ago and said you had big news. He wouldn't tell me what it was, of course."

Ramona looked at me. Her large eyes behind over-large glasses complement the hippie look she cultivates. She makes her own clothes, beautiful clothes, because she likes the kind of gauzy fabric and tie-dye look of the 1970s. She blends with the small store's vintage look of hardwood floors and wood bookshelves. Some have older, leather-bound books on them.

We stood next to the cash register and I lowered my voice to tell her about the jewelry. Though Ramona continued scanning the store for customers who might need help, I knew I had her full attention.

"How old are the bracelets?"

I shrugged. "How would I tell?"

"The diamonds would be really hard to date, but if you bring the bracelets in I could probably tell you when the style was popular."

I started to tell her I'd do that tomorrow when the bell above the door tinkled and we turned to look at the customer. Except it wasn't a customer, it was George. My stomach muscles tightened and I consciously relaxed them.

"Hey, you two." He used the casual tone he employs to greet me these days. George wore his typical khaki shorts and collared Hawaiian-style shirt, his uniform except in deep winter, when he wears long khaki pants.

We said hello and then stared at him. George doesn't need anything in the Purple Cow. The *Ocean Alley Press* has any supplies he could want.

"Scoobie called from the bus stop to say that Jolie had some big news, and he laid odds that you'd be in here." He nodded at me but mostly looked at Ramona.

"I hate it when he does that," I fumed.

"Knows how you'll act?" George smiled. "So, what's the big news?"

I was annoyed at Scoobie for telling George I had any kind of news. There would be no keeping George at bay until I told him. "Scoobie has a big mouth."

His smile broadened. "Come on, Jolie. It'll be like confession."

"You're the Catholic," I grumbled.

George kept staring at me.

"I found something in the house. Well, Scoobie and I found it."

George's tone turned bemused. "Damn. I thought he was just trying to make us talk to each other."

"Oh!" Ramona looked from George to me and flushed.

George and I had agreed we would not behave childishly about our break-up. We know all the same people, and it would be ridiculous if we had to see Ramona and Scoobie or our friend Bill separately. I just have to keep the butterflies in my stomach at bay, and George has to act as if he doesn't miss me. Which he maybe doesn't.

"Sooo," George said.

I shrugged. "It was just a few pieces of old jewelry. We found it behind the living room wallboard in my house. Probably not worth much."

Ramona looked away, seemingly not wanting George to figure I had told her I thought otherwise.

George looked disappointed. "Still, it's odd that someone would put a wall over some gold necklaces, right?"

"Ha! He didn't tell you it's necklaces," I said.

George grinned. "But you just told me it isn't."

"Don't you have more interesting stories?" I asked.

"Ooh, you'll like this," Ramona said. "George is looking backwards."

I feigned innocence. "What else is new?"

He apparently decided not to respond to that point. "You know how all the news was about Sandy in late October, early November?"

I looked at him with raised eyebrows.

"Yeah, yeah, rhetorical question. Anyway, I had a great idea. Somebody needs to look at what didn't make it into the paper then, or maybe just had a couple lines instead of a story."

"Isn't it kind of late to follow up?" I asked.

"Won't know until I do more leg work." Then he looked at me directly, something he does not often do these days. "You have any ideas?"

Between getting windows boarded up at the Cozy Corner and trying to find extra stock for the food pantry, I hadn't thought of much else at that time. "Hmm. Anything Halloween-related? Maybe tricks because there weren't too many treats?" Since Sandy had come ashore October 29th, many towns had canceled trick-or-treating, including Ocean Alley.

"Maybe you should check at the firehouse," Ramona suggested.

"Huh." He seemed to consider this. "I'm going to talk to our favorite sergeant at the police station this afternoon. I should go by the fire station after that."

"Didn't some mayor say there was so little crime for a couple of days after Sandy that it was almost like when there's a blizzard?" I asked.

"Atlantic City, I think." He looked at the clock on the wall above Ramona's head. "Gotta run." George left.

After a couple of seconds, Ramona said, "That was…"

"Awkward," I sighed.

"I figured you guys would have made up by now. It's been what, three months?"

"Closer to four, but it's no big deal." *As if.* I ticked George off well into December, and crocuses were already popping up around town. "You know, it is an interesting idea. Remember the day before Sandy? The mayor said they were going to introduce some new way to track crime?"

Ramona shrugged. "Kind of. Roland was talking about how dumb it was, because there's hardly any crime here."

I grinned and Ramona rolled her eyes.

"You know what I mean. Compared to Camden or something."

"It was an election year so the mayor had to say something. The only thing I know that's not solved is that stupid Peeping Tom." The guy had been peeking in windows for months, and he's always gone by the time police arrive.

Ramona sighed. "I'm glad I live in a second floor apartment."

We talked for a couple more minutes and I asked her if she wanted to go to dinner with me, but it was her yoga night. I figured that asking her was enough to mean I hadn't lied to Aunt Madge about dinner plans.

My car was in the lot on the side of the Purple Cow. Usually, one of the two parking spots in front of the store is open, but today they had been taken. The lot only has five parking spaces, since it's the size of a small store that used to be in the spot. It's also surrounded by buildings on three sides, so sunlight is sparse except at noon.

As I pulled my keys out of my pocket I felt someone touch my elbow. Before I could fully turn to face the person he (or she?) had tugged hard on the shoulder strap of my purse. I careened to my left and would have fallen over if my car had not been there to stop me.

Before I could regain my balance the person slid my shoulder bag down my arm and ran up the street.

I yelled, "Hey, hey!" and took off after him. I focused on his backwards-facing baseball cap. I knew there was a reason I didn't like the Mets. Under the hat was a ski mask. It only took me about twenty paces before I realized I'd never catch the guy. And it was stupid to chase him. *Who knew who had a gun?*

Chapter Three

I SLOWED AND LOOKED around. If it had been summer the streets would have been crowded, but on a chilly day in April, the wind from the ocean held a promise of rain. No one was on the street, and none of the two and three-story businesses that lined the street were visibly busy.

I glanced at my hand, which still grasped the car keys. "Crud! Crud! Crud!" I yelled this at the top of my voice. I had my keys, but lots of important stuff was in my purse. All my ID, a great picture of George and me, which I probably didn't need anymore anyway, and my calendar. I wished I had a bunch of rusty nails or something in the bottom of the bag. That would teach a thief.

No one had heard me yell at the thief when I was in the small parking lot, but now that I was on the sidewalk my bellowing had attracted several people. Roland hurried out of the Purple Cow toward me, and a woman from the beauty salon across the street gestured to me. I waved to her and pointed to Roland and walked toward him.

"What is it, Jolie? Are you all right?"

"I am. But my purse is about three blocks away by now."

He had reached me and had a sympathetic look on his face. Roland is in his forties. He has a full head of brown hair that is wavy when it gets longer, like now, so he looks closer to my age. Now he frowned. "Come back to the store. We'll call the police from there. I'm glad you weren't hurt."

I could feel tears of frustration welling, so I only nodded and fell into step beside him.

"It's ridiculous," Roland said. "I haven't heard of a purse snatching in the off-season in years. Maybe ever." We reached the store and he opened the door for me.

As I brushed my hand across my eyes I couldn't think of why anyone would target me. My Toyota was almost five years old and my hooded spring jacket and tan pants weren't ritzy. *What about the jewelry?* I pushed the thought aside. There was no way anyone knew about it.

THE JEWELRY WAS, OF COURSE, George's immediate opinion. Roland called the police but Ramona had called George. She would have called Scoobie, but knew he was at the college library.

"No one knew about it except the four of us and Aunt Madge and Harry. No purse snatcher would have known."

"I suppose," George said, but slowly. His gaze was unfocused, which I recognized as his look of concentration.

"Didn't you say that Scoobie called you from the bus stop?" Ramona asked.

I looked at Ramona with not exactly surprise, maybe more like appreciation. She's really smart, but her mind doesn't generally go to sleuth-type thinking. In fact, she abhors my occasional need to get to the bottom of something. "Good point. I'll have to ask…"

"You ask him who was around and he'll think it was his fault," George said.

"He's a big boy," I snapped. *I hate it when George gets something before I do.* I thought for a second. "I'll ask him if he has ideas about who might know about the jewelry."

George rolled his eyes. "Like that's…"

"Hi Dana," Ramona said. She had been scanning for customers, so she had seen Corporal Dana Johnson come into the store.

Dana is my favorite Ocean Alley police officer. It's not just that she's younger and a woman. She never treats me like an errant teenager.

"Jolie, we were just saying at the station that you hadn't been in for a while." Her eyes smiled.

I tried to paste a smile on my face. "Just can't stay out of your hair."

Dana was all business when she took down what little I had to say. "You've said guy a couple of times to describe the thief. If the person was wearing a ski mask, how do you know it was a guy?"

"I guess it was more of an impression, maybe the build."

"Okay, we're going outside. I want to see where you were standing so we can try to figure out where the person came from. You," Dana pointed her pen at George, "stay here."

"Free press," he said, fairly amiably.

"Yes, but not everything we do is freely available. I don't feel like making Jolie come down to the station so we can talk without you."

George raised his hands in mock surrender. I knew it was time for him to be writing his pieces for the next morning's *Ocean Alley Press*, so most of me hoped he would be gone when Dana and I were done.

Once we were in the parking lot, Dana told me to stand next to the car and she positioned herself in front of me. "So, if you were right there and I'm standing where the guy was, how do I compare in height?"

I turned and stared at her for a couple of seconds. "Hey, with you I can see all of the top of the handicapped parking sign on the wall. When the guy was there I think it was blocked."

We both stared at the wall, as if a measuring tape would appear and tell us how high the image was. Dana walked to it. "So, I can measure later, but I'd say that's almost six feet high. Maybe only five-ten."

I am five two, and I hadn't felt dwarfed by the guy. "You know, I think the height is right, but it reminds me he wasn't really a big guy, in fact maybe skinny. Hard to tell because he had on a windbreaker or some jacket like that. Oh, and a Mets hat."

Dana turned in a circle to take in all of the parking area. "There's only one way in and out of here. It's an odd place to plan a robbery."

"I almost never park back here. I didn't see where he came from. He must have hidden behind the car closest to the Purple Cow."

Dana was still making notes when her radio phone buzzed. "Johnson." She listened for a second, and then nodded at me. "Okay, we'll be down."

"We?" I asked, remembering that I was kind of hungry.

"Somebody turned in your purse. The handle was sticking out of a street trash can just beyond Java Jolt."

WE DROVE SEPARATELY AND I followed Dana into the secure area of the police station, which was behind the reception counter. Sergeant Morehouse stood in the hall near the small conference room. He did a little, I would say sarcastic, bow to indicate that I should go in before he did. Then he walked in behind me, letting Dana follow him.

Morehouse is only about ten years older than I am, but he dresses like a much older person. Always polyester pants, a plain shirt, and tie. And we aren't talking new ties. He keeps his brown hair, I think it's brown, so short he looks like an Army sergeant instead of a police sergeant.

My purse sat on the table, and I started to reach for it. "Just a second. Did the perp have on gloves?" he asked.

I thought for a couple of seconds and shook my head. "I don't think so, but it was so fast, I'm not sure."

He nodded and picked up two long pencils from a jar on the table and fished in my bag, pulling out the case that had my sunglasses, my wallet, whose change purse was not closed all the way so it spilled a couple of quarters, my pocket calendar, my small digital camera, tissues, and a ring that had the Cozy Corner front door and garage keys on it. I said a silent prayer of thanks that I hadn't had what commercials call feminine hygiene products in the purse.

"Oh, gosh. I forgot the B&B keys were in there."

Dana added the keys to her list of items I'd named.

"Anything obviously missing?" he asked.

"I don't think so. I had about thirty dollars in the wallet."

He inserted the two pencils in the part of the wallet that holds bills, separating the pocket.

I peered in. "It looks like the amount I had." I looked at him

Morehouse shook his head. "I'll have the guys look for prints before we take it out and count it. If it's all there, it raises the obvious question of what did a thief expect to find?" His look was accusatory.

Morehouse and I have, if not a love-hate relationship, a state of mutual tolerance that is sometimes more flexible than others. "I don't know. They wouldn't have had time to make a copy of the keys, would they?" Morehouse looked at Dana.

She shook her head. "Only if they ran right into the hardware store and got waited on immediately, but since the purse was a few blocks from there, no."

"Have a seat, Jolie." Morehouse turned to Dana. "I doubt it will do any good, but let some of the other guys know what the perp was wearing, and anything else you can think of."

She walked out.

I blew out a breath. "My guess is he's not walking around with the ski mask."

"Most crooks are kinda stupid, but that would be even dumber than usual." He sat across from me. "So, what were they looking for?"

I frowned. "No way anyone would know, but this afternoon Scoobie and I…" Morehouse gave me a look that said *you gotta be kiddin' me.* I ignored him. "Scoobie helped me pull down a piece of drywall that I couldn't pull myself. There was a small pouch of jewelry behind the wall."

"Jewelry?" He gave me a skeptical look. "Just sittin' there? Look valuable?"

"Not the crown jewels, but there were several loose diamonds and some kind of pricey looking bracelets." I kind of enjoyed his baffled expression. "I took them to Aunt Madge's."

"Smart. No security system at your new place."

And I hadn't planned on putting one in. "She has one of those fire safes. I thought I'd see who owned the house thirty or forty years ago, and then see if they maybe stored it there and forgot about it. Or maybe see if there were reports of stolen jewelry that looked like the bracelets."

This idea had just taken full form. For some reason I wanted him to know that I hadn't planned on keeping the jewelry if I could find out who owned it.

"And a course you woulda asked our help in trying to figure that out," he added.

"Um, yes." I had been thinking of the *Ocean Alley Press* microfiche that was in the library. In part because I was intrigued by the idea of looking, and in part I figured the paper's archives were a better source. Only police records from the last twenty years or so are digitized. And part of me was beginning to mull over asking George to help me.

"Humph. And you still think basically everything seems to be there?" He gestured to my purse and its now spilled contents.

"It looks it. If I think of something else I'll tell you. When can I have it back?"

"We have your prints from the various times we've used them for elimination."

I gave him what I hoped was a charming smile.

"I'll see if the guys can check your driver's license and credit card for prints this evening so you can have them back tomorrow. I doubt the guy looked at it, but you might wanna get a new credit card. Could take a couple more days for you to get all of it. Unless we find a suspect. Then maybe longer."

I did my best not to appear irritated. I knew in a larger town I might not have my stuff for weeks. "Okay. Bottom line, I can go?"

"As long as you aren't holding back from me."

This is more like the Sergeant Morehouse I usually deal with. "The guy found me, remember?"

"Yep. Tell Madge hello. And Harry." He looked at me intently for a couple of seconds, but didn't say anything else. However, as I got halfway down the hall he called out. "Can I see 'em?"

For a split second I didn't know what he was talking about, and then I realized he meant the jewelry. "Sure, I can bring them…"

"I'll come by in the morning." He said this as he answered his mobile phone, so I knew I was again dismissed.

RAMONA SAT IN THE SMALL waiting area, in one of those hard plastic chairs that are meant for people who weigh less than one hundred fifty pounds. Which she does.

She stood. "I know you weren't hurt or anything, but I thought you might want a hug." I'm not much of a hugger, but we did a brief one and walked out together.

"I'll give you a ride." Ramona doesn't own a car, and her regular walking keeps her very trim. I don't weigh too much more than I should, but my steady supply of Aunt Madge's muffins and Java Jolt pastries make me suck in my tummy more than I used to.

She glanced at her watch. "That would be good. I can catch the last half of my yoga class."

"Gosh, I'm really…"

"Don't be silly. You'd do the same for me."

I would, but she doesn't seem to get jammed up the way I do. "George go back to the paper?"

"Almost as soon as you and Dana went out to the parking lot." We had gotten to my car and I punched the key fob to unlock the doors.

We didn't talk as I drove. Ramona and I are very different, but we have a companionable friendship. It isn't like my friendship with Scoobie, who almost knows my moods before I do, but it's nice to have a girlfriend.

I had a lot of friends when I lived in Lakewood, which is thirty miles or so inland. They were couples friends, mostly. I exchange Christmas cards with a few people from that life and send gifts if someone sends a baby announcement. Mostly people aren't sure what to say. "Gee, Jolie, I see your divorce is final." Or maybe, "That was a good picture of you sitting behind Robby when they did his probable cause hearing."

"Jolie?"

"Yes?" I jolted back to the present.

"You just drove past the yoga studio," Ramona said, gently.

"Gosh, I'm sorry." I did a u-turn in the street.

"Is that legal?"

"Probably not." I pulled in front of the studio, which has dance classes and yoga for women only, and pushed the car button that unlocks all the doors.

Ramona got out of the car, but before she shut the door she looked back at me. "When you stop thinking about George you can move along." She smiled and shut the door.

Although I had not been thinking about George at that precise minute, I was still annoyed that Ramona was probably right.

I PULLED INTO THE parking lot at Burger King and sat in the car for a minute while I went over my day. It had to be a coincidence that we found the jewelry and then someone tried to snatch my purse.

I walked through the last couple of hours in my head. Scoobie left, the annoying bargain-hunter called, and I left for Aunt Madge's. Then I went to the Purple Cow.

Had someone been snooping in the yard and seen Scoobie and me find the jewelry? Did they know I was rehabbing the house and perhaps been looking for it themselves? Surely if a prior owner or an heir thought I might find hidden valuables in the house they would have had an attorney contact me.

Unless it was stolen jewelry. But that was ridiculous.

So, that put me back to being the target of a random robber. If that was the case, why didn't they steal at least the money in my wallet?

There was no obvious answer, so I walked into Burger King and stood studying the menu that was plastered on the wall behind the counter.

Lester Argrow's voice cut across the room. "Hey, Jolie! Got somebody who wants to meet you."

Nuts. I knew very well that Ramona's Uncle Lester met most of his customers in Burger King. He reasons that there is better parking than near his miniscule second story office in a nearby building. Probably it's also because his office is usually kind of messy. I should have realized he might be at a table here at dinner time.

The man with Lester was probably about forty and very good looking with wavy dark blonde hair and a square jaw. If you put a flannel shirt on him he could be a manly man advertising tools, but he had on a light brown shirt and a dark brown suede jacket over a pair of pressed blue jeans. *Why does anybody iron blue jeans?*

"How do you do?" I extended a hand. He took in my wind-tousled hair and yellow knit sweater under my hooded jacket. I felt like I was being x-rayed.

"Ms. Gentil, how are you?"

I figured Lester must have told him how to pronounce my name. The man didn't look like someone I knew, but his voice sounded familiar. "Fine, thanks."

He gestured that I should join them, and I slid into the booth next to Lester and he sat across from us. "I'm Clive Dorner. We spoke on the phone earlier today."

The guy who wanted hurricane bargains. "Right. Glad to see you found Lester." I tried to keep the disdain from my voice.

"Thanks for the referral, kid." Lester gave me an exaggerated wink. He's almost a caricature of a low level mob guy—short, pushy, and always with a wise crack. Most of them don't have a mole on the side of their face and, in all fairness, Lester does not seem to have an evil bone in his body. Lots of pushy ones, though.

"Have you found some property that suits your needs?" I asked this kind of coolly, since his *need* seemed to be to take advantage of homeowners who could not afford the repairs Sandy required them to make.

"Lester showed me several, most of them in…what did you call it, Lester, the popsicle district?"

The popsicle district is the informal name for a large neighborhood of smaller houses. A few years ago someone painted theirs chartreuse. Since then, almost every repainting has been in a vivid color. My new house is on the edge of the district, closer to the main part of town. It's light blue, so it wouldn't really fit in the popsicle district.

"Yeah," Lester said. "I pointed out your place. You got a helluva deal."

"Largely because of its condition," I said, dryly.

"Those are the best bargains," Clive laughed.

Oh, good, he laughs at his own jokes. I avoided looking at my watch. "It's taken work, but with any luck I can move in in a week or so."

"You were lucky," Lester said. "Some houses that lost a piece a roof took in a lot more water."

I nodded and directed my comment to Clive. "The biggest leak was above the kitchen sink, so a lot of the water went right down the drain."

"I bet a place that age has had a lot of remodeling," Clive said.

"It's had enough that I don't have to do anything major before moving in. I replaced some wallboard, but it was mostly to be sure there wasn't any mold lurking behind it."

"Ocean Alley was lucky to be eighty miles north of where Sandy came ashore," Clive said.

"Jolie's lucky she didn't have a lot of mouse poop," Lester said. "It bein' empty all winter."

"Are you saying you sold me a house with mouse poop?"

Lester was, for once, silent.

"I've rehabbed a bunch of places," Clive said. "You never know what you'll find behind old walls.

"I suppose that's true." *Was that comment a coincidence?*

"You free this evening?" Clive smiled broadly.

Lester choked on his coffee.

"Thanks, but I have a date."

Lester choked on the ice water he was using to wash down his coffee. I patted him on the back, and he squeezed out a few words. "Who ya datin' now?"

"Nosy, aren't we?" I stood. I had just remembered that I didn't have my purse, so I couldn't have ordered anything without borrowing money. "Gotta go get prettied up." I gave the two men my four-fingered wave and a smile. *Looks as if Aunt Madge and Harry get me for dinner after all.*

Chapter Four

"WHY DID HE have to word it that way?" I fumed.

The Tuesday *Ocean Alley Press* said that a local appraiser had been accosted outside the Purple Cow, and described me as an inquisitive citizen who had helped local police solve a couple of recent crimes. George's description of me was as good as drawing a map to the Cozy Corner.

I glanced further down the page and groaned. There would not normally be a photo with such a brief article but the Press had used the one of me holding the large underpants. The caption said, "Ms. Gentil at a recent auction."

"They named me in the caption," I grumbled.

"You don't look accosted," Aunt Madge said. "And it's obvious those aren't your bloomers."

She pretended to be serious, but I saw her smirk.

We were sitting in her kitchen, waiting for the two B&B guests to finish eating in the guest breakfast area, which was on the other side of the swinging door that separates her living area from the guests' breakfast room. It's my favorite time of day to be with Aunt Madge.

"He couldn't have said it was a simple purse snatching?"

"You know they write things that sell papers, right?" Aunt Madge asked.

"Gee, you think?"

The sliding glass door opened and Harry walked in with the dogs, who were on leashes. Aunt Madge is very happy that she married Harry, but Mister Rogers and Miss Piggy are ecstatic. Harry takes them for walks every morning and evening.

My cat, Jazz, got off my foot, her seat of choice when I'm at the kitchen table, and walked over to give the dogs a good sniff.

"Morning, Jolie." Harry blew a kiss to Aunt Madge.

"Hello, boss," I grinned at him. "I'm getting ready to go appraise that house at J and Conch."

"Looked for comps yet?" He poured himself a cup of coffee and joined us at the table.

"Checked to see if any recent sales looked similar, but I'll do the real work after I go to the house." It was going to be tough. There have not been a lot of sales since the hurricane, and housing values have really fluctuated since last October. Some people think the shore may be susceptible to more big storms, and that drives prices down. On the other hand, there's a housing shortage south of us, so that has driven prices up in some areas.

"I see George is picking on you again," Harry nodded at the paper, which he had likely read before his walk.

"He'll get his. Hey, can I borrow a digital camera from one of you for today? Mine was in my purse and Morehouse still has it."

While Harry got his camera from the top drawer of an antique washstand in the hallway outside their bedroom, I walked toward the dogs. They were on their rug by the sliding glass doors, still panting lightly. Each gave me a tail thump. I stooped to get Jazz. She deftly ran around Mr. Rogers and sat, very purposefully, at his side.

Aunt Madge laughed. "Remember when she wouldn't even get on the floor because she was afraid of them?"

"Yep. And then she terrorized him by jumping on his back for a ride all the time." I stared at Jazz and she twitched her tail and looked away.

"I'll take her up to your room in a minute, Jolie," Harry said. "You can get going."

As I opened my car door I thought that the hardest part of my move might be dislodging Jazz.

I FINISHED VISITING AND MEASURING the house at Conch and J and took pictures with Harry's camera. The house was in pristine condition, and I hoped that documenting its condition really well would help me appraise it at something close to the agreed-upon selling price.

Before going to the office to enter information into the appraisal software I stopped by my little house. Yesterday evening I had carefully closed and locked every window and door, but today I wanted some windows open. The mildew-resistant paint I used had a more pungent smell than regular interior latex paint. I wanted the smell of paint from the bedrooms out of the house.

I opened the door and stared with satisfaction at the living room-dining room combination area that led into the kitchen, which was not large but was fine for one person. The bath was behind the kitchen, and on each side of the bathroom was a bedroom. A small hallway connected them. By tomorrow night the two guys I hired from the veterans outreach center would have the drywall hung in part of the living room and it would be ready to paint.

The kitchen window that looked out on my back porch stuck a bit, and I had just gotten it open when someone knocked at the front door. Skittish after my encounter with the purse snatcher, I looked through the living room window to the small front porch. Auctioneer Norman Fitzgerald stood there with a cardboard box in his hand.

I opened the door, my surprise likely registering on my face. "Hello, Mr. Fitzgerald."

"Good day, Jolie. Your aunt told me I might find you here." He wore a huge smile.

"Aunt Madge knows all. Please come in." He walked in and I gestured to one of the canvas camp chairs.

"Oh, I'm not staying. Well, maybe for a minute. I thought you'd like this." He handed the box to me and moved to a canvas chair and sat down, very slowly.

I took it and peered in. "My drawer! Where did you get this?"

"It's the strangest thing. When I got in my van this morning it was on the front seat. Don't lock the van."

I took the drawer from the box and studied it. It fit only half of the top of the chest of drawers, and there was another drawer in the other half. Each drawer was only about eight or nine inches wide. I turned it over and then looked again at Mr. Fitzgerald. "Who would put it there? Heck, why would anyone take it?"

He looked around the room. "I haven't been in this house for, oh, at least thirty years. A cousin of my mother's owned it then."

"Except for the addition of the screened-in porch in the very back, it's probably much the same. Would you like to look around?"

"No thanks. Well, maybe." He glanced around the room for almost twenty seconds, taking in the bare studs that comprised three of the four walls and the wallboard stacked against the studs. "Looks better without the starfish wallpaper."

"I've been scraping that wall for days. The starfish paper was two wallpapers deep."

"Heavens to Betsy. You're a hard worker." He smiled.

"Yep. I wanted to leave one original wall, and that wall would have been harder to take down since it's plaster. Kind of silly, I guess."

"Not at all. People don't appreciate older things anymore, always buying new furniture or taking out perfectly good windows." He looked around again, and then back at me. "I felt right bad about someone taking your drawer. Guess it was some kind of joke or something."

I thought about Tiffany from the *Ocean Alley Press*. Not even George would encourage that kind of a joke from another reporter. "Don't know, and don't care. I'm just thrilled to have it back. Come on, I'll give you a quick tour."

"If I'm not holding you up." He stood.

"You're not. It's not a big house, so it's always a quick tour." I grinned at him.

He nodded. "Gotcha. Gee, I'd forgotten that this kitchen would be big enough for a small table."

We moved from there to the bedroom I planned to sleep in. "I love the closet. Somebody paneled it with cedar, so it smells great."

He peered in. "I think my mother's cousin did that right before she died. She said it made her clothes smell right good." He ran his hand over one closet wall. "Nice tight fit. If you sand the cedar lightly now and then it increases the scent."

"Right." I wanted to ask him if his cousin had died in this room, then decided I really didn't want to know. Instead, I asked, "Was your mom's cousin well-to-do?"

"Not so's you'd think. She was like a lot of people who grew up during the Depression. She was a good saver."

So, maybe she got a little paranoid when she got older and hid her jewelry.

I debated asking Mr. Fitzgerald if the woman's heirs thought that any of her valuables were missing, and decided not to. "From going through my papers at settlement, I think her name was Bridler, right?"

"Naomi Bridler." He walked into the bathroom. "Gee, must have been Mrs. Peebles modernized this bathroom."

"I'm not sure. I like having the storage space under the sink. And the lighting's good for makeup."

"You girls…well, I should probably let you get back to work." He moved toward the front door. "Maybe you'll let me come back when you get all your redecorating done."

This struck me as the comment of a very lonely man. "Of course. If I ever get up the energy I'm going to have an open house."

With a wink and verbal goodbye, Mr. Fitzgerald left.

I walked to the chest, which was covered with a plastic table cloth to keep it free of dust. I took off the tablecloth and shoved the drawer in place. Oddly, it didn't stick this time.

AFTER I FINISHED THE data entry for the house I had just visited, I left Harry's home office and headed to Java Jolt. The local coffee house is still in temporary quarters on D Street, and there is very little space. Joe Regan expects to move back to his boardwalk location any day.

"Morning, Joe. You getting ready to pack?"

"Yep. Thinking about a packing party. You want to come?"

From the usually somber Joe this comment bordered on hilarity. He knows what a klutz I can be. "Sure. You know when?"

"Next couple days." He grinned. "Nice undies, by the way."

"George is working on a first class ticket to hell." I studied the list of drinks. It was warmer today and I wanted something cold.

"You like chocolate. I have a new chocolate chip frozen coffee drink."

"It's on me," said a man's voice. Clive Dorner sat at a table in the back of the small shop. I hadn't noticed him. With him was a woman not too much older than I am, who looked somewhat familiar.

"Thanks, but I've got it." I said this pleasantly enough, considering that I thought of the guy as a bottom feeder, and turned back to Joe.

"Suit yourself." Dorner said this quite cheerfully. "How about joining us? I'm trying to talk Fiona here into investing in a house with me."

"I'm meeting my friend, uh, Scoobie here in a couple of minutes." Scoobie and I do meet here at this time some days, but I had no idea if he would stop by today. I glanced at Joe, who was being studiously disinterested.

I turned to face Dorner and then looked more closely at the woman. "Oh. We met at the auction, didn't we?" I hadn't paid a lot of attention to her then. Now I took in not only her auburn hair but her high cheekbones and bright green eyes. She could be an ad promoting Irish tourism.

"Yes, Fiona Henderson. You outbid me." She gave a tight smile.

It might have been my imagination, but Fiona did not look any happier to be with Clive Dorner than I was to run into him.

Clive got to his feet, and I noted his coffee cup was empty. "Are you still looking around with Lester?"

"Found a couple of places. Trying to consider which would net the most profit in a couple of years."

Fiona frowned slightly as she got up to leave. She pulled a dollar bill from her wallet and left it on the table as a tip.

Dorner looked at me steadily, and I realized that one reason he annoyed me was that he seemed to be one of those people who knew he was good looking and used it to push people to get his way.

"We got off on the wrong foot," he said, with a wide smile. "Let's see what we can do about that."

"We're good," I said, in a casual tone.

"We may be, but you think I'm here to take advantage of people by paying less for their houses than someone else might." He grinned and Fiona flushed, the color of her face now almost matching her hair.

As if he knows what I think. "It's not just that you do it, it's that you're so proud to do it."

He threw back his head and laughed. "I like you, Jolie. You've got ba…spunk."

"I do." I picked up a couple of napkins to take to my table.

"Okay, I'll head out. But if you need any advice on fixing up that little house you bought, I'm your man. I've bought a lot of fixer-uppers."

Dorner set his empty mug on the counter. As he did, a well dressed woman of about forty came in. I'd met her briefly when I dropped my Steele Appraisal business cards at real estate offices around town. With her reddish blonde hair and tailored tan pantsuit, Betty Fowler looked all business.

And she was delighted to see Clive Dorner. "I wondered what had happened to you, sugar," she said, all smiles. "I have two new listings that are just perfect…"

"I would, but I have to be back in Philadelphia before six." Dorner flashed her a broad smile. "We do need to pick up where we left off." He glanced at Fiona, seemingly expecting her to follow him.

"Call me," Betty gushed.

"Will do. Thanks, Joe. See you soon." Dorner carefully avoided looking at me. He was busted and he knew it.

"Next time I'll bid higher." Fiona gave me a small smile as she followed Dorner out the door.

As the door shut behind them, Betty turned her one hundred-watt smile on Joe. "You know what I like, don't you sugar?"

"Sugar-free iced mocha coming up," Joe said, without the wattage.

I paid Joe and moved aside so Betty could pay for her order, then claimed a table by the window while Joe finished mixing my drink. Idly I wondered why Fiona was with Dorner. She had struck me as a nice woman when I saw her at the auction. Given her cringe at one of Dorner's comments, she didn't like his methods any better than I did. *Maybe she doesn't know him any better than I do.*

Joe called my name and I walked to the counter to pick up my drink. There were only two other couples in the shop, quieter than it usually was in the late afternoon.

"Ta ta, all." Betty gave me a friendly nod as she walked out with her coffee.

Joe rolled his eyes in her direction and then looked at me directly. "You know Dorner well?"

"Nope. He called about looking at houses and I gave him Lester's name."

"He's kind of sure of himself."

I sensed Joe didn't like Dorner any more than I did. I carried my drink back to my table and thought about what I'd learned in the sixty seconds or less that Dorner had talked to Betty Fowler. It seemed that Dorner had been looking in Ocean Alley before he called me, meaning his request that I show him around was a pretense for…what?

I wasn't rolling in money, so I certainly wouldn't be an investor if he wanted cash for his lowball offers for properties. There was no way he knew about the jewelry. Scoobie and I had only just found it when he called. How would he have even known who I was?

The annoying voice in my head reminded me that I was mentioned in the *Ocean Alley Press* from time to time, but those articles never made me sound like someone who would be, to use Harry's phrase, a good catch.

The door opened and Scoobie greeted me with his usual, "Yo, Jolie."

"Don't even go there," I said.

He laughed. "Could have been worse. At least the picture wasn't in color. And no one would really believe they were your pants."

"I believe I said not to go there."

"'How are your walls?" He sat across from me. "Any new revelations?"

"Nope. I got the drawer back, though." I relayed Mr. Fitzgerald's visit. "He thought it must be some kind of joke. A stupid one if you asked me."

"Can't imagine anyone stealing that for a joke." He stood and walked over to Joe and paid for his large decaf coffee. As usual, no small talk between the two men.

He rejoined me. "At least you have it back."

"Did you see a couple leaving as you got close to Java Jolt? He was maybe forty, kind of good looking. She looks like thirty-fiveish, about five-five and had auburn hair."

"Trying to hone in on her boyfriend?" he asked.

"Yeah, like I have a lot of time for that right now. That was Clive Dorner, and the woman's name is Freda, no Fiona."

"Dorner?" he asked.

"He wants to buy some houses on the cheap. I referred him to Lester."

"That's pretty harsh." Scoobie took a sip of coffee and then blew on the steam rising from it.

"Lester's shown him a few places. I saw them at Burger King right after my purse was taken." I gave half a shrug. "You know Lester, if he smells a commission he can be quite easy to get along with."

"I don't think I know any Dorners, and I didn't take a good look at the guy."

"How about the woman?"

Scoobie looked at me intently. "She looks like somebody I might have seen around, but I never met her. What do you care?"

"I just don't like the guy." I decided not to mention that I thought Dorner was already looking for property with another agent before I sent him to Lester.

Scoobie half turned in his chair and looked at Joe. "People don't have to like each other to get along, do they?"

"Talk about living proof," Joe mumbled, and went back to the coffee mugs he was drying and stacking on the counter.

"Cleared up?" Scoobie faced me. When I didn't answer, he took a large slurp of his coffee. "So, you get a drawer and a purse stolen but get them back ASAP, and your money's still in your wallet. What do you think that means?"

"I think it means people think I have more money than I do."

Scoobie just looked at me.

"I don't know what it means. I think whoever took the drawer was either mad they didn't win the bid or thought Mrs. Peebles or somebody kept something valuable in that drawer." I had just realized that it might not even have been Moira Peebles' chest of drawers.

"When I called George to congratulate him on the photo of you and your bloomers…" Scoobie ducked as I threw a wadded napkin at him, "we talked about your purse snatching for a minute."

"And?"

"I was at that city bus stop near your house when I told him about the jewelry. There were other people around, so I wasn't specific about the type of jewelry or where you lived. But someone could have overheard, and they might have seen me leave your house before I went to the bus stop. And then you came out of the house a few minutes later."

"It's a stretch." I thought about it for a few moments. It seemed to me that the person almost had to know about the jewelry to understand what Scoobie meant when he talked to George.

When I didn't say anything, Scoobie changed the topic. "George said you might give him ideas for his piece on ignored news, or whatever he's calling it." His tone was nonchalant.

I don't think he cares one way or the other whether George and I are dating, but he's not big on tension. He has indirectly accused us both of being busybodies who should learn to share better.

"I told him I'd tell him if I thought of…" My phone chirped. I was frazzled and didn't even look at the display, just pushed the silence button. The call would go to voice mail. I hadn't said two words more to Scoobie when it rang again.

"Somebody's persistent," Scoobie said.

I answered it.

"Where you at?" Morehouse asked.

"Java Jolt. Where are you?" I asked, needling him.

"Your aunt's. I'm no jeweler, so I wanna take the stuff to somebody, see what they're worth. You gotta sign for me."

"Can I come to the station to do it?" I had just gotten my drink and didn't feel like heading to the Cozy Corner.

"I can't take 'em without youse signing for 'em, and you shouldn't be carrying the stuff around." When he's rushed or especially irritated, Morehouse's Jersey accent is more pronounced.

"Okay, I'll see you in a couple." I hung up and told Scoobie where I was heading. "Want to come?"

"Nope. You still want help painting the cabinets in your kitchen later?"

"Yep. I'm getting closer to moving in, I think. See you this evening?"

He agreed and I drove to Aunt Madge's.

Morehouse sat catty-corner to her at the large oak table and they each had a mug of tea in front of them. Neither one of them looked happy.

"What's up, you guys?" I asked.

"This all there was?" Morehouse asked, by way of a greeting. "Just diamonds and bracelets?"

"All I found." I sat next to Aunt Madge, more or less facing Morehouse. "Why? Do you think there would be more?"

"How would I know? These are likely worth somethin'. Shouldn't keep them at your place."

"Can you keep them at the station?"

He shoved a property receipt form toward me. "Do I look like a safe deposit box?"

I scanned his written list of the jewelry, and murmured. "You're really giving me a chance to say you have a square head? Your list misses the brownish bracelets."

He didn't reply, and I looked up to see that I had, yet again, irritated him. "You started it."

"They look cheap. You keep 'em."

"If you can't keep the rest until Jolie figures out what to do with them, please let her have a day or so notice before you return them, so she can open a safe deposit box."

"We'll hang onto 'em for a while." He took the form I signed and stood.

"How come you do it when Aunt Madge asks but not me?"

"Because your aunt isn't a pain in the backside." He looked at her. "Thanks for the tea, Madge."

He's been at the Cozy Corner enough that Aunt Madge let him show himself out. I regarded her for several seconds, taking in her blondish-red hair. Her one frivolous habit is to change her hair color every few weeks. She doesn't use permanent color, so it washes out pretty fast.

"Did he tell you why he's annoyed?" I only half-cared.

"Apparently he thinks a few of the loose diamonds could be worth quite a bit. It makes him wonder why they were placed behind the wall."

I shrugged. "If it was a crime it would have been a while ago. It's not like he's going to solve it."

"I think that's probably what bothers him."

Chapter Five

ALTHOUGH I am chair of the Harvest for All Food Pantry Committee, anyone on the committee can call a meeting. It's just that no one else does. While I was sitting with Aunt Madge, Reverend Jamison telephoned to say he'd been asked to phone me to set up a meeting for this evening. He said he had another call and hung up as I was asking him who had asked him to call me.

Mentally I went through the committee roster. Dr. Welby (who abides no teasing about his name) is our informal leader. He retired from active practice a few years ago, though he did some volunteer work after Hurricane Sandy. He would have called me if he wanted a meeting.

Sylvia Parrett is a very rigid person, but she's also a hard worker. With her buttoned-up cardigans and low voice, Monica Martin can only be described as mousy. Though they work as hard as anyone for the food pantry, it did not seem likely that either one of them took the initiative.

I know I shouldn't have favorites, but Lance Wilson, our treasurer, has become a dear friend. *Who knew I would have a friend more than sixty years older than I am?*

Aretha Brown is our only black member, and I finally got up the nerve to ask her to think about friends who could join us. I didn't say black friends, but I think she knew I meant that. Our pantry users are a diverse group and I think that our committee should be, too.

Megan Ortiz has been a regular volunteer during pantry giving hours, and I finally convinced her to join the committee. She's the one who most knows what she's talking about when we discuss what's needed. She's also almost shy when she comes to the meetings, so she wouldn't have asked Reverend Jamison to call me.

And Scoobie, who invited himself onto the committee. Scoobie would never have gone through Reverend Jamison. He would have blithely invited all of us to a meeting himself.

FIRST PRESBYTERIAN CHURCH, First Prez to locals, is red brick with white trim on the windows and at the steeple. Very traditional. I parked my car on the street by the side door that opens into the pantry, which is set up like a dry cleaning shop, except with shelves instead of rows of clothes. And it doesn't stink.

I entered the pantry and went through the interior door to the corridor that leads into the to the community room area of First Prez.

Laughter came from the small meeting room and I felt myself relax. This couldn't be some kind of emergency. I walked in and raised a hand in greeting. "Hi, guys."

Choruses of "hello Jolie" and "hi" came back to me, and I could swear prim Monica actually had a pleased expression.

"What's up?" I asked.

"We're waiting for Scoobie," Sylvia said.

Uh oh. To say that Sylvia and Scoobie rub each other the wrong way would be an understatement of some magnitude. In fact, they have only recently gotten back on sort of friendly footing after some unkind remarks (on both sides) about our last fundraiser, a hot dog eating contest.

"Hello, girlfriend," Aretha smiled broadly.

If Aretha's smiling it must be good news.

Megan winked at me.

As I sat, I heard footsteps coming down the steps from the main church area. Given the speed it had to be Scoobie. He walked in as I asked, "Is Lance coming?"

Scoobie shrugged and Dr. Welby said, "In a couple of minutes. Did I hear you had some excitement at your new house?"

Nuts! I looked at Scoobie, who said, "Not from me. Probably Sylvia."

She sat up straighter, but when he wiggled his eyebrows at her she relaxed, and asked, "What does Dr. Welby mean, Jolie?"

"You know I have to be really sure there's no mold. Scoobie helped me pull down a piece of wallboard and there was a small pouch of jewelry behind it. Nothing that looked especially valuable."

I rushed the last few words.

"Oh, that's disappointing," Dr. Welby said. "I heard it was quite the pile of loot."

I did an internal groan and Scoobie asked, "How did you hear?"

Dr. Welby considered this. If it had been anyone else, I would have thought they were pausing for effect, but he's a very direct person. "I ran into George Winters at Java Jolt. He said he'd love to do a story on it, but putting it in the paper would be like advertising a burglary opportunity."

"I can't believe that would stop him," Aretha said.

Slower footsteps in the hall were probably announcing Lance. I looked toward the door, but all I saw was his head as he peered in. "Scoobie's behaving, it's okay to come in."

He grinned more broadly than I've seen since the hurricane. He put his hand, which held several helium balloons, into the room. One said Happy Birthday.

"Ha. Fooled you," Aretha pointed a finger at me.

Megan added, "I didn't think we'd pull it off."

Dr. Welby literally beamed. "There's an idea for the next food pantry fundraiser."

"It's your birthday?" I asked Lance.

"Nope, yours. And Scoobie's."

"And Ramona's," Sylvia said. "You all work at the fundraisers, and you're all turning thirty this year."

"Jennifer Stenner, too," I said, referring to the high school classmate who had taken over her family's longtime appraisal business and usually helps at the fundraisers.

"And Bill Oliver's," Scoobie said, mentioning to a classmate who was now a dentist in Newark. "And Daphne at the library."

"Good! The more birthday people the more of their friends to come to the party," said Dr. Welby.

"What about George?" Megan asked.

"He was a year ahead of us," I said.

Lance passed out balloons. Scoobie's expression was hard to read. He is a lot more comfortable with groups of people than when we renewed our friendship a year and a half ago, but he is far more at ease creating situations that embarrass me rather than those that put the spotlight on him. He's in recovery from excess alcohol use and what he calls his love affair with pot.

Scoobie avoided looking at me.

"Now, we can get going." Sylvia pulled a small notebook out of her purse. "People don't have to pay to get into birthday parties, so we have to figure out what we can charge money for."

"The food, of course," Monica said. "I'll…"

"…organize the bake sale," Aretha said in tandem with Monica.

Monica always says she'll do the bake sales, but she can get quite flustered. Today, however, she looked very pleased with herself.

"And to play any games," Megan said, "Like at Talk Like a Pirate Day last year."

"We can charge a small admission fee," Dr. Welby said, "and waive it if they bring cans of food."

I let them all talk for a couple of minutes. Scoobie was uncharacteristically quiet, but after a minute or so he looked at me and gave a small shrug.

When there was a brief lull in the conversation, I asked, "Whose idea was this?"

There was a chorus of "I'm not sure," and "Do you remember who?"

For some reason, Aunt Madge's face came to mind. Despite her air of propriety, she can be a trouble maker sometimes.

Chapter Six

THE NEXT FEW DAYS WERE a blur of activity and I tried to put the jewelry, the annoying Clive Dorner, the purse snatcher, and the so-called birthday party out of my mind. Scoobie and I finished painting the kitchen cabinets and two guys from the VA Outreach Center had put up dry wall in the living room-dining room combo a couple of days ago. I used the fact that I needed to pay them as an excuse to get my purse back. Morehouse said that there were no prints other than mine on it. I hadn't really expected any.

Ramona and Scoobie and I were going to paint the newly hung walls this evening. Tomorrow afternoon, Sunday, I would move in. Rather, friends and family were moving me in.

I sat in my car, eyes closed for a minute before I walked into the small store I was about to appraise. We don't often do appraisals on Saturday, but the owners said it worked better for them.

I was beat, and my arms felt as if they'd been lifting heavy boxes. That would be tomorrow, so it was probably from reaching above my head to paint the top-level kitchen cabinets.

I got out of the car and studied the knick-knack and beachwear store more closely. Harry and I mostly do residential appraisals, but there are several small stores for sale around town. Most have elderly owners who made post-hurricane repairs and don't care to have to do it again.

The owners of this store had not formally listed it for sale yet. They wanted to get a sense of its value before they set a price. Lester had suggested me. He usually tries to get people to list high, but I figured he didn't have a clue what to suggest, because he would usually be afraid that Harry and I would suggest it was worth less than he wanted to list it for.

New plate glass windows gleamed, as in many stores around town, and I smelled a fresh coat of paint. The store had some stock in it, but not much. They probably lost most of it when the hurricane blew out the old windows.

I was about to open the door when a man's voice called, "Jolie, Jolie!" in a very excited tone.

Max walked hurriedly across the street. He used to be homeless but now has a very small cottage at the far end of town. It's paid for with his VA benefits, since he had a fairly bad traumatic brain injury in Iraq. Physically he's fine, but his judgment has become more like that of a teen instead of his thirty-ish years, and he talks rapidly, often repeating words.

"I'm helping tomorrow, helping. I saw Scoobie, and he said I could."

"Thanks so much, Max." I worried that he might get hurt trying to lift things he shouldn't. "We're having subs for lunch."

He pulled a wool scarf tighter around his neck and continued beaming at me. He was dressed oddly for an April day in the sixties—light windbreaker, but also the scarf and gloves. "I'm happy to help, happy to help. Will you have something chocolate for snacks?" Before I could answer, he gave an abrupt wave and turned and walked toward Mr. Markle's small, in-town grocery store.

I stared at his back for a second, and then put my hand on the door handle.

"Jolie, what a surprise." Clive Dorner walked toward me, cup of Java Jolt coffee in hand.

Great. I let go of the door. "I see you're imbibing."

He laughed. "It's halfway warm. Join me for a walk on the boardwalk?"

"Can't, thanks. I have to do this appraisal," I nodded to the store, "and then get it written up so it's not on my mind for my move-in day tomorrow."

He had stopped a few feet from me. "Got her fixed up the way you want it?"

"It's fine for now. Over time I'll do more." I put my hand back on the door handle.

"Damn shame about your purse."

I silently cursed George Winters. "I was really, really lucky. Somebody dumped it in a trash can."

His eyebrows shot up. "You are lucky. Did they take much?"

"Nothing of consequence." I didn't want to get into an involved conversation. If I said nothing was taken he might ask me why I thought that to be the case and I'd have to listen to his ruminations. George's theory had been that the thief thought someone saw him take it and wanted to dump it before he got caught.

"Guess I'll let you get to it." He raised his coffee cup as if toasting me.

"Have a good afternoon." I took a deep breath as I opened the door. The only person in the store, Ocean Alley Swimwear and Gifts, was one of the two women who had bid against me at the auction. She seemed to be staring at Dorner as he walked away.

"Hello," I said, in mild surprise.

She looked at me directly. "Ah. My bidding buddy. I'm Patricia, in case you don't remember." She was petite and dressed casually in denim capris and a lightweight knit top. Her auburn hair was pulled back into a pony tail that made her look about twenty instead of early thirties, which is what I thought when I met her at the auction. I decided my early estimate was probably correct.

"I'm Jolie. I do remember, but thanks for the reminder." I glanced around the small store.

She explained that she was a teacher's aide in the winter and worked part-time in the summer, and that the owner had asked her to come down to let me in. "We aren't open in April."

"Thanks for being here." I looked around the store some more.

"I think they want to refinance so they can make the store look more up-to-date before they open Memorial Day weekend."

"They're lucky they had some equity in the building." My guess was that Patricia had been told this so she wouldn't think the building would be sold. Or maybe refinancing was the owner's intent and Lester was only hopeful he would get a listing. *Not my business.*

"I'm worried that if they find out it isn't worth enough to get a loan that they'll close. I worked here every summer in high school and college. I used the money to pay for my band instruments, now I use the money for my kids' soccer stuff."

"I hope it works out." I smiled as I pulled a tape measure and notebook from a canvas shoulder bag that holds stuff that won't fit in my purse.

Patricia took items off shelves and dusted them as I measured. I wanted to ask her if she had taken the drawer from my chest of drawers, but I couldn't think of a way to do it. It didn't seem likely that she would have done something as daring as steal the drawer, not with all those people around. In fact, with their easy bantering, the auction foursome seemed like people I'd like to get to know sometime.

It didn't take long to take measurements of the main room and small storage area and half bath in the back. I pulled my newly returned camera from my purse, hoping the photos would help me increase the appraised value. The store had been nicely decorated. I figured if it had sold last year it might have been worth a lot more than it would bring this year.

I aimed the camera toward the back of the store and pushed the shutter, but nothing happened. No batteries? Then I realized that it would not have turned on if there were no batteries.

"Problems?" Patricia asked.

"I hope not." I looked at the bottom of the camera, trying to find what to push to eject the data card. Maybe the police had put it in wrong when they were inspecting the camera.

The data card was gone. If I'd been alone I would have cursed Sergeant Morehouse. Instead I looked at Patricia. "I just lent it to someone. They must have taken the card out and forgotten to put it back in."

"You can use my phone camera." She reached for her purse on a shelf behind me.

I started to say that the quality would not be sufficient, but decided against it. If the photos were okay it would save me a trip back. If not, I'd just have to return. "And you can email me the photos?"

"Easy as pie."

I took several pictures and then wrote down my email address. I could take exterior pictures anytime. I put my tape measure in my purse and started to ask her something.

Patricia beat me to it. "Are you enjoying the chest of drawers?"

"Getting ready to. My friends are moving me into my house tomorrow afternoon."

"That's great. Where is it?"

"It's a couple of blocks south of the popsicle district, on Bay Street."

"That part of town is really changing," Patricia said.

I nodded. "I think a lot of the older residents are leaving and there's more energy with the younger buyers. Present company excluded."

She laughed. "I'm always really wiped out when I have to move."

"If you worked here in high school you probably haven't moved too often."

"I married a guy I met in college and we moved to Texas for his job. The job lasted, but the marriage didn't, so my kids and I moved back here."

"Ouch. I got divorced not too long ago."

"Kids?" she asked.

"Nope."

"I was going to say I might see you on the soccer field. Two of mine are in grade school and they live to play soccer."

I moved toward the door. "I'm sure I'll see you around town."

After a couple more pleasantries I walked to my car. I liked Patricia. Maybe I'd see if she and her kids wanted to come to whatever the heck the birthday party was going to be. But first, I had to swing by the police station.

It was Saturday, so I didn't really expect Sergeant Morehouse to be there. It was too complicated to explain it all to someone else, so I left a brief note at the front desk asking him to call me when he figured out where my data card was. I wasn't even snotty about it.

SUNDAY AFTERNOON WE gathered at the Cozy Corner in fifty-degree temps to collect my things. My sister Renée came down from Lakewood. I had told her there wasn't that much to move, but she said she was here for support and fun, not work, and she brought a huge tin of homemade chocolate chip cookies.

"How come you learned to cook and Jolie didn't?" Scoobie asked.

"She didn't like my mother standing over her shoulder," my sister said, cheerfully.

"Damn, Jolie. I thought you just got stubborn when you got older."

"She was pretty stubborn in eleventh grade," Bill Oliver said. I stuck out my tongue at him.

Before I could say anything else, Aunt Madge produced a list of items she thought we were moving. "All of the furniture in Jolie's bedroom goes, except for the chest of drawers," she began.

"That rocker's not mine," I said.

"It is now." She smiled at me, and I blew her a kiss.

"There are a couple tubs of houseware-type stuff you put in the basement, and Harry and Lester drove out to your small storage locker to get lamps and a few boxes. Up to you whether you go back later today to get your exercise bike and heavier boxes of books and all that."

"Harry and Lester?" I almost groaned. "Lester will talk his ear off."

"And probably insult him about appraisal prices," Ramona added.

"Lester wanted to help," Aunt Madge said, "and Harry said now you owe him."

I grinned at her. Lester would help, and he would probably bug me about the appraisal I was working on of the small store.

It didn't take long to load my possessions in the cargo van I'd rented and I told Aunt Madge I'd be back in a few hours to vacuum my old room. Scoobie and Ramona rode in Bill's car and Renée and I were in the cargo van.

"I bet you never thought you'd have your own place this soon," she said. Renée is several years older than I am, and she was my biggest supporter when my husband was arrested for embezzling from his bank. I haven't seen her much the last eighteen months. At Christmas she told me she had been giving me space, but she expected to see more of me in the future.

"You're right. Sometimes I feel guilty that I got the money for helping to solve a murder. It kind of feels like blood money or something."

She shook her head, firmly. "You gave that guy's parents peace of mind."

And that conversation was the most peaceful moment of my day.

Scoobie had told Max to meet us at my house, and he was on the porch swing as Renée and I pulled in front of the bungalow. "Jolie, Jolie, I told your friend to come back later." He literally ran up to the van.

"What friend?" I asked.

"Um, I don't know." He had seen Scoobie getting out of Bill Oliver's car and headed in that direction.

Renée gave me a questioning look.

"Traumatic brain injury. He loves chocolate."

She picked the tin of cookies off the floor of the van and I ran up the steps to unlock the door to my house. The condo Robby and I owned in Lakeview was elegant and worth many times what I'd paid for this storm-damaged little house. I knew I'd be much happier here.

Scoobie carried a tub into the house. "You want anyone to unpack your bloomers?"

"Only if you put a picture in the paper."

"You need to get some curtains," Ramona said, a few minutes later.

"She's got blinds," Bill said. "So no huge rush."

"There's still that Peeping Tom," Ramona added.

"Why does Tom peep? Tom peep?" Max asked.

"It's an expression," Renée said. "It means someone who looks in a window when it's not their house. Not a good thing."

This was apparently all the explanation Max needed. He stood and wandered back to the kitchen to get part of a sub sandwich.

"Someone told me about that. Maybe George," Bill said. "Why the hell can't they catch him?"

"Kind of hard to know where to look until they get a call, and by the time the cops get there, he's gone." Scoobie took a bottle of water from the full-sized fridge I had just had delivered.

Bill frowned. "Are you comfortable being here alone at night?"

"You offering to stay?" Ramona grinned.

Bill flushed. "You're a pain, Ramona."

"What you need is a couch," Scoobie said, "so I have a place to watch the Discovery Channel." He sat on one of the dinette chairs.

"You know, kid, you got that great cedar closet and the kitchen's not bad. You put in new windows and enclose that back porch, you could sell it in a year and get double what you paid for this place." Lester leaned against the door jamb that opened to the kitchen, surveying the house as if he was planning to list it.

"Except I'm looking for a place to live in, not an investment."

"Yeah, but…" Lester began.

"Lester." My sister and I said this together.

"Give up while you're only a little bit behind," Scoobie advised.

HOURS LATER, I WAS ABOUT to fall asleep when I realized I still didn't know the name of the friend Max said had stopped by just before we arrived with the furniture. *They'll come back.*

Chapter Seven

I SLEPT IN twenty minute increments the first night Jazz and I were in our new house. I had expected the smell of fresh paint to be a bother, but it wasn't that. Every time I got Jazz settled down and I fell asleep, Jazz was awake and rushing through the house in no time at all. I called the vet and had an appointment for eight-thirty Monday morning. I'd be tired all day, but I'd know she was getting care for whatever illness this was.

Dr. Holly was a kind man of about sixty. I had not met him until I brought Jazz in for an annual check-up a few months ago but, of course, Aunt Madge had known him for years. He had deftly wrapped all but Jazz's head in a towel and I was now holding her while he peered into her ears. She objected strongly, but was in no position to scratch me.

"She certainly looks healthy, and I don't detect an elevated temperature. She's been eating, and drinking plenty of water?" He put his thumb on one side of Jazz's jaw and forefinger on the other and forced her mouth open. I had no idea a cat could growl so deeply without having control of its mouth. He shone a small pen light down her throat and let go of her.

"Judging by her water bowl, I'd say she's drinking normally. I gave her a more expensive brand of food last night, and she gobbled it."

"Special occasion?" He shone the pen light into her eyes. Jazz aimed her mouth at his finger, but missed.

"We just moved into my new house." I felt almost silly saying "we," as if Jazz was a person.

Dr. Holly looked at me directly. "Did she used to live with other pets?"

"Yes, Aunt Madge's…"

"Retrievers, yes, of course. She seemed to get along with them?"

"The last year, especially. She sometimes slept between them." It had never occurred to me that Jazz might miss the dogs that much. I'd had her for several years before we moved in with Aunt Madge. She was used to being alone when I was working, and I had never had other pets.

"Unless the blood work shows something, my diagnosis would be that she is simply very upset." He put my cat carrier on the exam table and opened the door. It took me about fifteen seconds to wrestle Jazz out of the towel and into the cage. She gave a really long hiss and then tried to swat my fingers while I locked the carrier.

"So, what do I do?" I asked.

"You could give it a week or two to see if she calms down, maybe take her back to the B&B for a visit. I don't attribute true thinking skills to animals, but seeing the dogs might reassure her that they aren't gone forever."

I thanked him and carried Jazz to the car. Aunt Madge had let me bring Jazz and been kind to her, but she is not a big fan of cats. Jazz tried to wander through the B&B, and Aunt Madge did not want her hair or dander to be a source of allergens for guests. Jazz had been relegated to my bedroom unless she was with me in the great room.

I drove to the Cozy Corner, an idea slowly taking form. Jazz seemed more fond of Mr. Rogers than Miss Piggy. She wound herself around his legs if he stood still for more than a minute, and she followed him around like a puppy.

Miss Piggy is more laid back than Mr. Rogers. I figured Jazz could take or leave Miss Piggy. And two retrievers would take up a lot of room in my small cottage if we planned an overnight visit.

I parked in the B&B's small lot and left Jazz in the car in her carrier. I left the windows down to let in the fifty degree air. Her yowl carried to the side door of the B&B as I inserted my key. I could hear the vacuum above me.

Aunt Madge is technically my great aunt. Her late sister Alva was my grandmother. My mother visited Aunt Madge every summer until she was old enough to want to spend all her time with her friends. She often said the bungalow Aunt Madge and her late husband, Uncle Gordon, lived in at that time was always so clean you never saw as much as a grain of sand on the door mat. The B&B is also spotless, but she tolerates a bit of mess from guests. Not too much from me.

I went up the main stairway, which is in the foyer, and yelled hello. I didn't want to startle her.

"Good morning, Jolie." Aunt Madge wrapped the cord around her vacuum. "Surprised to see you this time of day."

"I have a special request that involves Mr. Rogers." As we walked down the back stairs into her great room, she listened as I recounted my conversation with Dr. Holly. "So, I wondered if I could borrow him, maybe over night. If she sleeps when he's there, I'll know she's not sick."

"Hmm. I never thought of the dogs as diagnostic tools, but I suppose it's worth a try." She turned on her electric kettle. "I reserve the right to call you at three in the morning if Miss Piggy starts running through this house."

I RACED THROUGH an appraisal at a house in the popsicle district. It was as if I wanted it to be nighttime so I could see if Jazz really would sleep when Mister Rogers was in my house.

I was on the courthouse steps when my phone chirped. "Where you at?" Sergeant Morehouse almost growled.

"In my favorite building."

"So, you're here then?" He actually chuckled.

"Courthouse. Did you get my note?"

"Yeah. You sure you had the card in it? Evidence people here said the purse was out of your possession for such a short time they didn't look at your camera. Didn't even dust it."

I stopped on the courthouse steps and a man almost ran into me. I waved him a sorry. "I rarely take it out. I just plug the camera into Harry's or my computer. You know what this means?"

He sighed. "I hope that your memory ain't so good."

"It means someone, somehow, wanted to see if there were any pictures of that jewelry on the camera."

"And…?"

"There were."

"Crap."

I waited a couple of seconds, and then asked, "Now what?"

"Now I check to see if the damn camera card is here somewhere." He hung up with his trademark lack of goodbye.

I sat on a bench just inside the courthouse. Before I further insisted that the card had been in the camera I owed it to whatever evidence tech might be getting his tailbone chewed to be sure it had been in the camera. I couldn't remember taking it out since I developed Christmas pictures at the drug store in early January. It definitely was in there.

I looked around the main floor of the courthouse, wishing that one of the two police officers who just came in would walk up and hand me my camera card.

The Miller County Courthouse is not large, in keeping with its status as the smallest county in the state. The hardwood floors needed to be refinished, but a recent coat of paint made it look if not modern, at least fresh.

The previous courthouse on the site burned in 1919 or thereabouts. Uncle Gordon's mother was the county elections clerk at the time. She snuck into the burning building and shut a couple of heavy oak doors. It kept the fire from spreading to the area of the building that housed most of the records. Everyone who has to pay for a title search or does family history research owes her thanks.

My thoughts went back to the camera. After another minute I decided to put some of the Twelve Step teachings to work and stop thinking about something I could do nothing about. I walked into the Registrar of Deeds Office, not having much luck with that. Ten minutes later, I was concentrating so hard on the folder the Registrar of Deeds keeps on recent sales that I didn't hear George sidle next to me.

"It can't be that interesting."

I jumped. "Just disappointing. The buyer agreed to what seems like a fair price, but I can't find any comparable sales to support it."

"Other sales are for a lot less, you mean?" he asked.

"By several thousand dollars."

"Do you have to do it today?"

I turned to fully face him. "You doing an article on housing prices?"

"I was just thinking, with so many houses on the market, there could be a few sales in the next week or ten days that would let you support the price." He studied the thin spiral notebook he uses to make notes as he talks to people.

"That's not a bad idea. Maybe I'll wait until Friday." I felt like a sixteen year old waiting to get asked to prom.

"I wanted to see what you thought of a story idea," he said.

From the other side of the Formica counter, there was a decided cough. The clerk met my eyes and gave a tiny jerk of her head, indicating the office behind her, where the Registrar of Deeds sat. I nodded thanks and got off my stool.

George followed me into the hall. "It's like a Kindergarten class in there. You open your mouth and they tell you to pipe down." He opened his notebook. "There're a couple of stories that maybe got short shrift during Sandy."

Of course. His idea about things that may have been neglected because of the storm.

"One was a fire on Sand Castle Way, and the other was a pick pocket that paid visits to the last two auctions that Fitzgerald held just before Sandy." George cleared his throat. "You hear anything about either of those?"

"I remember the fire. What's so special about that?" I asked.

"Cause wasn't determined. State fire marshal thought it looked suspicious, but they couldn't document any accelerants or anything."

"Suspicious, how?" I asked.

"It started in the kitchen, which is pretty common. But they couldn't link it to a faulty stove or anything. In fact, the gas was off. Then a lot of what was left got blown away by the hurricane the next day, so they couldn't do as full an investigation as they normally would."

I couldn't imagine why he'd think I would have heard anything about the fire. "I don't even remember anyone talking about it, just that there were a couple paragraphs in the paper the morning of the day Sandy came ashore. And it was vacant, right?"

"And you didn't see anything in other vacant houses you appraised?" he asked.

I looked at him directly. "Like what?"

"Like when you found cigarette butts and soft drink cans in a house one time."

"Nope. What are you thinking?"

"There was a fire in another vacant house just last week. Usually the fire marshal can figure out a lot more than he can with these two. All he can tell is where they started, and there's no reason for a fire to start there either time."

"What part of the recent house?" I asked.

"That time in the living room, with curtains probably being the point of origin. There were curtains above the stove in the other house." He flipped a page in his notebook. "The fire marshal said the houses burned because they were old and frame. In a newer house, the curtains probably would have burned and then the fire might not have found any other fuel."

"Insurance, you think?" I had read about several suspicious house fires further south of us, but they were in houses that Sandy severely damaged. There were media speculations, never proven, that owners were wary of rebuilding and were trying to get insurance money.

"Didn't seem likely," he said, looking at a nearby wooden bench that was meant to hold people waiting to enter the small courtroom down the hall.

"Hey, why were there curtains if the houses were vacant?"

"The first home was for sale, and they had taken out almost all the furniture, but they were leaving blinds and curtains. Sandy damaged the second one and they didn't bother to take everything out."

"It doesn't seem like a lot to go on, especially with so much time between the fires."

"Yeah, that's what the local firefighters think. Still..."

"Unanswered questions," I said, smiling. "You hate those."

He flushed and started to say something, but I cut him off. "If I see anything I'll let you know."

"Okay, thanks." George turned and walked quickly toward the large oak doors that led to the street.

He was out the door before I could ask him about auction thefts, or whatever it was. Nothing he knew would likely explain why someone took my empty drawer, or whether he thought a purse thief took my camera card. I decided to keep that to myself for now.

I turned to go back to my notes, which I'd left in the Registrar of Deeds' office, when a thought occurred to me. This was the first time George had initiated a conversation with me in months. *He must really want something, and I'm not crazy enough to think it's me.*

MISTER ROGERS WAS very uncertain about getting in my car without Miss Piggy. They have ridden with me to go to the vet for shots or for a drive to the dog park at the edge of town. Always together. He gave me what I interpreted to be a questioning look.

"No vet, no shots." He didn't move. "You want to see Jazz?" He wagged his tail and gave a short bark.

"I'll be darned." I gave his back side a small push and he clambered onto the beach towel I had placed across the back seat. He sat very regally, as only a part-retriever can, while we rode the six or eight blocks to my house.

When the car came to a stop I turned to face him. "I have to put your leash on in here, so you don't get spooked and run." His tail thumped the back seat.

We were in the house in less than a minute. Less than ten seconds after we walked in, Jazz ran into the room so fast that she skidded on the hardwood floor and ran into Mr. Rogers' leg. He leaned over and gave her a huge lick, something she has never permitted. It was a struggle to get the leash off, because Mr. Rogers seemed as excited as Jazz was.

Jazz turned and walked toward the kitchen and he followed her. "Giving a tour?"

Ten minutes later they were both sitting on her round cat bed so I put a plastic table cloth next to it on the floor. Mr. Rogers got onto the tablecloth and laid his head on Jazz's bed and Jazz settled in next to his head.

So, I knew she really missed the dogs. The test would be when I tried to sleep the night through.

THE EXPERIMENT WAS successful. Jazz and Mister Rogers had let me sleep all of Monday night. *Now what?* I couldn't have a dog at the house every night. I had to hope that Jazz would calm down now that she knew she could continue to see the dogs.

The breakfast dishes were piled in the sink and I had the back door propped open so Jazz and Mister Rogers could wander in and out on this sunny Tuesday. Jazz could probably jump up to the top of the yard's chain link fence, but she likely would not. There were enough new things to explore in the small yard. And she's not stupid. She knows where she eats.

I blew dry my hair, still thinking about what to do to make Jazz happy. "It's ridiculous," I said aloud. "She's a cat. They adjust."

The back door banged into the wall and I turned off the hair dryer and walked into the kitchen. Mr. Rogers was sitting inside near the door, tail wagging. Jazz had her head in the small coat closet that was just inside the back door.

I suddenly remembered Mister Rogers' affinity for chipmunks. He had brought them, uninjured, into the Cozy Corner a couple of times. They stayed for quite a while. "Nuts." I edged Jazz out of the way with my foot and opened the closet door fully.

I didn't think I had put a black bag on the closet floor, so I bent over to look at it. If skunks can smile, I'd swear this one was grinning at me.

Chapter Eight

THE ANIMAL CONTROL officer did not laugh when he arrived. He said he had seen people sitting on their kitchen tables several times. He also said he thought he knew this skunk, and that she'd had her scent glands removed.

"How do you *know* a skunk?" I glanced at his name tag. Sam York, Animal Control.

He reached down to pet her, and I inched away. "Her name is Pebbles, and she belonged to Mrs. Peebles," he said.

"So…she used to live here?" *That's all I need. A skunk that wants to reestablish residency.*

"Mrs. Peebles was very sad about leaving Pebbles, so I told her I'd see if she could get acclimated to the wild again." He looked up at me from his position crouching next to the skunk. "She wouldn't have her defense mechanism, and she was used to being fed, so I wasn't sure if a release would take."

"So, where has she been?" I asked.

Jazz tried to poke her head under the skunk's tail, and it obligingly lifted its rump off the floor. Mr. Rogers kept his distance, head cocked.

"I took her home with me for a few days, to be sure she'd eat, and then I dropped her at that small wildlife refuge a couple miles from town. I went by every day and fed her once. They're used to eating two or three times a day. I figured if she got thinner, I'd know she couldn't hack it."

I looked at Sam. His worn blue jeans and multiple tattoos did not make me think of someone who made sure pets were safe. Then I looked back at the plump skunk. "Obviously she ate well."

"One day she didn't show up to be fed. I went back a couple of evenings. Once I thought I saw her with another skunk, but I couldn't be sure."

I stared at him. "I'm not sure I've ever seen a skunk in the wild. Except after they've been squashed and are on the shoulder."

He grimaced. "They aren't exactly nocturnal, but they keep out of humans' way. Anyway, Sandy came not long after that, and I was so busy trying to match dogs and cats with owners, stuff like that, that I couldn't look for her for a while."

He kept stroking her, and reached down so Jazz could smell his hand. Mr. Rogers kept sitting on his haunches, panting lightly. "When I went back, I figured she'd either died in the storm or found some skunk buddies."

"So, she survived the winter."

"Guess so. Female skunks tend to burrow together. They don't hibernate, but they go into torpor and just come out a few times to eat." He grinned up at me. "And then I guess she found her way back."

"Are you saying I have to keep her?" I realized I had almost shrieked. "Sorry."

"No, but they can be litter trained. Pebbles was, and I'm almost sure this is her." He frowned. "It's odd, because they don't really have a homing ability. I'm amazed she found her way back here. It's about three miles."

"Maybe she's been making her way slowly, or maybe she's been here for a while and just came in because of Jazz and Mister Rogers."

"They often make a den under a house or shed," he said. "You could look around."

I made a face. Pebbles had settled back down, sitting with her front paws in front of her. Jazz sat next to her, and I looked up at Mister Rogers. He was not as sure of the situation, but he went a bit closer and then looked up at me.

I stared at Jazz. Could Pebbles be a solution to Jazz's loneliness? *And what in the hell do you feed a skunk?* "Does she stay indoors all day?"

"You'd pretty much have to keep her in unless you were here and aware of her. Kind of like today, when the door was open." His face acquired a grim expression. "There are always people who would freak if they saw her out there. Somebody might hurt her. Mrs. Peebles always kept her in during the summer."

I sighed. "And if it doesn't work, just take her back to the sanctuary?"

"If it doesn't work, call me. I kind of like her, and she didn't seem to mind being alone while I was at work."

"You want her?" I asked, hopeful.

"I'd rather not unless I have to. I'm always bringing some injured dog or cat home." He stood. "If she gets scared, instinct will have her raise her tail to spray, but nothing comes out."

"A bit of good news," I muttered.

Sam told me that pet skunks ate a lot of vegetables and something called Skunkie Delight, which was a mixture of various grains. He also told me that it was important to keep the litter clean. "They won't go in a dirty box. I think Mrs. Peebles kept the box in that closet." He nodded to the closet where I had found Pebbles.

I groaned and retrieved Jazz's very small litter box from the bathroom and put it on a plastic trash bag in the closet. Pebbles immediately used it. Used it waaaay more than my little cat would.

"You probably need a bigger litter box for her." Sam left.

I DECIDED TO GO for all or nothing, and drove Mr. Rogers back to the Cozy Corner. Aunt Madge was still laughing when I left, and it honestly sounded like a cackle. Then I stopped at the store for a large litter box and a huge tub of litter. Jazz might like the skunk, but no way would she share her box.

By the time I was done I also had some unsalted rice cakes and cheap frozen vegetables. I was not about to buy her fresh broccoli. Then I realized I had better find some articles on skunk care. Maybe they could only eat fresh food.

"Crud!" I yelled and pounded the steering wheel with my fists. I didn't need a skunk traipsing through my new house.

The man in the car next to me waved, and I realized it was Bill Oliver. *Probably here visiting his parents.* We were sitting at a stop light. He used the button to roll his window down, so I did the same. "Have some kind of issue, Ms. Gentil?" He looked amused.

"Other than having to adopt a skunk for Jazz to play with, no."

Bill threw back his head and laughed. The light turned green and the car behind him honked. He was still laughing when he drove away.

At least I'd given Bill a laugh. He lost his younger brother not long ago. And he hadn't cackled the way Aunt Madge did.

I was anxious to see the condition of my house after Jazz and Pebbles had been alone for about forty-five minutes. They seemed very calm with one another, so I was hopeful.

There is no garage, but I had a small off-street parking area. It hardly qualifies as a driveway, but at least it gets my car off the street. I squinted at the porch as I took the litter and pan out of my trunk. Much of the small front porch was hidden by an overgrown honeysuckle bush. It looked as if someone was sitting on the porch swing, but at dusk I wasn't sure who it was.

At first I thought it might be Max, but a closer look told me it was Mr. Fitzgerald, and he appeared to be dozing. Perhaps he had decided he'd like to see how his cousin's former house looked now that I'd fixed it up more.

I left the heavy tub of litter next to my car and went up the short set of stairs. I was trying to think of how to awaken Mr. Fitzgerald without startling him when I saw the blood. A lot of blood. It ran down the side of his head onto the porch swing cushion.

Chapter Nine

I SAT IN MY CAR trying not to be sick. Mr. Fitzgerald's face had not looked peaceful. His grimace led me to think the blow that killed him really hurt. Not that it made much difference. He was dead either way.

"You doing better?" a woman's voice asked.

I looked into the concerned face of Dana Johnson. "So so, but definitely better than twenty minutes ago."

Dana had apparently been on patrol when the call came in, because she was at my house within two minutes of my finding Mr. Fitzgerald. By that time I'd been standing by my car, crying and trying to dial 9-1-1. My hands shook, and luckily someone else had beat me to the call. I supposed they heard me scream and saw me run off the porch looking freaked out.

"There's no need for you to sit out here. I can drive you to the station, or to your aunt's if you want. I think Sergeant Morehouse would be willing to talk to you there."

"I need to check on my, um, pets."

"It's just your cat, right?" she said this in a tone that implied there was no way I was going in my house.

I sighed. "Do you know Sam, the animal control guy?"

"Sure. Half the unmarried women in Ocean Alley have tried to snag him."

"He just introduced me to a skunk that used to…"

"Oh, good! You found Pebbles." Dana called over to Sergeant Morehouse, who seemed to be directing a patrol officer to look for something. "Pebbles showed up here." She looked back at me. "Just today, you mean?"

I nodded. *Am I the only person in town who didn't know Mrs. Peebles had had a pet skunk?*

Morehouse walked over. "You said you were only gone about forty-five minutes?"

"If that. Just enough time to drop off Mister Rogers at the B&B and get some food for the skunk."

"Did Fitzgerald bring the skunk earlier today?"

"No. Well, if he dropped her off he didn't tell me. She came in from the backyard with Jazz and Mister Rogers. Why would he have had her?"

"You know how on TV the cops say they're the ones who ask questions?"

I gave him what I hope he recognized as a look full of sarcasm.

He stared at me for a few moments and I could tell he was running through potential reasons I might be angry with Mr. Fitzgerald. I was fairly sure his gut would tell him I didn't kill the poor man, but he'd have to be sure.

"You know him well?" he asked.

"I don't think I met him before the auction last weekend, but if Aunt Madge said I met him when I was a kid I'd believe her."

"And you weren't expecting him?"

"No. Can I go see about Jazz and Pebbles? And I need to give Pebbles a bigger litter box."

Morehouse began to look amused, a side of him I rarely see. "I think Mrs. Peebles used some sort of tray she bought at the hardware store. Bigger than a litter box."

"How come everybody knows this skunk?" I asked, irritated.

"How many other pet skunks you know in Ocean Alley? And no, you can't go in yet, but in a few minutes you can go in the back door."

He walked away and Dana looked at me. "I'm going back to the guys to help look for whatever someone used to hit the poor guy. Did you call your aunt or Ramona or…somebody?"

She had been about to say George. "I'm calmer now. I'll call Aunt Madge."

Of course, there was no need. Harry's car honked and the tires screeched as he came to a stop. *I didn't know Aunt Madge could sprint.*

She stopped a few feet shy of me and looked at me critically. "Charlotte Evans called me. Why on earth didn't you?"

"Thanks for coming." It was better than saying something like, "Would you like to know how I am?"

"I'm going back to the guys," Dana said, and walked away quickly.

Aunt Madge moved to me and leaned down to kiss my cheek.

Harry walked to us. "You're okay. What on earth happened?"

I told them about finding Mr. Fitzgerald and that I'd been sitting in the car since the police arrived.

"When Charlotte called she said you were crying hard. You didn't even cry when you broke your wrist," Aunt Madge said.

"Which one is she, anyway?" I nodded to the small knot of people, mostly neighbors it seemed, who were behind police tape that had hastily been run from my porch to the street and across the yard to a tree at the corner of the small lot.

In response, Aunt Madge turned to the small group and called out, "Thanks, Charlotte."

The woman, who looked to be in her mid-forties, was trim and very attractive, with perfect blond hair. Her dark pink slacks and cream top indicated expensive clothes habits.

"No problem. Come over if you need to." She turned and walked toward the bungalow across from mine. Except it's not a bungalow anymore. It has a second story, with balconies in the front and back and a huge deck.

"She and her husband own that beachwear and souvenir shop just off the boardwalk," Aunt Madge said.

"Jolie!" A short woman who looked to be in her mid-sixties waved at me from the police tape and I walked over. I thought her name was Virginia, and I knew she lived behind me and over one. "How are the pets?"

"They're okay as far as I know. Did you hear Pebbles came back?"

She just stared at me, and a thin boy of about twelve who stood a few feet from Virginia said, "I thought she got snuffed in the storm."

"Apparently not. She showed up earlier today."

"I fed her when Mrs. Peebles was in the hospital for a couple of days," he said.

"Gee, I may talk to you about that sometime." I was anxious to get closer to the house. "Maybe…"

He interrupted. "I bet you don't know how she got her name, do ya?"

"I did kind of wonder." I studied him more closely. He had the look of every kid who wants you to guess a secret or answer a dumb knock-knock joke.

"Mrs. Peebles liked to tell everyone the vet mixed up her name and wrote Pebbles instead of Peebles on her chart, so she started calling her that."

"Nicholas…" Virginia said.

"But that's not true. Me and my brother started calling her that. We said when she pooped it looked like Pebbles." His grin was catching, and I smiled back at him.

"So she went with it, huh?" I asked.

"Yep, but we weren't supposed to tell why she called her Pebbles. She laughed at fart jokes, too."

Virginia looked mortified.

I asked, looking from one to the other. "Your grandson?"

"Oh yes. Visiting for spring break." She gave a weak smile.

"Thanks for that, shall we say nugget?" Nicholas whooped and I looked at Virginia. "I have to get back to Aunt Madge."

Virginia looked relieved when I walked away.

I walked toward Aunt Madge, glad to have had a diversion in the form of skunk naming protocols. She watched the police intently as they moved through the yard, and I touched her shoulder. "They said I can go in in a few minutes. I want to check on Jazz and Pebbles. Do you think they're all right with all those people in the house?"

"If not, Jazz is welcome at home, but I'm not sure about Pebbles." She eyed the medical examiner's van as it pulled up.

"I really don't want to watch a bunch of people peer at Mr. Fitzgerald's body." I felt suddenly cold, a reminder that April at the shore has no warmth when the sun gets low.

Harry came toward us. "Sergeant Morehouse will come by the Cozy Corner if you want. You can go in the back door and check on Jazz."

"And Pebbles," I added, as I got up.

"Pebbles?" he asked.

As I walked toward the back of the house I heard Aunt Madge say, "You aren't going to believe this one."

Two weeks ago, I had had the local locksmith, Margaret, rekey the doors and make them all work with the same key, except the back door. It had some kind of antique lock with a fancier key. The only copy was in a drawer in my kitchen, so I hoped the police had opened the door for me.

A uniformed officer, very young, had apparently been assigned to escort me. He walked in step with me as I moved to the back of the house.

"I'm Edgar Quinn." he said. "We met briefly when a bunch of us were carrying in all that donated food, you know, last fall."

No one needs to say "after the hurricane." We all know what we mean when we talk about things like home repairs or disaster assistance. He was referring to a truckload of supplies that the food bank in Lakewood had sent down two days after the storm.

"Oh, sure. But thanks for reminding me."

"You met a lot of people back then."

We had reached the back door, and I felt a lot calmer as I thought of the volunteers who had poured into the New Jersey beach towns last November. I took a deep breath. "There's nothing bad in here, is there?"

"Nope. The house was locked until you gave Sergeant Morehouse your keys, so we don't think the perp went inside. But if something looks out of place, tell me. Later on you'll probably want to go through everything to be sure your stuff is all there."

We entered through the unlocked back porch door. Jazz perched on the kitchen counter and made quite a fuss as I walked in. She's not allowed up there and she's not much of a meower, so

I could tell by her plaintive noises that she was very unnerved by the police who'd walked through the house. *Thank God I didn't have dirty clothes and dishes strewn around.*

I picked her up. "It's okay. Where's your friend?"

"Who…" Quinn began.

"Did they tell you about the skunk?" From his pained expression, I could tell no. "Sam said she doesn't have scent glands."

His expression cleared. "Sam would know."

There was a soft patter of additional paws and Pebbles appeared at the entrance to the kitchen. She looked at me and walked to the fridge.

"Got you trained," Quinn said.

"Actually, not yet. She just showed up today."

"Boy, you are having a day," he said.

"Not as bad as Mr. Fitzgerald," I said, softly. "I just picked up some food for her, but it's in my car. Sam said raw veggies and some grain stuff." I set Jazz on the floor, and received a quick swat in return. Tail in the air, she walked a few feet away from me.

I had some cauliflower in the bottom drawer of the fridge and pulled it out. I had no idea of portion size or how big a piece she could eat, so I took several florets and quickly crumbled them into one of Jazz's food bowls and set it on the floor. Pebbles walked over, smelled it, and began to eat.

"I guess I should look around."

The front door opened and Sergeant Morehouse walked in. "Where is she?"

I nodded to the kitchen floor, and he stared at her for a moment and shook his head. "We had more calls than you could ever guess about that damn skunk."

"She got out?" I asked, almost hopeful.

"No, people just saw her and thought she was wild and could spray. " He looked at Edgar Quinn. "You walked around yet?"

"No sir, just starting."

"Have a look." Morehouse glanced at me. "You doing better?" When I nodded, he started to say something else, but then his phone rang and he answered it.

Officer Quinn followed me through the living room and two bedrooms. Someone had closed all the blinds, for which I was grateful. At dusk, all the lights in the house glared. I didn't want half the town seeing every detail of my house.

The small rooms had little furniture. All I had in the second bedroom was a futon and the small card table with a chair in front of it. "Everything's here, as far as I can tell."

"Kind of what we expected," he said.

"Jolie." Morehouse's voice can be very authoritative.

I rolled my eyes at Quinn and he turned slightly so Morehouse wouldn't see him smiling.

Morehouse walked to the door of my bedroom, which I had just been inspecting. "Lieutenant Tortino said you could stay here tonight, but we both think there could be gawkers, so it might not be a good idea. Which means you will, of course."

"Hey. Speaking of gawkers, where's George?" I knew Scoobie worked in the college library and Ramona worked until six, but George never missed a big story, even if he wasn't the reporter on duty when the call comes in.

Morehouse grew somber. "Fire down at Perch and H Street." His phone rang again.

"Another vacant one?" I asked Quinn.

"Think so," he said. "You staying?"

"Yes." It was suddenly very important to me not to be driven out of my house the first week I moved in.

Chapter Ten

I DID LEAVE FOR A WHILE. I dropped Jazz at Aunt Madge's and told her I'd be back to get her later that evening. Pebbles and Jazz seemed okay together, but I didn't want to find out later that Pebbles was a bully if she'd been stressed. With any luck, Pebbles would remember where the litter box was.

I love Aunt Madge and Harry a bunch, but I didn't think I could sit and talk one-on-one to anybody for a while. Instead, I parked on a street just off the boardwalk and wandered down to Java Jolt, now back in its boardwalk location. I knew there wouldn't be many people in there at almost dinner time, and probably no one would ask me about Mr. Fitzgerald.

"Jeez, Jolie." Owner Joe Regan stared at me for a couple of seconds and then turned toward the large thermos on the counter. "Every time I turn around I gotta give you free coffee because you got into some kind of trouble."

Word travels fast. "Ah, the world is normal."

He looked at me, puzzled.

"If you're scolding me things aren't totally wrong. You're extra nice to me when I really mess up. Not that this was my fault."

He handed me a mug. He'd already put the right amount of cream in it and passed me a sugar packet. "It never is, according to you. I just talked to Fitzgerald a couple of weeks ago."

"Really? Did you know him well?"

"Nope, but right before I opened Java Jolt I asked him to look for coffee collectibles, you know, like an old grinder or mugs or something. Thought he might see something at one of his auctions and I'd head over there."

I looked around the coffee shop, and realized that in addition to moving the counter back so there was more room for customers, he had added several decorative things on small shelves that were now behind the counter. "You've done more just in the last couple of days. It looks good." I wanted to talk about anything but Mr. Fitzgerald.

"Ever since Father Teehan chewed my ass for cussing Sandy a lot, I've tried to remind myself it's worse south of here."

Joe is known for his sometimes grumpy view of the world, and for some reason he likes to give Scoobie a hard time, so I've never gotten real chummy with him.

I was about to reply when the door banged open. George, followed by Scoobie, came in.

"Where the hell have you been?" George asked.

I tamped down my anger. "I went down to Atlantic City to hang out in the casinos."

Joe grunted and Scoobie walked over and hugged me. It felt good.

"Sorry," George said, gruffly. "We were worried."

"You were," Scoobie said, as he gestured that we should sit at a table by the new glass picture window that faced the boardwalk. "I told you she always lands on her feet. Unless she's falling down the stairs, then I have to help her."

"Very funny." We sat at one of Joe's new tables.

George walked to the counter and ordered coffee for himself and hot tea for Scoobie.

"You are okay, right?" Scoobie asked.

"No." I wasn't going to pretend this was like getting a tooth filled. I could still see poor Mr. Fitzgerald's body in the porch swing.

George came back as Scoobie gave my shoulder a squeeze. "Morehouse said you looked okay," George said.

"Oh, I will be. It just, well, looked like it hurt." My voice was a whisper by the end of the sentence.

"He was a nice guy," George said, apparently not sure what to say if I was going to choke up. "A bunch of times a year he'd let people use him for charity auctions without charging them."

"Hey, there was another fire?" I asked.

"Yep. Same deal." In a low tone he gave Scoobie a thirty second summary of his efforts to see if the fires in vacant houses were linked. He turned to Joe. "If you want to hear, just walk over."

"Try not to be too big a jerk," Joe said, more like his usual self. He poured the dregs from a dirty mug into the sink behind the counter.

"But no obvious link?" I wanted to be distracted for a few moments. I thought George's idea of a connection between the fires was a stretch.

"Not yet." He looked at me directly and looked away.

"Hey, your other idea was the auction thefts."

"Yeah, but Fitzgerald wasn't too keen on that story going anywhere."

"That doesn't usually stop you," Scoobie said.

"Fitzgerald sort of implied he'd take legal action if I published something that deterred people from using his services, so I went into watch and wait mode," George said.

"So, was stuff still being taken?" I asked.

"Don't know. I heard about it originally from Lester, and I've been asking other people." I groaned and George continued. "One of Lester's customers had put a bunch of stuff in one of the group auctions and swore that he didn't get paid for all of it. Fitzgerald just kept telling the guy it must have gotten stolen or mixed in with another lot, and it would be found and credited to the guy. Either way, Fitzgerald wasn't willing to fork over any cash right then."

"I guess Lester would have told you if it had been resolved," I said. "Still…"

"I know where you're going with this, Scoobie said. "The drawer."

"More like the murder. Maybe some other people lost stuff and…"

My cell phone chirped and I looked at caller ID. "That's Morehouse's cell." I wished I didn't have it memorized.

"Jolie," he said, brusquely. "I think you better come back."

"Why...?" He had hung up.

"I hate it when he does that." Since he was speaking at full bellow, George and Scoobie had heard him.

"I'll go with," Scoobie said. "You coming?" he asked George.

"He already threw me off the property. He'll just say I went looking for Jolie to get around him."

I raised my eyebrows in amusement as we all stood and gathered up napkins and mugs.

"Okay, I did want to see if you were okay, all right?" George more or less stomped out ahead of Scoobie and me.

SCOOBIE AND I walked up the back steps and saw Sergeant Morehouse in the kitchen. "What's wrong?"

"What's wrong is Norman Fitzgerald got killed on your front porch." He saw my look of shock at his harsh tone, unusual even for him, and had the decency to look chagrined.

"But I called because Pebbles doesn't seem to want to be left alone."

I glanced to the floor to see she had her head on his pant leg.

"Isn't that special" Scoobie said.

"It ain't special. This skunk thinks it's a person. Always has." He scowled at me. "Anyway, you probably should take it with you, or stay here tonight." He looked at Scoobie.

"Yeah, yeah, I can bunk here." Scoobie glanced at me. "Like when Madge and Harry were on their honeymoon. Pretty soon people'll talk, you know."

"Not likely." Morehouse bent down to gently push Pebbles away and walked out.

"I think one of us was insulted," I said to Scoobie.

He grinned. "I wonder what Morehouse would say if I spread it around that he has a soft spot for skunks?"

I looked around my small kitchen, which I had painted a bright yellow. "I'm not sure I can ever walk in the front door again."

"I bet it'll be a while. Can I use your car to get some books from my place?"

"Sure." I dug the keys out of my purse. "Oh, I have food and a new litter pan for Pebbles in the car. Bring them in when you come back, would you? The police already brought in the new tub of litter for me."

"I bet there's a picture of Pebbles in the paper tomorrow." Scoobie left.

I wandered through the house, Pebbles at my heels. I supposed she was hungry, so I went back to the fridge and gave her some more cauliflower. She gave me what I interpreted to be a dirty look, and started eating.

Automatically I washed the couple of dishes in my sink, thinking all the while. Why would Mr. Fitzgerald stop by? *Maybe he found out who took the drawer.* But that didn't make sense. He would have dealt with the thief, not come to see me. Suddenly I remembered that he said he had not been in the house for years, but Morehouse had asked me if Fitzgerald had brought Pebbles to the house.

I called Morehouse. "Did Mr. Fitzgerald know Mrs. Peebles very well?" I asked.

"And you need to know this *now*, why?"

"Because you thought he might have brought Pebbles, and I think he told me he hadn't been here for…maybe decades."

"Humph." He paused for a couple of moments. "When did he tell you that?"

I relayed Fitzgerald's visit to return the drawer.

"You didn't tell me that." His tone was accusatory. "Who took it?"

"Don't know. Someone left it on the front seat of his truck, or van, whatever he had. Hey, where was his van?"

"Couple streets over," Morehouse said, slowly.

"Don't you think that's kind of odd?"

"Maybe, maybe not. Dana's asking people on that block to see if he was visiting them."

"What if…?" I began.

"Jolie, it's been a long day," Morehouse said.

"Oh sure. I suppose I'll talk to you tomorrow."

He grunted and hung up.

I looked at Pebbles, who had walked to where I sat on the rocking chair Aunt Madge had given me as a housewarming present. "Maybe you could teach him some manners."

She stared at me and wandered toward my bedroom. It occurred to me I didn't know where she used to sleep. It darn well was not going to be on my bed. I followed her.

Pebbles sat in a corner of the room and stared at me intently, if a skunk can do that. I pulled a towel out of the linen closet and placed it on the floor near her. She immediately sat on the towel and rooted around for a couple of moments to get comfortable.

I sat on my bed and kept thinking. If Mr. Fitzgerald, Norman as Morehouse had called him, parked a couple of blocks away, maybe he didn't want it to be obvious that he was stopping by.

But it wasn't dark then. If he really wanted to be low key he would have come later. Maybe he was walking by and realized someone was following him and came onto the porch looking for help.

I put my hand over my mouth. *Would he be alive if I had been home?*

There was a knock at the front door and I jumped. I stood slowly and peered out the front window. Aunt Madge stood there with a shoe box. Jazz!

I opened the door quickly.

She stooped and opened the box and Jazz ran out. She looked around the room and ran into my bedroom.

"She's been in almost a panic. She chased Miss Piggy to the third floor, and the dogs know not to go up there."

"Wow." My eyes had followed Jazz and returned to Aunt Madge. "I wasn't going to use that door for a while."

"I thought you'd say that. There's police tape around the swing but not on the stairs. It's like riding a bicycle." She sat her purse on the small table by the front door.

"What? Oh. I get it. Well, I hated riding a bike."

She shook her head slightly and looked around the room. "Looks the same." She sat at my small dinette table and I sat next to her.

"They don't think anyone came in," I said.

"What could he have been doing here?" she mused. "If I remember correctly, Norman's cousin or someone used to live here."

"I think he said his mother's cousin, and about thirty years ago."

"That makes more sense. She was quite a bit older than we are."

"Mr. Fitzgerald was about your age? I thought he was older."

"You're buttering me up." She patted my knee. "I know you'll be fine in a day or so, but are you sure you want to stay here tonight?"

"Scoobie went to get some books, and then he's coming back." When she looked relieved, I added, "But why would he be here today?" Aunt Madge always knows. I stared at her.

She shook her head. "Norman was outgoing in some ways. You'd have to be to get in front of a crowd all the time. But in his own way he was a very private person. I don't even think he went to St. Anthony's all that much."

Scoobie walked in as she was finishing her sentence. "Bet he wished he did when he got to the Pearly Gates."

I screwed up my nose at him. "Ugh."

Aunt Madge frowned, and then shook a finger lightly at Scoobie.

"Sorry." He placed his pile of books on the couch. "You doing okay, Madge?"

"Yes, Adam, thanks." Aunt Madge is the only one who calls Scoobie Adam. "Now that you're here, I'll head home." She pulled a tooth brush out of the side pocket of her purse. "I was actually going to offer to stay over if you needed me."

AT ELEVEN O'CLOCK, MY eyes closed as I read Sue Grafton's latest novel. Usually I stay up half the night with her books, which told me I was more tired than a boardwalk carnival worker on Memorial Day weekend.

Scoobie had shut the door to the other bedroom so Pebbles would stop wandering in. I got out of bed to turn out the light, and noticed that Jazz seemed to be fascinated with something near the bottom of the chest of drawers. There was a tiny corner of a piece of paper sticking out from behind the chest of drawers. She tried to paw it out.

I stooped to pick it up and had to fight her for it. When I finally had it, I saw that it was Norman Fitzgerald's business card, and my address was written on the back. It was a couple of seconds before I realized that the person who had killed Mr. Fitzgerald must have been in my house. I sat on the edge of the bed and then lay back and looked at the ceiling. After a few seconds Jazz jumped on the bed and stuck her nose on mine.

"No wonder you were scared." I moved her face away from mine and softly stroked her. I looked again at the card. It didn't seem likely that Mr. Fitzgerald would need to write down the address for himself, so he must have told someone else where I lived. Morehouse could probably compare the handwriting on the card to Mr. Fitzgerald's.

"Crud." If there had been fingerprints I'd probably obliterated them.

Chapter Eleven

WEDNESDAY MORNING I drove to the police station and waited for almost fifteen minutes before Morehouse came to the door that led back to the offices and waved me in.

As I walked into his office I thought it looked even smaller than other times I'd been there. Then I realized that another four-drawer file cabinet had been wedged into the room so that his desk now sat between two of them. My knees bumped into the desk as I sat in one of the two chairs across from it.

Before I went to bed last night I had put the business card in a plastic sandwich bag. I placed it on his desk without saying anything.

He looked at both sides of the card. "Where'd you get this?"

"A tiny corner of the card was sticking out from behind my chest of drawers last night."

"Son of a…my guys should have found that."

"I think Jazz had worked a bit to pull it out more."

"Maybe, but how did it get behind there in the first place?" He seemed to ask this more to himself than me.

I answered anyway. "Do you suppose it means they moved the chest of drawers?"

Morehouse didn't answer, but picked up the baggie and walked out of his office toward the open area where more junior officers sit. I figured someone was going to get chewed out, and took the moment to look at the notes on a small pad of paper on his desk.

There were three names. Two were crossed out so thoroughly that I couldn't read them. Not upside down anyway. The third name was underlined. *Clive Dorner. Why did that sound familiar?*

Morehouse walked back in and sat down. "Who is Clive Dorner?" I asked.

"Don't read the crap on my desk. That's police business."

"Then don't leave it on your desk when you have a guest."

He snorted. "Guest, are you? More like a pest I'd…"

"Hey, he called me the other day."

"What the…What do you mean he called you?"

"That telephone invention thing."

"Don't be a smart ass."

"It was at least ten days ago. I could check my phone. Clive Dorner said he wanted me to show him around town, he was looking for property." My tone of derision was probably obvious. "He wanted to buy houses and flip them, I think."

"You ain't a realtor." Morehouse stared at me intently.

"I am, but I haven't worked as one since I moved here. I referred Dorner to Lester, and then later I ran into the two of them at Burger King."

"So Lester knows this guy." He drew a circle around Clive Dorner's name.

"Just to show him around, I think. Who is the guy?"

"Norman Fitzgerald's nephew. Grew up in Ocean Grove, but moved away about twenty years ago, maybe more."

"Mr. Fitzgerald's nephew! What made him call me?"

"If I knew things like that I wouldn't be looking for him, would I?"

"But who is he?" I persisted.

"He buys properties, fixes them up fast, and tries to sell at a big profit. Flipping, like you said. Not usually here, though, as far as we know."

This still didn't tell me anything about the man. "Sooo, he was looking at houses here not just because of the hurricane, but because he lives near here, or something?"

"Only address I can find for him is in Philadelphia. Haven't found anyone here who knows him well. Who told him about you?"

I shrugged. "I don't know. Maybe he told Lester that. Did you know him before today?"

"Not me. One of the guys who knows him saw him at the courthouse the other day," Morehouse said.

"The courthouse. I suppose he could have been researching properties."

Morehouse grew impatient. I wasn't telling him anything he didn't know, apparently. "Dorner told the guy he was looking up houses with liens on them, looking for bargains."

"What a sleaze."

He shrugged. "We all wish things was how they were, but it's better to get the places fixed up than have them rot." He flipped a card in his Rolodex, apparently ready to get back to work.

Who still has a Rolodex of phone numbers? "Sergeant," I waited for him to look at me directly. "Someone was in my house."

"Maybe," he said, quietly. "Or maybe Fitzgerald wrote your address down so he could find you with that drawer thing, and it fell out of the back of the drawer or something."

"Or maybe not. I need to know…"

"I get that," he said, not being grouchy. "You want to know, but you are not to go poking into this. If someone was in your house, you don't want to run into them on your own." He pointed his finger at me. "I'll send some print guys over to check out the immediate area where you found the card."

"I touched everything." I felt frustrated at every turn.

He stood as if to dismiss me. "Somebody smart enough to get in without leaving evidence of entry probably wore gloves."

"That's comforting."

I DROVE BACK to my house and walked in the back door using the special key for its antique lock. I knew I'd have to use the front door again, but not yet.

Two sets of feet, eight altogether, padded across the hardwood floor in the living room into the kitchen. Jazz and Pebbles stopped at the edge of the room and then Pebbles walked to the fridge.

"You ate already." Jazz rubbed my ankle and I looked down at her. "Can you teach her to be less of a glutton?" In response, Jazz walked to her bowl.

With a sigh, I poured a few pieces of dry cat food into her bowl and a few Cheerios into Pebbles' bowl. Then I went o my bedroom.

I stared at the chest of drawers for about ten seconds, and then opened the top right drawer. I removed the scarves and gloves and placed them on top of the chest and took out the drawer.

It was not a big drawer, so I lifted it above my head and looked at the bottom. Nada.

I carried the drawer to my small dinette table and set it on the table and stared at it. Nothing looked odd, so I decided to get the other top drawer, which was on the left side of the chest of drawers. After emptying my underwear from that drawer I sat it on the table next to the right-side drawer.

The difference was immediately apparent. The drawers were the same length, but the drawer on the right side, that of the vanishing act, was almost half an inch less deep. A thin piece of balsa wood had been fitted into tiny slots that had been carved down each side, at the back of the drawer. An equally thin lid fitted over the extra space, probably with a hollow space beneath it.

It would be easy to hide something back there. Something like diamonds.

I wiggled the bit of wood that I thought covered a hollow space. It moved a little, but there was no way to raise it. There was just the slightest space between the side of the drawer and the inserted piece. Maybe my metal nail file would fit. I took it from my purse and slid it between the balsa wood and the side of the drawer.

Jazz now sat on the table top to inspect my work and Pebbles leaned against my leg. I pushed Jazz back, gently. She was interested enough in what I was doing that she didn't swat me. She moved to the edge of the table and stayed just out of easy reach.

After a few seconds of gently wiggling my nail file, the wood loosened and slipped into the recess. A glance told me it had been glued to the other piece, not fastened with a nail or screw.

I peered into the small space. If you put marbles in there they'd rattle, but a thin necklace or bunch of gems could be wrapped tightly in cloth and would not make a sound.

I sat on a dinette chair and stared into the drawer. Jazz was now sitting in the other one. It seemed that someone took the drawer from the auction site so they could check it. I'd probably never know who took it or if anything had been in the space. Or if Mr. Fitzgerald was killed because the murderer thought there was something still in the drawer and wanted to be sure they got it rather than Mr. Fitzgerald. It was maddening.

I SAT IN BURGER KING with Lester. I had looked for him, though I didn't tell him this. He had a cup of coffee and his traditional six packs of sugar. I had an iced tea and was really glad to have something cold to drink.

I could not get Clive Dorner out of my mind. If Dorner was related to Mr. Fitzgerald, maybe he knew something about whether his uncle had been on my porch because of the chest of drawers. But that didn't make sense. When Fitzgerald had the drawer, whether he'd been the person who originally took it or not, he could have looked at it. Maybe even taken something out of it.

On the other hand, if Mr. Fitzgerald knew something had been removed from the drawer, the murderer might not have known that. He (or she) may have wanted something valuable they thought was still hidden and been willing to kill to get it.

Speculation is pointless.

Lester had not known that Dorner was related to Mr. Fitzgerald but, as usual, he had something to say. "Haven't heard squat from the guy in more than a day. We was about to make an offer on a house on Ferry. Then nothing, blatto." He took his unlit cigar out of his mouth and pointed it at me. "You gave him to me. I took him to six places."

I am very familiar with Lester's work ethic. In fact, I admire it, especially because when he makes sales I usually get to do an appraisal. "I'm sorry, Lester. He sounded like someone who really wanted to buy."

Lester waved the cigar at me. "I know you wouldn't do me wrong, kid. We gotta find this guy."

I hate it when he says *we*. Lester fancies himself some sort of detective. He has helped me out a couple of times, so even if

I want to blow him off, I'm polite. "If I figure out where he is, you'll be the first to know." I did not say *we*.

"I even bought the guy a burger," he groused, and then changed tacks faster than a sailboat on a windy day. "Still pissed off at George?"

"Didn't Ramona tell you? It's the other way around." I grinned at him. "Unless you want to tell him to get over it."

"Guy's nuts. You're a great dame, Jolie." He didn't look at me as he said this.

Lester is maybe ten or twelve years older than Ramona and I, and he's a little too rough around the edges for me. "Thanks, Lester. I haven't even been divorced for eighteen months. I'm not really in the market."

"So, where should we look for this Dorner creep?"

I shrugged. "Maybe he just got busy. He could be the person who has to make his uncle's funeral arrangements."

"Didn't you say he was in your bedroom?"

"I said he *might* have been. It seems like too big a coincidence that he called *me*, his uncle is dead on *my* porch, somebody seems to have dropped Mr. Fitzgerald's card in *my* house, and Clive Dorner's not around."

He chewed on his cigar for a moment, and a woman two tables down said, "There's no smoking, you know."

Lester eyed her. "Which is why it ain't lit, lady."

Such tact.

He looked back at me and in a low tone said, "She must know my ex-wives."

I stood. "Thanks for talking to me."

"Where ya goin'?"

"Probably to the office." This was not true. I planned to go to the library, but I wasn't going to say that to Lester. He'd tag along.

"Gettin' a lot of work?" he asked.

"Some, but not enough. Sell Clive Dorner something and I'll get more."

THE LIBRARY HAS PAST issues of the *Ocean Alley Press* on microfilm, which is helpful because it isn't online. It Is also a quiet place to think. It's not that the Cozy Corner and my new house are noisy, but Jazz, and now Pebbles, can be quite the distractions. Plus, if there were dishes in the sink or the bathtub was dirty, I felt compelled to clean.

As I walked into the library I was again struck by how different it was than when I went to school in Ocean Alley in eleventh grade. Huge file catalogs had been replaced by two computers that had searchable indexes for books or whatever else the library had to offer.

More computers, these for patrons to use to access the Internet, stood along one brightly painted wall. In eleventh grade, there were just a couple of computers, and the Internet connection was really slow.

Before I checked the *Press's* digital index, my guide to the microfilm copies of older papers, I did a quick web search for Clive Dorner. His name came up as a licensed realtor in Pennsylvania, which I didn't think Morehouse knew but would surely find out.

However, I couldn't seem to find Dorner affiliated with a particular real estate agency.

I switched to the *Ocean Alley Press*. Dorner was on the *Press's* short list of New Jersey residents who graduated from LaSalle University the year he finished. That explained why he moved from Ocean Grove to Philly. *Not that an explanation was required.*

That was all there was in the *Press*. I didn't expect much, since he'd lived in Ocean Grove. The one helpful thing was his father's obituary. It mentioned that Clive was the only child of Stanley G. Dorner and his late wife, Norma (Fitzgerald) Dorner.

It also named two Fitzgerald brothers-in-law as survivors, one of whom was Norman. Both of the in-laws lived in Ocean Alley. I glanced at the date of the obit, which was fifteen years ago. Though the auctioneer had been alive until last night, the other man could have passed away. And I found his name in the *Press's* obituary index, so there would be no information from him.

So, Norman Fitzgerald appeared to be Dorner's mother's brother. *Norma and Norman. Maybe they were twins.*

I had spent a lot of time each summer with Aunt Madge, perhaps Dorner was here a lot with his mother's relatives. He had never mentioned any ties to Ocean Alley, but there really wasn't any need to do that. Still, when I sold real estate in Lakewood I spent a lot of time with potential buyers. Usually they would mention something if they knew the town or any people in it.

Dorner had something to hide. But what? And where is he?

Getting my house ready for move-in and then finding Mr. Fitzgerald had pushed the purse thief to a back corner of my mind. Clive Dorner made me think of the diamonds and gold bracelets and whether the purse thief knew about them. Dorner had called soon after I found the jewelry. He was slim enough to have been the purse thief, but could he move that fast?

"That's ridiculous." Then, since there was nothing useful about Dorner in the newspaper's archives, I used search terms like burglary and stolen jewelry.

There were too many items for burglary, even when I narrowed it down by searching for diamonds and dates of twenty to forty years ago. I thought that could be when the stuff was placed behind my walls.

I stared at the screen, my thoughts flitting from jewelry to Jazz and Pebbles to Clive Dorner to poor Mr. Fitzgerald. The chest of drawers was from Fitzgerald's auction of Mrs. Peebles' things, and Fitzgerald brought the seemingly stolen drawer back to me. The auctioneer had been related to Clive Dorner. A distant cousin of Mr. Fitzgerald's had lived in my house. He could also have known Mrs. Peebles. *Damn.* I had forgotten to ask Sergeant Morehouse why he thought Mr. Fitzgerald may have had Pebbles.

I did another search of the *Ocean Alley Press* index, this time looking for Norman Fitzgerald's auction company. I didn't know the formal business name, but it popped up quickly— Beach Treasures and Trash. *No marketing consultant helped with that name.*

Since the first article was from almost forty years ago, the business could have been formed about then. Aunt Madge would probably know. What was more interesting was that he had had a partner, Francis Xavier Murphy. The only local person I knew named Murphy was an elderly woman who had a good sense of humor and liked to read mysteries. I had visited her in her apartment more than a year ago. Mrs. Murphy was a widow, but had two daughters who I thought lived in or near Ocean Alley, with their children.

"That would be too big a coincidence."

George slid into the chair in front of the second microfilm machine. "But you won't know until you check it out."

"True." I spoke carefully, not wanting to seem overly pleased to see him.

"I might be able to help you on the Fitzgerald thing," he said.

"Oh, are you okay?"

"As much as a person can be the day after finding a nice man dead on her front porch." I crossed my arms in front of me and kind of hugged myself. "Help how?"

He pulled out his ever-present reporter's notebook. "You know who his partner was, before that guy died?"

"Francis Xavier Murphy."

He gave me a look bordering on respect. "Not bad."

"Is Mr. Murphy's wife in that really small assisted living building that's in town?" I asked.

"Yep. You know her?"

"I visited her last fall." I avoided saying I sought out Mrs. Murphy because I thought George was all wrong on a story he was doing at the time.

George gave me a slightly quizzical expression and continued. "I talked to Father Teehan this morning. He said that the two guys were in business for decades, but that the last few years before Mr. Murphy died, which was maybe ten years ago, Father thought they'd had some sort of falling out. After some point, you never saw them work together at an auction, and they never sat together at coffee after Mass."

In a town like Ocean Alley, those were strong hints of disaffection. People usually put aside disagreements at church. "Did Father Teehan know why?"

"People don't gossip too much to a priest. You could talk to Madge or, since you know her, Mrs. Murphy."

I raised an eyebrow at him. "Are we friends again?"

He appeared to have hoped this question would not arise. "We're always friends. Sometimes I'm just more pissed off at you than usual."

"Now see," a woman's voice said, "that's why you have to keep it low in a library." Daphne shook a finger at him. "Not everybody wants to hear who you're mad at, George."

"Plus," I grinned at her, "a lot of people already know he's mad at me."

George rested his head on his folded arms for a moment. "This is almost like when you and Ramona gang up on me."

"I love a challenge," Daphne said, but very quietly. She sat on the edge of the table I was in front of. "I heard a couple things about Mr. Fitzgerald and Mr. Murphy."

George raised his head, on full alert.

"Like what?" I asked.

"Seems Mr. Murphy thought he might not be getting his full cut from some of the auctions. But I don't think there was proof."

"Seems like something they could have proven one way or the other," George mused.

"They have a full inventory of everything when they start bidding. And if you win a bid they give you a receipt that shows not just what you paid but the inventory number for what you bought." I knew this from seeing the list of items Mr. Fitzgerald had worked from at the recent auction, and from my own receipt.

"And it's probably audited," Daphne said.

I remembered that she was not only the only black cheerleader in high school, but the only girl on the math team.

"And there's not likely a chance they'd let me look at old records," George said, glumly, "if they even exist."

"Maybe Mrs. Murphy can authorize something," I said. "But, it still seems a stretch to see a link between them falling out years ago and Mr. Fitzgerald's murder."

There was a ding from the area near the check-out desk, and Daphne left to wait on a library patron.

After about fifteen seconds, George asked, "So, who calls her, you or me?"

"If you don't know her, better be me. As long as Aunt Madge doesn't find out. Morehouse always tells her when he orders me not to look into something."

George grinned. "Never stopped you before, did it?"

Chapter Twelve

MRS. MURPHY WAS AS pleased to have a visitor when I stopped by on Thursday as she had been a year or so ago. She looked a bit more stooped with age, and her small apartment in the assisted living building was more cluttered, but not messy. There were several books on the small dining table and sweaters were draped on her recliner and a couple of dining chairs. The overall impression was one of coziness.

"And how is Madge? I kept meaning to send a card to them when they were married, but you know how it is. Best laid plans of women and wombats."

I was again reminded that I liked Mrs. Murphy's independent nature. "I'll tell her and Harry that you said hello."

She offered me iced tea. "But you'll need to pour it yourself. These old hands aren't too steady." Mrs. Murphy made her way to a recliner, her walker making gentle thumps as she raised and lowered it with each step.

I declined the tea and sat across from her. "I wanted to ask for your help with something, but if the topic is too uncomfortable, just say so, okay?"

"Norman Fitzgerald died on your front porch," she said, in a quiet tone. "I despised that man, but I don't wish murder on anyone."

I wasn't surprised that she had figured out what I was interested in. Mrs. Murphy had more of her faculties than some people half her age. "You're right, that's my topic. It's okay?"

She nodded, but I couldn't read her passive expression. I plowed ahead. "A couple of weeks ago, when I was fixing up the house I bought, I found a small pouch of jewelry behind one of the walls."

She looked at me more directly. "I can't say I'm surprised."

"Really? I was." I gave her a quick smile. "I wondered…"

"Could you tell how long it had been there?" she asked.

"I have an idea, but it could be way off. That section of wallboard was newer than some of the rest. Scoobie and I thought it was maybe twenty years old, it could have been older."

She looked thoughtful. "That could mean he was skimming a lot earlier than my Francis thought. If Norman was the one who put the pouch there. Who owned the house before you?"

"Moira Peebles, but only for about fifteen…"

"Oh! Did you find Pebbles? I heard she might have bought it during the hurricane."

What is it with this skunk? "Actually, she found me." I described how Pebbles had wandered in with Jazz and Mister Rogers. "And Sam, the animal control guy, said it was really funny, because they don't usually find their way back, like a dog could."

"She probably didn't. Did you talk to Virginia Mulligan?"

"Virginia? Oh, a Virginia lives in the Cape Cod sort of behind me. Is that who you mean?"

"Yes. She turned the top floor into an apartment and rents it out. She always liked that skunk."

"But she didn't have it, did she?" I asked.

"Virginia gets around just fine, and everyone knew that Sam fellow took Pebbles to the wildlife area. I bet Virginia went out and got her before Sandy got here. Pebbles would have gone right to her."

I stared at Mrs. Murphy for a moment. "I guess I'll have to ask her."

"Now, you said it was Mrs. Peebles' house. That makes sense, because some aunt or cousin or somebody related to Norman owned it before Moira."

"Mother's cousin I think. He told me."

She spoke sharply. "You talked to him the day he died?"

"No, Ma'am. He stopped by to return, well, it sounds funny, but return the top drawer of a chest of drawers I bought at an auction. Someone had stolen it after I won the bid. Or at least taken it, whether they meant to keep it I don't know." I did not tell her about the hidden space.

She shook her head slightly. "So many shenanigans at that auction house."

"Shenanigans that would make someone angry?" I asked.

"Humph. Francis and I were certainly angry. Francis was convinced that a few things that seemed to have been pilfered from the auction tables actually ended up in Norman's pockets. Ultimately, his bank account."

"What kinds of things?" I asked.

"Usually small things. A Cartier watch, which should never have been on a table. Things on the tables were generally not all individually inventoried. Valuable items were generally in a locked case so no one could walk off with them before the bidding started. Francis said later he thought the watch was listed as being on a table so it would appear that someone took it. And let's see, an engagement ring, a child's comb and brush set made of ivory. Lots of little things."

I thought about this. There were probably many items that Mr. Murphy did not know about. Maybe the diamonds in the small pouch were taken from several rings. "And your husband discussed this with Mr. Fitzgerald?"

"Discuss would be mild," she said, grim expression grim. "My Francis was not a violent man. He was going over some paperwork at home one day and realized that watch had not made it to the auction block. He was so angry when he left to find Norman that I was afraid he would get in trouble for hitting Norman, or doing something worse."

"Did your husband compile any list of vanished objects?" I asked.

"Not that I know of. After he died I sorted through Francis' personal files myself. I didn't see anything like that, though I didn't go through every piece of paper."

That reminded me that I wanted to ask Mrs. Murphy if she had any old auction files. "Could I possibly see…?"

"What was in your pouch?" Mrs. Murphy asked.

"Several loose diamonds, three gold bracelets, and some others that were some kind of plastic," I responded.

She nodded. "Probably bakelite. Popular, oh, twentieth century, up until the war. It's an odd form of plastic, and it's not worth a lot, though you should check eBay or something to see what it's selling for now."

"I never heard of it."

"Why would you? Unless Madge or your mother had some. Ask Madge."

"Um, I might."

She laughed. "Madge doesn't know you're here, does she?"

"No." I gave her a weak smile. "I'm not going to ask you not to mention it, but…"

She waved her hand to interrupt me. "I won't see her, and she won't ask me. What are you trying to find out?"

"Why someone killed Norman Fitzgerald on my front porch. It was a very hard thing to see him sitting there like that."

"I'm sure it was," she said, quietly.

"The thing is, a lot of people talked about him as this nice guy who did charity auctions, and donated to St. Anthony's and other places. It makes sense that he might be the one who hid the jewelry, but no one seems to say negative things about him."

She shrugged. "People change, I suppose. Maybe he stopped stealing from his clients, not that anyone except Francis figured it out. Or maybe he just kept his ill-gotten income really quiet."

"Do you know if there was any old paperwork related to the business that I could look at?" I asked.

"You know, my daughter reminded me that if Norman ever sold the business we were supposed to get something." Her smile was bitter. "I hadn't thought much about it because that business provided a good income for us for years, but there weren't assets other than what was about to be auctioned."

"And that wouldn't be much, unless he had a big sale coming up. Just whatever commission or whatever you called it after the sale…Oh. I suppose the business could be sold based on its reputation. There could be money from that sale."

"Ah, yes," she sighed. "I'm to a point where I just don't want to stay angry about it all, but I suppose I need to check."

"And if there is some paperwork, could I, uh, maybe look at it?"

She smiled. "You're as smart as your aunt. But a bit more devious. I think any auction files Francis had are long gone. I have no idea if Norman Fitzgerald had heirs or if they get a portion of the business. My daughters can look into it."

That reminded me of one more thing. "Did you know Mr. Fitzgerald's nephew, Clive Dorner?"

She thought for a moment. "I don't think so. There were a couple of Dorners in Ocean Alley many years ago, but I don't recall a Clive."

Mrs. Murphy didn't ask me why I wanted to know, and she was beginning to look tired. I thanked her for talking to me and had stood to walk out when I noticed a photo of a woman and three young children on her bookshelf, one of many framed pictures. This one was a bit bigger than the others, so it stood out. "She looks familiar."

"Oh, that's Patricia, my daughter, and her children. You might have met her after that funeral, the first time we met."

I nodded slowly. I had steadied Mrs. Murphy on a walker after a child had knocked into both of us. I'd ended up throwing away a silk blouse because red Jello is not forgiving. "There were a bunch of people there. I remember you of course." *And I just met Patricia in the store where she works sometimes.*

"Oh, it was a work day for her. She was in the hall some of the time. On her phone thing that gets the Internet."

"I used to have one. Kind of felt like it was tattooed to my hip when I lived in Lakewood." On impulse, I stooped and kissed her cheek. "Thanks for talking to me."

Chapter Thirteen

I AM NOT A BIG FAN of funerals, but I'm even less a fan of finding dead people on my porch swing. Norman Fitzgerald's funeral was to be held on a balmy Friday, and he was certainly someone I knew, even before the porch swing. Besides, maybe something someone said would give me a hint about why someone killed him. Or at least what he was doing on my porch when he was killed.

Catholic Masses are very long, so I adapted a habit of George's and took cookies with me. I could already feel the Fig Newtons crumbling in my pocket. *I should have brought dried apricots.*

Aunt Madge had declined to attend. She said nothing about me going to the funeral of someone I barely knew, likely figuring a death on my porch would trump any charge of me not minding my own business. Scoobie was in class and Ramona was working, so I sat in a pew near the back of the church by myself.

St. Anthony's is the largest church in Ocean Alley and its new building is only a few years old. Its main section has about thirty long pews on each side of the center aisle, with fewer pews in the two transepts that go off to each side near the front. No other church in town has the side sections, which I thought of as wings.

I was trying to read a plaque near the Baptismal Font saying who had donated to it when George slid partway into the pew with me. He whispered, "You need to move further up. You stick out like a dead fish on the beach."

"You could have left out the dead part," I grumbled. I saw him give a small smile, which was immediately gone, probably because smiles are not the best things to wear to a funeral.

We settled in a pew about ten rows back from the altar. It was the last row of mourners now, but probably would not be in a couple of minutes. I glanced at George. Even at Aunt Madge and Harry's wedding and a prior somber occasion I had not seen him wear any kind of shirt other than a collared Hawaiian-style shirt. He did own a couple in darker colors.

Today George had on a rust colored, long-sleeved dress shirt, plus a tan tie with letters on it. Another sideways glance told me the letters were OAHS, which stood for Ocean Alley High School. "School spirit at a funeral?" I asked, quietly.

He gave a short grunt. "Hand painted. She sells them on the boardwalk some summers, and it's my only tie."

The she had to be Ramona, and I wondered why I hadn't seen anyone else wearing them. *You're at a funeral. Quit thinking about other stuff.*

An altar boy lit candles, so it would not be long before Father Teehan started the Mass. I looked at the backs and profiles of the people in front of me, several of whom talked to the people next to them in low voices. Many were older.

"Move on over," said a man's voice.

"Lance, hi," I whispered. George moved further into the pew, and I followed.

A glance at Lance told me he still looked more tired and worn than he had before Hurricane Sandy. An online article I read said that recovery could take a more emotional toll on the elderly than younger people. Something about knowing they might not be around long enough to recoup all they lost, even if they rebuilt.

The article didn't talk just about money. In some of the harder-hit communities, many people moved inland, if only until homes were rebuilt. Friends would scatter, and life could be very different when they returned.

Lance patted me on the knee and glanced around the church.

He surely knew a lot of people. I saw the owner of the hardware store, the woman who worked in the office at Silver Times Senior

Living Complex, my friend Jennifer Stenner, several people from First Prez, and Dr. Welby. There were few others I could name. More that I could not name but had seen around town or picking up food at Harvest for All. One thing you could say about Mr. Fitzgerald, he knew people from all walks of life.

Just before Father Teehan came to the altar, a small group of family came down the aisle and sat in the first two rows. Clive Dorner was among them, looking very solemn. Apparently he had not been as hard to find as Sergeant Morehouse thought he might be. Idly, I wondered if Lester had badgered Dorner about buying a house, or if Lester gave potential buyers a break if a family member died.

I knew none of the others in the first two rows of pews. From Mr. Fitzgerald's obit I had learned that his wife had died more than thirty years ago and they had lost an infant daughter, but had no other children. His only survivors were several nieces and nephews and their children. That seemed sad, but when I remarked on this to Aunt Madge she said she had decided it was better to outlive your friends than to have a lot of them around to mourn you.

A couple of minutes later I remembered her only family survivors, besides Harry, would be nieces and nephew and their children. *Good one, Jolie.*

A throat cleared behind me, and I turned to see Sergeant Morehouse and Lieutenant Tortino. I knew they both worshipped at St. Anthony's, and I remembered that Sergeant Morehouse sold Christmas trees on the church lot every holiday season. I wondered if Mr. Fitzgerald had also done that.

I gave the two police officers my four-fingered wave before I turned to face the front of the church again. Lance shifted his position and I noted his small smile.

George whispered, "They could probably get you thrown out if you don't behave, you know."

I figured he was kidding.

Father Teehan said a number of short prayers and such. Masses were way longer than services at First Prez, and it was some time before he went to the pulpit to give his brief sermon. I could feel the Fig Newtons getting soft in my pocket, but with Sergeant Morehouse behind me I decided to let them get gooey. Besides, if I made a mess George would never let me forget it.

"As we gather to celebrate the life of Norman Matthew Fitzgerald," Father Teehan began, "let us take time to remember the many good deeds he did in our community. Some you know about, such as his willingness to use his auctioneering skills for many local charities, including St. Anthony's."

"Others you may not know. And if he were here, Norman would be red-faced because I am going to name a few of those. And the red would be anger at my telling of his good deeds, not embarrassment."

There were a couple of quiet chuckles, and then Father Teehan began listing Mr. Fitzgerald's efforts on behalf of children who had no school supplies (large annual donations to the Salvation Army, which distributed backpacks of supplies each August), donations to a large group home about ten miles away that housed young women who were pregnant and had no other means of support, and a formerly anonymous donation to the hospital when it needed to refurbish its pediatric wing.

George took notes, and I discreetly glanced around the church, at least the church I could see without turning around. There were looks and murmurs of surprise as Father Teehan named the many recipients of Norman Fitzgerald's largess.

Lance said, softly, "I had no idea."

I bet Mrs. Murphy would have an idea of why Norman Fitzgerald had so much money to give away.

I thought Mr. Fitzgerald's anger would be because people might question where he got the money. Unless there was substantial inherited wealth, and I hadn't heard anyone talking about it, it seemed that Mr. Fitzgerald must have hidden diamonds in a lot of places.

But how would he have gotten cash for the things he stole? It didn't make sense that he had gotten the money locally. Surely someone would have wondered where he had gotten all that jewelry or any other expensive item he wanted to sell.

Really, this was no different than laundering drug money, just perhaps something on a smaller scale. So who did Norman Fitzgerald know who did not live here and might have the ability to essentially serve as a fence? As this question meandered across my brain, Clive Dorner stood in response to Father Teehan's request that others could feel free to offer comments on Fitzgerald's life.

Philadelphia would be a larger market to sell stolen goods. Heck, most antique stores would take valuables on consignments, and there was always eBay. Of course, that made the sales more public, but if the seller used an assumed name…

"Thank you for gathering in Uncle Norman's memory," Dorner began. "There was no more generous soul than Norman Fitzgerald, and I'm not just talking about the many financial donations he made to various groups."

So what are you talking about?

Dorner said that his uncle had lavished attention and occasional financial assistance on his nieces and nephews. He described summers spent with "Uncle Normy and Aunt Gertie" and how he would never forget those happy times.

I felt nauseous. It wasn't just the idea that a lot of Fitzgerald's donations could have been made at others' expense, it was the syrupy tone that Dorner, and later a cousin, used to discuss their uncle. It was more like they were talking about someone nominated for Catholic sainthood than a kind uncle.

There was a general shuffle in the crowd, and people got to their feet to begin the post-sermon rituals. I followed George's lead about when to kneel *(I should have brought a cushion)* and when to stand to let others go to the front to get Communion. I knew Lance and I could not partake here, though I was getting kind of thirsty and would not have minded a sip of the wine.

George returned from Communion and knelt for a moment in silent prayer, and then sat down, fairly close to me. I had given up on the kneeling thing; Lance had not even tried. "Pretty big donations, don't you think?" he whispered.

I nodded. "More than I would have thought possible. And all to groups related to kids." That thought had just moved to the front of my brain. *Does that mean anything?*

Sergeant Morehouse and Lieutenant Tortino returned from Communion, so George and I did not talk again until the service was over.

"A very generous man," Lance said, as we walked into the bright sunlight of a warm late April afternoon.

George had moved away to talk to a few mourners, probably getting a couple of staid quotes if his editor wanted an article. Because of the murder, and now the surprise of the number of donations, he probably would.

"Did you know him well?" I asked.

"He was a good bit younger than I am, maybe fifteen years, and of course he didn't go to First Prez." Lance nodded at two women who passed in front of us. "We both used to belong to the Lions Club here, but neither of us was terribly active."

"Were you surprised at, well, I guess you'd say his wealth?" I asked.

"Surely. He did a lot of nice things for local charities, but I thought he gave more of his time than his wallet."

I thought I had learned all that I could from the funeral and declined George's offer to ride to the cemetery with him. Sharing information was one thing, but pretending like we were dating again would just encourage some of my wishful thinking. Though I had to admit, I had much less of a sense of loss than I had even a few weeks ago.

Chapter Fourteen

SATURDAY WAS EIGHT-THREE degrees and the air felt as if a swamp had descended on Ocean Alley. In August, a day in the eighties would be a treat. But in April?

I opened the windows in the office I shared with Harry and then looked around on the first floor of his house to see if I could find a fan. Nada. I decided that even if he was married to Aunt Madge, it was too intrusive to go to his second floor. Harry's former bedroom and a small study were up there, plus two other rooms he was still refurbishing.

I periodically used a file folder as a personal fan as I sat at the computer entering data into the software. I loved that I could enter measurements and the computer would spit out floor plans far more professional looking than any I could draw by hand.

Despite feeling clammy and wishing Harry would come over so he could turn on his central air for the first time this year, I was in a good mood. Lester had faxed information on two houses I could appraise this week, and another real estate agent had called to say she thought she would have one at the end of the week. After months of slow sales, things were looking up.

The last person I expected to see when I answered the doorbell was Clive Dorner. "Well hello." I stepped aside to let him in. Hardly anyone comes to Harry's and my home office. There is no need to. Our work takes us to the houses we appraise.

"Thanks, Jolie. Harry around?"

That relaxed me. Dorner wasn't looking for me. "He's supposed to get here anytime. I can call to see if he's left the Cozy Corner yet."

"No need. Do you mind if I wait?"

"No problem. You're in luck. He just bought a sofa for the living room." Harry had had almost no furniture on this floor except in the office. Why he bought a sofa now that he mostly stayed with Aunt Madge was one of those questions I didn't bother to ask.

I joined Dorner on the couch, two cushion-lengths away from him. "I hope yesterday went as well as it could for you."

"Funerals are never something you look forward do. Because of the way he died, Uncle Norman's was especially hard."

And yet you're calling on Harry only one day later.

"Of course," he continued, "it would hardly have been easy for you."

I nodded. "It is a…difficult memory."

"I hope you lose it quickly." His tone was very formal.

As if.

He looked around the large room. At some point what had once been a formal living room had been divided, but Harry had taken down the dividing wall and had someone patch the floor and sand the entire room.

"Is Harry about to refinish the floor?"

What I wanted to do was ask what he was doing here, but instead I simply said, "Yes, as soon as he can find someone. So many of the local contractors are working further south." Then I thought of something. "Did you go south, to Philly I mean, after he died?"

His look said he thought I was minding his business. *He should talk.*

"I did leave for a day. It seemed so unbelievable. He was such a gentle man, to die that way…"

His voice trailed off and I felt like an idiot. *What do you care if Morehouse couldn't find Dorner immediately after his uncle's death? Or if Lester was ticked because he couldn't get hold of Dorner?*

"I'm sorry," I said, meaning it. "I was in Sergeant Morehouse's office the next morning, and he wanted to be sure you knew about your uncle."

"He has been very helpful." After a few seconds of awkward silence, he seemed to get to why he was here. "Does Harry ever give bulk discounts?"

It was such an unexpected question I almost laughed. "You know Lester. He's never been able to talk Harry into a cheaper rate. I kind of doubt Harry would do it for someone else, but by all means ask him." Before he could say anything, I added, "We are less expensive than Stenner Appraisals."

"Lester did tell me that." He flashed what he probably thought was a disarming smile. "Never hurts to ask."

"Are you thinking of buying a number of houses?" I asked.

"I am. I'm getting tired of living in Philadelphia, and Ocean Grove houses are ridiculously over-priced." He frowned. "It has some beautiful neighborhoods, which Ocean Alley really doesn't."

I kept myself from responding. All of the property in Ocean Grove is owned by the Methodist Church, and homeowners essentially buy long-term leases rather than the property itself. To compare real estate in Ocean Alley to Ocean Grove is like comparing Philadelphia slums to San Francisco.

"Of course, Ocean Alley has its charms." He said this quickly, as if he sensed my internal defense of the town.

I gave him a tight smile. "Still on the lookout for those bargains, are you?"

"Lots of houses for sale. Someone has to buy them."

I sensed false cheerfulness on his part. "I guess it's better that someone buy them than they continue to deteriorate."

He nodded. "Exactly. It can't always be people who want to live in them while they work on them."

I decided to push this conversation toward something I wanted to know about. "I didn't know your uncle at all well, but from what I heard after the funeral yesterday, no one seemed to know what a wealthy man he was."

Dorner adopted a somber expression. "He was generous with family members, but none of us knew he had that kind of money."

He flashed a smile. "Better to find out that than learn you have to pony up for the funeral."

I wanted to tell him to have some respect, but since I sometimes have none, I simply asked, "Where do you think he got it?"

Someone else might have told me to mind my own business, but Dorner just shrugged. "Don't know. I'm his executor, so I may know later."

"Not that it's my business." When he didn't say anything, I added, "I wish I had had a chance to know your uncle better. He came by my house the other day, but it never occurred to me that would be the only time I'd really talk to him."

Dorner raised his eyebrows. "Really? I didn't realize he had talked to you recently."

"I bought something at one of his auctions, and a piece was missing. He found it later and brought it by."

Dorner gave me a broad smile. "That's just like Uncle Norman…oh, you're the woman who had the drawer taken from the chest. He told me about that."

"He mentioned he had family who used to live in the house, and we had a nice chat." I was babbling inanely. I wanted to see if Dorner had much reaction to anything I said.

He frowned. "Hmm. I'm not sure who that was."

"His mother's cousin, I think he said."

"Must have been before my time."

Bologna. If he knew his uncle well enough to spend time here and serve as executor, he knew who had lived there.

Before I could say anything else, he asked, "Interested in a little proposition?" He apparently saw my cool expression. "Investment proposition."

"No. I'm happy with my new house, and looking forward to doing a few things to improve it." After a couple of silent seconds, I asked, "Are you going to live in one of your new purchases?"

"Probably," he said. He stood and walked over to examine the fireplace mantle. "I may live in Uncle Norman's house for a while."

"He must have all kinds of stuff in there." *Maybe more jewelry?*

He shrugged. "He got rid of a lot when my Aunt Gertie died. I haven't been in there since he died. I think the police are done with the house and I can go this evening."

As he said this I heard Harry's steps on the front porch.

"I hope they didn't leave you a mess." Of course the police would have been through the house. I realized I didn't even know what part of town Fitzgerald had lived in.

Harry came in and I made introductions before walking back to the kitchen to make coffee. I figured Harry would need a second cup after spending time with Clive Dorner. Their conversation was over before the coffee finished dripping, and Harry came into the kitchen with a puzzled look.

"Did he really want a discount on appraisals?" I asked.

"That's what he said. Given that he's been in real estate for a while I was surprised he asked. It's not at all a common request. And investors usually don't care that much."

I shrugged and took two mugs from a cabinet. "How many houses is he thinking of buying?"

"He thinks six or eight. It would be good to get the business, though who does the appraisal is up to the bank doing the financing, of course."

Harry and I both knew this. We also knew that real estate firms usually have a role in picking the appraiser, especially if it's an out of town bank financing the sale.

Harry shrugged. "Since the buyer pays for our work I don't know why Dorner cares."

"He told me he might live in his uncle's house for a while."

"Hmm." Harry took a mug from me. "He didn't mention that. No reason that he should."

"I don't like him."

Harry looked surprised. "That wouldn't stop you from doing the work, would it?"

I grinned. "Heck no. As long as he doesn't try to come with me."

Harry gave me a sort of knowing smile. "I thought he might be more interested in you than the appraisal."

Yuck.

AFTER I'D FINISHED working at the computer I drove down to the police station and asked to see if Sergeant Morehouse was working on a Saturday. He was.

"What can I say this is about?" asked the very young officer.

"When he hears my name, he'll know."

"I still need to be able to tell him."

I thought for a moment. "Please tell him it's about his jewels."

"His jewels?"

"His jewels," I repeated.

I didn't bother to sit in one of the very uncomfortable plastic chairs in the small waiting area, and it was less than a minute later that Morehouse opened the secure door that leads to where the officers sit. "Get in here." When he stood back to let me in he added, "You aren't nearly as funny as you think you are."

"And yet you let me in." I followed him into his small office and sat across from him.

"You shoulda just called. I don't know anything new," he said.

"No fingerprints on that business card?"

"Just yours. And lots of unidentified ones on the chest. Probably from the auction. Don't you dust?"

I bristled. "I've been busy, and…"

"I saw you at the funeral. Stay outta anything to do with Fitzgerald."

"Did you figure out why he was on my porch?"

"It don't matter how many people we talk to, no one saw Norman Fitzgerald walk up to your house the night he was killed."

"What about fingerprints on the porch swing or someplace else near, um, Mr. Fitzgerald?"

His look was shrewd. "If someone else asked I could just say murder investigations are not public business."

"But it's me, and he was on my porch." I tried not to sound as churlish as I felt.

His look softened a bit. "I know this has been rough for you. There were some prints, but none matched anything in our database or the federal one."

"I guess that would be too easy," I said.

He just looked at me.

"I was thinking maybe it would help if we started to tell people what I found. Maybe someone would recognize…"

"Maybe someone would think there was more where that came from and visit you in the middle of the night to find out." He used his most surly tone.

I just looked at him.

"Yeah, yeah, it's your stuff. You can take your jewels wherever you want them. They aren't officially part of any investigation."

"I was thinking of wearing the bracelets."

"Go to Target and buy something new."

"Not because I like them, because someone might recognize them and ask about them. That might help us figure out…"

"There is no *us*. Besides, the stuff isn't here." He looked a bit uncomfortable as he said that.

"You told Aunt Madge…"

"That I'd hold it here for a while. I am. I asked Mark Foster at the downtown jewelry store to look at them. When he saw the stuff he said he could do a better estimate if he took them to his store. Guess he has some special thingamabobs to use to look at the diamonds."

"Oh, that's okay." Part of me wished he had asked me about this, and the other part knew that since the diamonds and bracelets were not part of a crime that he was doing me a favor by having anything to do with them. I'd probably have to pay a pretty penny for an appraisal, but Mark Foster would probably look at the diamonds as a favor to Morehouse.

"He also said his store safe might be a lot safer than keeping them here, but I told him I'd have to talk to you about that." He looked at his watch.

"Why do you suppose he thought that?"

"I don't think anybody would steal them from our evidence room, but a lot of people have at least some access to the place."

"I don't think anyone would either." No way would I imply I thought any of Ocean Alley's finest would steal. "But if you would be more comfortable if he kept them, that's okay with me."

"I got work to do. You hear anything about Fitzgerald I want to hear it."

I got up and turned back from the doorway. "Clive Dorner said he might live in his uncle's place for a while. Where is that, anyway?"

"Lookin' for a new boyfriend?" He was going through a couple of papers on his desk and looked up when I didn't say anything.

"No."

"Hey, listen…" It was the first time I've seen him look almost stricken.

I kept moving. I wasn't sure whether my eyes burned because I was mad at Morehouse or missing George.

Chapter Fifteen

BETWEEN PAINTING THE INTERIOR window trim at my house and working one afternoon at our twice weekly food pantry distribution, I had little time to think of diamonds or my front porch swing. A professional cleaner had taken out all the stains and applied a coat of primer so it looked unsoiled. I still hadn't used the front door.

Despite a to-do list that included two appraisals, I wanted to talk to the jeweler who was storing the diamonds and bracelets. I had seen Mark Fisher around town, but didn't really know him. When I walked into his store on the following Wednesday he was with another customer and gave me a nod of recognition.

His small store was five blocks back from the ocean. While there had probably been relatively little storm damage, it looked as if the ravages of the damaged economy had hit his business. Jewelry and crystal figurines were spread somewhat sparsely among the display cases. That told me that sales were not good and he was not replenishing his inventory as he might have in previous years.

The tinkle of the door chimes marked his customer's exit and I looked up from a glass case that contained gorgeous watches.

"Guess you know I have some things of yours," Mark said. He had a pleasant expression, reinforced by a round face and dimples that reminded me of a cherub.

"And I really appreciate you keeping them here. I wondered, is there anything distinctive about any of it? Something that might help me figure out who it might have belonged to?"

He looked surprised. "Isn't it rightfully yours?"

"Probably, but someone could have been looking for it. Maybe it was even stolen a long time ago. If it belongs to someone else I want them to have it."

"Good of you." He shook his head slowly. "The diamonds used to be in settings. You can tell because there are some minute scratches on a couple of them. Likely made when someone other than a jeweler took them out of a ring or earrings, or whatever. If you had the item that used to hold them you might come up with a match, but even then, maybe not."

I nodded. "Kind of what I figured. Are the diamonds worth a lot?"

"Two are quite nice, possibly worth several thousand dollars. The smaller ones are lovely, but a jeweler would call them imperfect stones."

"I was curious…" I began.

"Now, the bracelets are more distinctive." He warmed to his topic. "If someone had taken pictures of them, say for insurance purposes, that would make identifying a prior owner fairly easy. Even without photos, someone might be able to describe them well enough for you to feel certain that you'd found the owner."

It didn't seem likely that someone had taken photos decades ago, but I didn't say that. "Do you think I could wear a couple of the bracelets?"

He smiled. "They are yours."

"I know. But, I don't want all of it. I mean, if you don't mind keeping it for a while longer, until I can find where it came from. Oh, do you need storage fees or something?"

"No, I hope you find who used to own it. When you decide what you want, I'll write up an informal receipt, so it's clear you have it."

"Of course." I thought for a moment. "The wide bracelet, I think, and a gold one."

Mark walked into a room behind the display area, and in about three minutes he was back with the bracelets and a handwritten receipt for me to sign.

I thanked him and looked at the bracelet on my wrist as I walked to my car. It was elegant, my knit top was not. I took off the bracelet and stuck it in my purse before I drove to Java Jolt for a dose of caffeine.

Lester gave me his usual enthusiastic greeting. "Hey kid. Got some appraisals for you soon."

Lester was no longer mad at Clive Dorner, who had contacted him soon after his uncle's funeral and made offers on two of the houses Lester had shown him. "And the guy says he wants to get another couple before the end of the summer. I told him the sooner the better, of course."

"Of course," I smiled. "It seems like I see more for sale signs than a month ago." I didn't mention that I'd seen two that had Betty Fowler's name on them. Apparently Lester still didn't know that Clive was also working with her.

"Yeah," he frowned, "I've got about the same number of listings as before, but I guess some of the high-fallutin' agents got a few more recently."

I tried for tact. "Probably more summer dwellers selling. You have more all year round."

"Yeah." His expression brightened. "Your buddy Dorner…"

I rolled my eyes.

"…says he'll use me to sell the houses he's goin' to fix up."

"Why? Doesn't he have a New Jersey license?"

"Yeah, but he's mostly used his Pennsylvania license, and he says if he tried to sell them himself buyers'll think he's not being truthful or something. He said he wants third party involvement." Lester said the last words as if making fun of Dorner.

"So, you make money twice on the same house."

"Except," he lowered his voice, "since he's giving me all his business he wants me to charge a reduced commission."

I laughed. "He's a piece of work." I started to tell him that Dorner wanted Harry to charge less, but stopped, realizing Harry would say that was confidential. Again, I chose not to say anything about Betty.

"You back with George?" Lester asked.

"You asked me that before. You need to give it a rest."

He flashed me a quick grin. "Can't blame a guy for asking."

I did an internal groan, but smiled just the same. "I suppose I could take it as a compliment."

My phone chirped. "Jolie." It was George, and I knew Lester could hear the voice.

"Yesss." I drew out the word.

"I've been hearing some stuff. Meet me at Java Jolt."

"I'm already here. When are you coming?"

"Now." He hung up.

"He don't say goodbye?" Lester asked.

I shrugged. "He's not as bad about it as Morehouse."

"Gotta get back to the office." Lester picked up his mug and placed it on the counter. "Whaddya doin' Joe, making it weaker?" He didn't wait for an answer.

Joe hollered to his back. "You want the enamel to come off your teeth?" He looked at me and shook his head. "At least he stopped bringing his real estate clients here. He'd buy two cups of coffee and they'd each have three refills."

"He is unique." I stood, giving Joe a smart ass attitude. "You don't' mind me getting a refill, do you?"

"You know I don't."

Since it was still before Memorial Day the coffee thermoses were on the counter instead of behind it, so I helped myself. By the time I had put cream in my coffee George had come in the door.

He nodded at Joe. "You have any more of that hazelnut stuff?"

"Just got it in. Have a seat. I'll bring it to you."

George sat with me and almost whispered, "He wants to hear what we're talking about." He pulled out a notebook. "I heard some interesting stuff about Dorner."

"Why do you care about him?"

"Because," George's tone implied the answer should be obvious, "I can't ask his uncle any questions, and I think it's kind of funny Dorner is going to be living in his uncle's house."

Joe put the coffee on the table. "I heard he lost a house in Philly, to a foreclosure."

"Yeah," George said. "I heard that, too. Thanks." His expression was anything but grateful.

I watched George seem to have an internal argument with himself. Should we stay in Java Jolt where Joe might try to listen to what we said, or should we go to the boardwalk?

"He'll get busy in a minute," I said, quietly.

"I shoulda ordered something he has to make in one of those loud machines."

"I heard that," Joe said.

"Surprise." George turned his chair so his back was to Joe. "So, I found the foreclosure information in court records in Philadelphia. It's not a finished process yet. If he gets a bunch of cash within the next few weeks he could probably get it back."

"So, he really needs to live at Uncle Normy's?"

"It's more than that. Uncle Normy had a lot of antiques and some other valuable stuff. Seems he told a couple of people that he sometimes bought items that didn't sell at some of his auctions."

"I guess he had to have some way to explain why he had stuff that he couldn't steal by sticking it in his pocket," I mused.

"The interesting part is, Dorner took some to your favorite pawn shop."

"So?"

"Your good friend Elmira Washington pitched a fit because she said a pair of candlesticks at the pawn shop was part of her mother's estate, and Fitzgerald supposedly sold them at an auction about ten years ago."

"And Elmira figures he kept the candlesticks so she got less from the auction. That'll tarnish that reputation everyone talked about at Fitzgerald's funeral. Can she prove it?" I never thought I'd be on Elmira's side about anything. She goes to First Prez, and she's such a gossip people even hate to talk to her after the Sunday service.

"She has pictures that have the candlesticks in them." George grinned. "I heard she was waving them around the waiting room at the police station, demanding to talk to the officer in charge."

"I can hear her now. So, did you talk to Dorner yet?" I asked.

"I figure he likes you. Maybe you could invite him for coffee…"

As I gave a firm no, Joe laughed.

"Shut up, Joe," George groused. He lowered his voice. "Okay, sorry. But Lester's selling him houses, maybe Lester knows something."

"I don't think credit problems are something you tell your realtor about."

George looked at me very directly for a couple of seconds and I returned his stare. "I guess you're right. Kind of odd that he thinks he can buy when he's losing his house."

I shrugged. "He could be buying as a business."

"I should've thought of that." He sighed. "Bottom line is I can't find him to ask about it. I mostly thought he'd return your phone call even if he ignores mine."

I took my last swallow of coffee. "You're on your own, pal." *In more ways than one.* I made to stand up.

"Stay with me while I finish my coffee," George said.

"Nope. Have a place to appraise, and it's supposed to rain. I want to get done." I gave him my four-fingered wave and said goodbye to Joe as I left.

Chapter Sixteen

I STEPPED INTO a Wednesday afternoon that had clouds hovering over the boardwalk. It had stayed warm for a couple of days, but the humidity had been lower until just a bit ago. The planet needed to remind itself that it was springtime in our hemisphere, and spring was supposed to be cool in New Jersey. A glance up told me April showers were definitely in my immediate future, so I hustled to the popsicle district.

The house was newer than some in the neighborhood. I'd have to remember to ask Aunt Madge if she knew whether the lot had been divided or if the house replaced an older one. I could find this out at the courthouse, but since somebody else gets paid to do a title search, I wasn't willing to spend the time on it.

I had just wrestled the front door open when there a car horn beeped twice. Clive Dorner pulled into a parking space behind mine on the narrow street. *Now what does he want?*

"Jolie. Just who I'm looking for." Dorner gave me a mega-watt smiles as he walked up the sidewalk.

"I guess you found me." I tried to keep my tone pleasant, since it seemed I would see him around town a lot. "What's up?"

"Mind if I come in with you?"

He had climbed onto the stoop with me, which was a bit close for my comfort zone. "It's really not appropri…"

"Somebody beat the price I offered for this house. I want to figure out how I got beat."

I did a mental shrug and stepped into the house. "Don't like to lose, do you?"

Dorner walked in after me. "Nope." He looked in the kitchen and quickly walked back out. "I didn't remember anything special about this little place and I want to see what I missed."

It seemed best to allow him to prowl by himself, so I began measuring the front room. The tiny house had an efficient traffic flow. The bedrooms were to the left of the front door, and the kitchen was straight ahead. No formal dining room, but the breakfast bar would be sufficient for most meals.

As I measured, I thought about how to ask Dorner about the items he was selling. It occurred to me that Elmira Washington had probably let half the town know she thought Norman Fitzgerald had kept candlesticks that she thought had been sold with her mother's other things.

"Heard you had a run-in with Elmira Washington."

He gave me a blank look. "Who?"

"She goes to First Prez with Aunt Madge. She thinks some stuff you took to the pawn shop should have been in her mother's estate sale, or something like that." I wrote down the living room measurements, being careful to avoid his eyes.

"Gee, I guess I should call her. Uncle Norman would sometimes buy an item before a sale started. I bet there's a receipt or something."

I looked up. "That would certainly explain it."

Dorner walked quickly through the rest of the house. Since it seemed he had been prepared to follow me around while I worked, I took this to mean that what I'd said worried him.

"I guess I'll head out," he began.

"How's it going, living in your uncle's house? Personally, I'd find it hard to be in Aunt Madge's house so soon after she died."

He flushed. "I've spent a lot of time in that house through the years. I'm familiar with every nook and cranny, so it almost feels like home."

"I can relate to that." I gave him what I hoped was a winning smile. "Did you ever spend time in the house I just bought?"

"You asked me that earlier. I don't think I've been in it." He studiously examined a window sill as he spoke.

"I knew your uncle's cousin lived there. I thought you might have gone over there with him."

"If I did I would have been very young. Don't remember it at all." He seemed in a hurry to leave. "I have a couple more houses to look at this afternoon, better hit the road."

I looked up from the clipboard on which I was writing measurements. "Tell Lester I said hello."

"Will do." He almost sprinted to his car.

I figured I had made him uncomfortable, which should tell me something, though I wasn't sure what. My guess would be that he knew good old Uncle Norman had hidden jewelry behind what were now my walls. He was probably snooping around his uncle's house trying to find things to take before he had to do the formal inventory of the estate.

WHEN I FINISHED TAKING photos and measurements I headed for the Purple Cow. In my mind everything that had happened in the last couple of weeks started with the jewelry, and Ramona had said she would look at it.

After she finished with her customer Ramona walked over and I pulled the rust-colored bracelet out of my purse. "The two like this are kind of funny. They sort of look like heavy plastic and sort of don't. They were in the pouch with the other stuff."

As she took it, she said, "Bakelite, I love these." She slid it over her slim wrists and held it at arm's length.

I pulled up my sleeve an inch and held out my arm, which sported the gold bracelet. "Your clothes would probably go better with this one."

She almost squealed, and I took it off my wrist and handed it to her.

"This is beautiful," she breathed.

"How old do you think it is?"

"It kind of looks like one you would see in pictures of the 1920s flappers. But I don't know that they were often gold." She held it to the light. "It's not solid gold, I think it's gold over some kind of metal frame. Tin maybe? Still somewhat valuable."

"It looks as if it's in really good condition."

Ramona nodded. "What makes me think it's from the 1920s or 1930s is the size. You're pretty small, and it just fits you. Women are bigger now, so bracelets have been made bigger for decades."

"It reminds me of the metal wrist bands that Roman soldiers wore."

"So," she concluded, "all you need is a Roman soldier and you're all set."

We both laughed, but I quickly stopped. Every now and then Mr. Fitzgerald's image came to me. Sleeping and yet very much not sleeping on my porch.

"What's the matter?" Ramona asked.

"Sometimes I can separate finding the jewelry from finding Mr. Fitzgerald. Right now I can't."

She studied the bracelets again. "The Bakelite ones were popular quite a while ago, maybe even before World War II. Anyone can buy them at an antique store or on eBay today, but the lack of any wear means these could have been put in that pouch not terribly long after they were popular."

"Maybe." I hesitated, thinking. "That might mean they were put in there in the 1950s which would make that wall older than I thought."

She shrugged. "Or they could have been in an estate sale much later, and Mr. Fitzgerald thought they might be worth something at some point. An auctioneer would think about future value more than you or I would."

"I feel as if I'm back to not knowing much."

Ramona smiled. "Maybe you need something else to occupy you, so you don't think about this all the time."

THAT'S JUST WHAT that night's Harvest for All meeting did for me.

"We need a place where we can make a mess," Dr. Welby said. He had essentially taken charge of planning for the so-called birthday party. His rationale was that I shouldn't have to plan a party for myself. When I reminded him that it was not just a party for me he ignored me.

"Why would that matter?" Sylvia asked.

"Have you heard of liquid string?" Scoobie asked.

I wanted to slide under the table.

"That should be an oxymoron," Lance said.

"Or just moronic," Sylvia said, in quite a sharp tone.

Scoobie gave her an engaging grin. "You spray it from a can. It's not something he usually orders, but Mr. Markle said he can get us a few cases really cheap. We could have contests. Like who could spray it really far without it touching the ground, or who can empty a can fastest."

Aretha laughed. "If you have more colors you could try to make pictures, maybe on the sidewalk, and give a prize for the best one."

"That would argue for an outdoor venue," Dr. Welby said, dryly.

"How do you spray it?" Monica asked.

"It's like a thing of whipped cream," Megan said, "but in more colors. It's actually a foam, and I think it's made of soap. It gets used a lot at the high school on April Fool's Day."

"So, you can wash it up easily?" Lance asked.

"Yeah," Scoobie said, "but it probably would be easier with a hose, so outdoors would be good."

I DROVE SCOOBIE BACK to his rooming house after the meeting. "You couldn't think of something less messy?"

He was unfazed. "You want a lot of people to come. There has to be something really different from a regular birthday party."

"Won't everybody be all gooey after they get sprayed? They're supposed to go on a scavenger hunt after that."

"We're all going on a scavenger hunt." He looked thoughtful for a second. "I guess people should bring a change of clothes."

We had decided to have the birthday party at the local tennis club, if they'd have us. I had thought of using the courts as a place to spray the so-called liquid string freely, but Dr. Welby pointed out it would make the courts slippery and offer a lot of business for his orthopedist friends. So, we would use the parking lot and people could clean up or change clothes in the locker rooms. Megan said her daughter Alicia and her friends would enjoy hosing down the parking lot when we were done.

I sighed. "I hope we have good liability insurance."

Scoobie shrugged. "Make them sign a waiver. Like before an operation. You agree not to sue unless they accidentally cut off a foot or something."

Chapter Seventeen

THE HOUSE I WAS to appraise on Thursday was one of Lester's properties. He was hot where prices were generally lower, and this neighborhood certainly was one of the lowest-priced in Ocean Alley. I asked him about this once, since he's always pushing Harry and me to appraise for more than we think a house is worth so he gets a bigger commission.

His reply was, "Get 'em while they're young and they'll buy their McMansion from you later."

Crafty guy.

Usually I take exterior photos after I look at the interior of a house, but in the interest of not getting soaked, I grabbed my digital camera and took a couple of quick shots from across the street. I thought I heard a crack of thunder in the distance and hurried to the side yard.

I took one, and since I couldn't get to the back yard without going through the house, I took one more picture in front and was about to go in when a car horn gave a light beep.

The woman in a BMW put the passenger window down and took off her sunglasses. "Hey, Jolie."

"Jennifer. Hi." I walked toward the street and she pulled up to the curb. A couple of drops hit my head. Since her family owns the town's far larger appraisal business, we were kind of edgy around each other when I first moved to Ocean Alley, or maybe it was just me. She's also realized that with low interest rates and the size of Steele Appraisals, we aren't really competition.

"You have the popsicle district sewn up with Lester," she said. "And you know how he is."

She smiled. "I love any business of course, but I don't miss his faxes when he doesn't like what we come up with." She looked toward the house. "I didn't even know this one was on the market."

"And you know how hard it'll be to assign a decent value."

She grimaced. "Don't I ever."

On the spur of the moment, I said, "You want to come in? Maybe you'll have some ideas about what would bring up the value."

I didn't need her help, but I thought it would be good to hear what she thought. She and her staff are the only other people in town besides Harry and me who have to figure out house values in the ever-changing post-Sandy market.

She glanced at what looked to be a very expensive watch. "Sure. I'm heading to the far north end of town, but I'm in no rush."

I stood on the narrow sidewalk, typical for this low-rent side of town, while she parallel parked. Expertly, of course.

As she locked the car, rain drops plopped more quickly on my head. We both looked up at the darkening clouds.

"Oh well, this is supposed to pass quickly." She smoothed her linen slacks.

We dashed for the porch and I pulled out the key Lester had provided and jiggled the lock until it opened.

I never expected to see a fire jump toward me as I opened a door. I only looked at it for a second or so. The yellowish orange flames climbed up the stained paneling and across the likely recently refinished floor. It moved really fast.

After my initial jump from the porch to the ground, I crouched and rolled maybe fifteen feet away from the house. Jennifer had been behind me, and she had jumped back before I did and was sitting on the lawn about ten feet from the porch.

"Get over here, Jennifer!"

She scrambled to her feet and we stood on the sidewalk about twenty-five feet from the house. My palms were so sweaty I dropped my phone. I had more success the second time I dialed 9-1-1.

"Fire! Hurry, hurry!" I yelled.

"Are you at 549 Ferry Street?" the dispatcher asked.

"Yes, I'm here! We're here!"

"Are you in the house?" he asked.

"No, no, I'm outside. It's supposed to be vacant."

"Move as far from the house as you can," the dispatcher said, calmly. "Alert neighbors if you can do so with no danger to yourself.'"

By this time neighbors had run outside and I could hear sirens. Two boys about middle-school age came toward us on bicycles and jumped off them. "Is anyone in there?" one of them yelled

"No, it's vacant," I tried to inject calm into my voice.

"I'll move my car," Jennifer said, walking faster than I've ever seen her. She peeled rubber and made it to a parking spot a few houses down the street just as the fire trucks came roaring toward us. I didn't feel calm enough to drive, but luckily my car was not directly in front of the fire.

The boys and I were getting soaked, but they were oblivious. "Pick up your bikes, move back," I ordered.

They obeyed, not taking their eyes off the fire, which had just blown out a window on the side of the house. "Wow, another vacant house on fire," one of them said, almost reverently.

BY THE TIME GEORGE showed up ten minutes later the fire fighters had two hoses on the small house and were spraying the roofs of the houses on either side. The nearby houses had probably been helped by the four-minute downpour that had moved through. The sun was already peering out behind grey clouds.

George and I stood in silence watching the hoses soak the hole in the roof that a few seconds ago had been the escape hatch for a huge plume of smoke above the small frame house. The air held a pungent odor of burned wood.

"Why are you here?" he asked.

"I'm supposed to be appraising it."

His head turned around so fast he could have expected a whiplash injury. "What's that supposed to mean?"

"I have this job, you see," I began.

"That's not funny," he snapped.

"I unlocked the door, and there was this kind of whooshing sound. I almost dove off the porch. Oh, Jennifer."

"What? She was here?"

I looked down the street. She had been next to me for a couple of minutes, but her car was now gone. "I think she probably went home to change." I was careful not to sound too bitchy as I pushed my soggy hair behind my ears.

George looked at me for several seconds and then back at the fire. "This doesn't look like curtains on fire," he said.

"The realtor's listing says it's vacant with no furnishings." I stared at the fire, mesmerized. "I think they may have just varnished the floors, because the fire was tearing across it."

"What would get that started?" he murmured.

We stood without speaking, shoulders almost touching, for another minute. At some point I had dropped the small notebook I use to jot measurements when I visit a house. If it didn't burn it was squished under firefighters' rubber boots.

I did have the listing sheet folded in my purse and I pulled it out, grateful that I had not lost the purse when I dove off the porch. "Utilities were supposed to be off."

"Deliberate," George muttered, taking the page that described the number of rooms and had estimated measurements and other information. He glanced at it and handed it back to me.

Squealing tires made us both look halfway down the block, beyond a couple of sawhorse barricades that firefighters had placed a few houses away. Sergeant Morehouse got out of a car and walked briskly toward the chief who had been directing the fire fighters. Since the water was having its intended effect, the chief now talked quietly to a guy in some sort of fire uniform, but not in the heavy coat and triangular hat worn by those actively fighting the fire.

Morehouse spoke to both men for a couple minutes, and then his posture straightened and he looked around until he saw me. He pointed a finger at me, which I took to mean not to go anywhere.

"I bet he accuses you of meddling or something," George said. I could tell he enjoyed the idea.

George walked a couple of feet away and started talking to some of the bystanders about when they noticed the fire.

One of the middle school boys said, "It was freakin' big, I'm telling you. Me and Eddie were the first to see it."

I thought my eyeballs were first, but I wasn't going to quibble.

Morehouse walked toward me and jerked his head to one side, indicating we should move away from the most dense area of gawkers. "Chief said that dispatch identified you were one of the first to call this in."

I nodded. "When I opened the door, it…"

"You opened the door," he said, slowly.

"I was going to appraise it." Surely he would have figured this out. I pulled the listing page back out of my purse. "This tells you everything I know about the place."

Morehouse scanned it and gave it back. "You see anything?"

"Other than the fire jumping toward me as soon as I opened the door, no. I had just gotten here. I took a couple of exterior pictures and…"

"I'm gonna need that camera card." He held out his hand.

"Not again. I'll make you copies in your office, but I've got pictures of my house and Jazz and Pebbles on there."

"Some of them are pretty racy, from what I hear." Scoobie had appeared behind me.

"Where were you?" Morehouse asked, none too nicely.

"Not my week to watch her." Scoobie looked at the charred remains of the now smoldering house and gave me a brief one-armed hug. "Besides, even if I wasn't at school, I wouldn't have been with her."

"I'm right here, you know." I scowled at Scoobie. "Oh, and Jennifer was with me. I think she went home to change."

"Home to change," Morehouse said.

I pointed to my head and let my hand fall down my torso. "Rain. Rain. Did not go away. She'll be back." I had no idea of this, nor did I have her phone number with me. Surely she would return.

"All right, Jolie," Morehouse said. "Come down to the station and we'll copy the photos. You take any after the fire started?"

I shook my head. "I never even thought of it."

"Which is why she'll never be a reporter," George said. "I took a few, but it was well underway by then."

"I got nuthin' for you, George," Morehouse said. "But you got photos for me. Email 'em. I won't release them to anyone else."

Morehouse is so charming.

"You think this is related to any of the others fires?" George asked.

"What part of nuthin' don't you understand?" Morehouse looked at me. "See you down there in two minutes."

"See you where?" George asked, as Morehouse moved away.

"Shut up, George," he called over his shoulder.

MOREHOUSE STUDIED my pictures without saying anything, and then called down the hall.

"Corporal Johnson, come look at these, will you?"

Dana came in with a questioning expression and he pointed at the pictures of the house that we had loaded onto his computer. "You patrol this area a lot, right? Anything look out of the ordinary?" He stood up so she could sit in his chair to look at the screen more closely.

She scrolled through the few photographs slowly, looking at each one for ten or fifteen seconds. I looked at them, too. It was a typical older beach cottage, which had four rooms with a hallway that connected them and kitchen and bath in the back, both added on, probably in the 1920s or thereabouts. There were off-street parking spaces for two cars, and the graveled area took up much of the small front yard.

"There's something different about the first and fourth one," she said. They were both the front of the house, one taken when I first got there, one about a minute later, after I took a shot from each side of the house.

I looked more closely. "Is that a glare from the sun or fire, in the second shot?"

"Fire, I think," she said. "It must have just started, or just moved to the front of the house, anyway."

"Or just gotten hot enough to flame." Morehouse turned to me. "Did someone know you were going to that house?"

"It was with Steele Appraisals for the work, but no one would have had any idea of when I would go there."

"Coincidence, I guess," he murmured. "Why was Jennifer with you?"

"She was driving by and stopped. I asked her to come in with me." I shrugged at his raised eyebrows. "It's harder to establish values these days. After Sandy. I asked her to come in."

"Who owns it?" Dana asked.

"A bank, I think. Harry can tell us if you can't get Lester. I recall the prior owners had it for maybe fifteen years." I looked at the photo again. "It wasn't updated much, you can see from the listing sheet. Wouldn't bring a lot in insurance if someone set the fire."

"There are a lot of deteriorating properties on that street," Dana said. "The real estate bust kept people from spending more on upkeep recently, and a couple were foreclosed."

I thought about the street's location, about six blocks from the beach. "I wonder if someone wants to encourage people to sell."

"Like who?" Morehouse asked, sharply.

"I don't know, it was just a thought."

"Pretty extreme," Dana said.

Morehouse's phone rang and he stepped into the hall.

"Did you get into this many predicaments when you lived in Lakewood?" Dana asked.

"Just the loser husband." I studied the screen.

Morehouse walked back in. "Clive Dorner."

Dana and I both looked at him, puzzled.

"Firefighters found his body in one of the bedrooms."

Chapter Eighteen

I SAGGED AGAINST MY CHAIR. "Clive Dorner!"

"Was he the buyer?" Morehouse asked, sharply.

I shook my head slowly. "Like I said, I think a bank that owned it hired us to do the work."

"What in the hell was he doing in there?" Morehouse picked up his phone as he spoke, and dialed.

I felt numb, and Dana looked incredulous.

"Lester?" Morehouse barked. "You're working with Clive Dorner, right?"

I could not hear Lester's reply, though I got the tone, which was one of caution. Lester, likely not having heard of the death, wanted to know why Morehouse asked the question.

"Dead." Morehouse said.

Now I could hear Lester. "The hell you say!"

"You know why he'd be at 549 Ferry? You show him that house?"

Lester's voice grew quieter again. I'd have to go find him.

Morehouse listened, then said thanks and hung up, with his usual lack of goodbye. He looked at Dana. "Lester said he thought Dorner was most interested in that house, of the ones he saw lately, but he hadn't made an offer and probably shouldn't a been in there. Ask around at the motels, see if he came back into town before he went there."

"He was staying at Norman Fitzgerald's place." In response to Morehouse's look, I added, "Dorner came to see Harry a couple of days ago."

"Corporal, head over to Fitzgerald's old place, see what you find."

She left, with a brief nod to me.

Morehouse pulled a notebook toward him. "What else do you know about Dorner?"

"I know…I think he was selling things from his uncle's house."

"Some reason you think there's something wrong with that?" he asked.

"I'm no lawyer, but he said he was executor of the estate. He didn't say it was all left to him."

"Ah," Morehouse said, clearly thinking. Then his tone became accusatory. "Why'd he tell you that?"

"When he stopped by Harry's, Dorner mentioned that he was executor… Hey. You might want to talk to Elmira."

"Now why in the hell would I want to do that?"

"Didn't you hear she thinks he's pawning stuff she thought was in her mother's auction?"

"Yeah, but it was Elmira." Morehouse pointed his finger at me. "You think of anything else?"

I felt edgy. "Point that somewhere else."

"Humph." He lowered his hand. "Do not go find Lester."

I stood up and picked up my purse from the floor. "I'm not going looking for him. I'm going home to change." *But it won't be my fault if he finds me.*

TALK ABOUT UNEXPECTED. Clive Dorner had been nothing short of sleazy in my book. I had briefly wondered if he had killed Mr. Fitzgerald, but only because I knew they were related and I thought Dorner was a heartless jerk. Now it seemed that their deaths could be linked.

After I cleaned up and changed I called Jennifer. "You okay?"

"It was terrifying. How do you get into these messes?" Her tone was more hysterical than accusatory.

"You should probably go talk to Morehouse before he looks for you."

"What will people think?" Jennifer asked.

For a second I thought she meant about Dorner being found in the house, but then I realized she didn't know that. "Think about what?"

"About us both being there. We're competitors." She stressed the last word.

What a silly thing to worry about. "Our names may not even be in the news. There are probably bigger things to worry about."

I wanted to get off the phone and focus on some of those things, so I told her I hadn't changed yet and needed to do that.

I drove to Java Jolt hoping to see Lester, but he wasn't there and I didn't know his other hangouts besides Burger King, which I also checked. Finally I stopped at Mr. Markle's Midway Market on the way home and bought a pan of frozen lasagna. After I cleaned up I had invited Ramona and Scoobie over for supper. I thought about George, but figured I'd let him find me.

LATER, IN MY LIVING ROOM, Ramona sat on the rocker and Scoobie had stretched out on the floor, studying the ceiling. The lasagna was in the oven and smelled wonderful.

"How did they know it was him?" Ramona asked.

"The radio said he was dead when the fire started and they put it out quickly. He still had his wallet." I always hated the phrase "burned beyond recognition" in newspaper stories, and was glad not to have to think of Dorner that way.

Scoobie played with a paperclip. "He's probably got a couple of Fitzgerald cousins still kicking. Don't know if any of them are in town, though."

I frowned. "I wonder if he went in to look at the house? It's the kind of bargain he was looking for. And there wasn't a sold sign, so he wouldn't have known it was off the market."

"You might want to lose the *he had it coming tone*," Scoobie said.

"Just because I thought he was pond scum doesn't mean I wanted him dead."

Ramona winced. "I don't think any of the Fitzgeralds he was related to still live here. His parents died ages ago, so there were just the cousins you said were at the funeral."

"I wish I never bought this house!"

"Yeah," Scoobie said, "because none of this would have happened if someone else had bought your house."

"It might have happened, but I might not know about it."

"I'm sure Mr. Fitzgerald and Clive Dorner would feel a lot better about that." Scoobie glanced around the room. "Hey, where's the skunk?"

"Under my bed. That's where she goes when there are strangers in the house."

"And Jazz doesn't mind?" Ramona asked.

A meow came from the hallway. I turned and saw Jazz sitting there. "Come here, baby." She strutted over and let me pet her before she moved on to Scoobie.

"You like your new roommate?" he asked. She swatted the back of his hand. "What's with this cat? She never swatted me at Madge's."

"Who knows? The vet said she was lonely, but I think she's a little better since Pebbles showed up." I walked into the kitchen to check on the lasagna.

Just as I pulled open the oven door my phone chirped. I shut the door and took the phone from my pocket.

"Hi Aunt Madge. I called you." I wanted to be certain she knew I had not wanted her to hear about Dorner on the radio. Or that I had been the one to come face-to-face with the fire.

"It's Harry. Madge is right here. What the hell happened?"

"I tried to call you, too," I said, quickly.

"I saw you on caller ID. We left the phones in the car while we took a walk on the beach."

He must think I'm really naïve. "The beach, right."

"What happened?" he repeated.

"There isn't that much to tell." I gave him a brief summary of what had happened, and then remembered what I wanted to be sure of. "Who was the buyer?"

"The bank. Jersey Sun Trust has bought a couple houses lately. My guess is that they want to do what Dorner was doing. Get some kind of run-down houses and fix them up."

"Why on earth..." I began.

"I think they're anxious to protect the value of some of the other houses they mortgaged." He said this with impatience, unusual for him. "Could you tell how the fire started?"

Scoobie stood in the doorway, listening to the conversation, brow furrowed.

"Unless there's something really obvious I bet they have a hard time figuring it out," I said. "The place went up like dry wood in a campfire."

"Hmmm. The important thing is you're okay." He must have turned his head from the phone. "You get all that?"

Aunt Madge got on. "This is ridiculous."

At least she sounds relieved, not angry. "I know. But I really am okay."

After a couple more comments about taking it easy and me reassuring her that Ramona and Scoobie were with me, they hung up.

"She had a much calmer life before you moved back here." Scoobie walked back to the living room and told Ramona who was on the phone.

To myself, I mumbled, "So did I." The lasagna still needed a few more minutes, and I took a notebook from what had quickly become my kitchen junk drawer. Usually I make thinking lists by myself, but I didn't know enough about Fitzgerald or Dorner to have much of a starting point.

"Okay." I sat at the small dinette table in the living room and opened the notebook so there was a blank page on the left and one on the right, and wrote Mr. Fitzgerald's name at the top of a page and Clive Dorner's on the other. "What do we know?"

"I guess I don't need to remind you to butt out," Scoobie said.

"Next time you find a dead man on your porch you can butt out," I said, feeling churlish.

"Jolie." Ramona waited until I looked at her. "I feel like I'd be encouraging you if I helped you with that list. Two people are dead. In case you haven't realized it, you met them both in the last couple of weeks or so, which could make you the common denominator."

"And your point would be?"

"Excuse me?" She stood, face reddening. "I'm not somebody who ticked you off in the grocery store. I'm your friend, and I'm trying to help you!"

I was stunned. Ramona never raises her voice or even acts ruffled. "I'm asking you to help by giving me ideas for…"

She stood, adjusted her crocheted vest, walked to the front door, jerked it open, and left.

I looked at Scoobie, "What…I only meant…"

"I think I'll head out with Ramona." At the door, he turned. "It's just too dangerous, Jolie. I don't know any other way to let you know that."

"What way? Where are you going?" I could hear the near panic in my voice.

"Probably see you tomorrow at Java Jolt, or something." Scoobie did not jerk open the door when he left, and I heard him call Ramona's name as he went down the short walkway toward the street.

I sat, motionless, with my mouth partway open, for about thirty seconds. Then the timer on the stove went off and I walked to the kitchen to get the lasagna out of the oven. I placed it on top of the stove and turned off the oven, all the while feeling numb. *What am I supposed to do? Pretend none of this is happening? Wait until something else happens?*

I felt Jazz brush against my leg and started to bend over to pet her. Instead, Pebbles looked up at me, brown eyes staring into mine.

"Ugh. Why did I even let you stay here? I don't need a damn skunk!" Seemingly nonplussed, she walked to the fridge. A mewing noise from under the tiny kitchen table made me look at Jazz. She hissed at me. Apparently I was not to talk to Pebbles in an angry tone.

I sighed in frustration and opened the fridge to get some raw vegetables and Skunkie Delight, a present from Harry. I put it in two separate pet bowls and set them on the floor. Jazz walked over and swatted my foot. It seemed that her defense of Pebbles did not go as far as letting the other rug rat get fed first.

"You had yours." She meowed loudly, and I obeyed by putting a few more pieces of moist cat food in her bowl.

The lasagna was too hot to put in the fridge, and I didn't feel like eating any. I set the timer again so I didn't forget to put it away after it cooled and walked to the living room and sat in the rocker with my notebook on my lap.

I don't need anyone to help me. I numbered the lines on each man's page, one through ten, and started making notes.

Mr. Fitzgerald
1. Had a cousin who lived in my house.
2. Took things from auction customers. I crossed out 'took' and wrote 'stole.'
3. Found the drawer on his seat.
4. Not sure who left it, or did he take it?
5. Grew up in Ocean Alley.
6. Did he know Mrs. Peebles well?
7. Dead

Clive Dorner
1. Spent time with his uncle here
2. Lived in Philadelphia
3. Grew up in Ocean Grove
4. Real estate investor
5. Took advantage of people
6. Called me instead of a realtor. Why?
7. Dead

I alternated items, adding one to Mr. Fitzgerald's list and one to Dorner's. I was about to write that Mr. Fitzgerald did things for charities when there was a light knock at the door.

"Nuts. I should have locked it." I peered out. George Winters gave me the peace sign.

"Don't tell me Scoobie called you."

He grinned. "Okay, I won't." He came in and looked around.

"Scoobie said you painted flamingos on one wall."

"And you believed him?" I gestured that he should sit at the small dinette table and sat across from him, my notebook closed in front of me.

"Since I didn't think you could draw, I figured it was at best fifty-fifty." He looked at me directly. "What is it you want to do?"

"Maybe nothing."

He snorted.

"But I like to make lists of what I know and don't know. I think better that way."

"Can we eat first?" he asked, sniffing the air.

I went to the kitchen and he stood in the doorway as I silently took two plates from the cupboard and cut two pieces of the lasagna and put one on each plate. *So, now he eats with me again?*

He carried the two plates to the table and I got ice water. After he took his first bite, he said, "This is a high-visibility deal. You think the cops won't do everything?" He did a gimme gesture.

I opened the notebook and handed it to him. "I expect they will. I just want to be sure they connect all the dots. I don't want to find anybody else on my porch swing, and I want to know who used to own that jewelry so I can return it and no one else comes looking for more."

He glanced up from the list as he pulled out his narrow reporter's notebook and took the pencil from the spiral binding. "And those dots would be?"

"First, the drawer vanished from the chest of drawers I bought at the auction…"

"And you got it back."

"From Fitzgerald, who says he doesn't know who put it on his van seat, but maybe he did know."

"And…?"

"The jewelry." I raised my hand and closed two fingers. "Three." I closed another, "is the obvious one. Mr. Fitzgerald on my porch. Four, he's Clive Dorner's uncle and now Dorner's dead."

"Luckily not on your porch." George looked at me steadily.

"Five. At some point Fitzgerald's mother's cousin lived in this house. Maybe she put the jewelry behind the wall."

"Be a pretty big hole," he said, bemused.

"It was newer wall board. What if she was remodeling? Or maybe she didn't know that Fitzgerald put it there, if he was helping her, or something."

When George said nothing, I continued. "Dorner was looking for bargain property here. I'm going to see if he bought anything before. What number was that?"

"You're on six. You need another hand."

I stuck out my tongue at him and he touched the small camera he always carries in the breast pocket of his Hawaiian-style collared shirt.

"Any pictures and I throw *that* in a swimming pool." I was alluding to treating his camera similarly to his mobile phone, which got damaged that way. It was not my fault. At least, not intentionally.

"Ha! You admit you drowned it!"

I ignored him. "If Dorner told other people he was looking for hurricane bargains, they could have been as annoyed with him as I was. People hate those vultures."

"But not enough to kill them. Especially Lester."

"Because he would lose a commission?" I usually don't like dark humor, but this struck me funny. "Lester would have made sure the contract was signed and there was an estate to manage the deal before he killed him."

George grunted and looked at his notes. "I checked at the courthouse. Dorner didn't own any other property here and I couldn't find old records. Unless he bought it under a business name or something. So, the question is not just why here, but why now?"

I nodded slowly. "Because there are more inexpensive properties further south." I had forgotten that George and I thought a lot alike. *I miss that.*

He caught my expression and looked away for a moment. "Right. He did live up the road in Ocean Grove a lot of his life, but I talked to some real estate people in Philadelphia and…"

"When did you do that?"

"As soon as I found out he died. Kind of tricky, because I figured I'd be telling the people at the firm he worked with about his death. And I was."

"What did they say?"

"When I first said I was calling about him, I got a kind of snotty tone from the guy who talked to me. Said Dorner did not work there regularly and he had no immediate way to contact him. When I said why I was calling he was shocked and wanted more info. When I tell them something they tell me something."

I nodded. "Like what?"

"Like Dorner never mentioned to anyone that he was looking for property up here, though the guy hadn't talked to him in a few weeks. He said Dorner was a wheeler dealer, but he didn't know that he'd ever out and out cheated anyone. Said Dorner sometimes followed leads that maybe should have gone to someone else."

I was in commercial real estate in Lakewood for years. It's a cutthroat business, especially after the housing bubble burst a while back. "Hmmm. People who work together regularly don't usually do that."

"Yeah. Reporters at competing papers'll do it, but if you work at the same outlet the bosses want you to work together."

"Okay," I said.

"Okay what?"

"What part do you want to do?"

"It's probably easier for me to get background stuff. People expect a reporter to ask a lot of questions. Especially after two murders." He tapped his finger on his notebook and then looked at me. "The jewelry was here. It's the most concrete thing we have."

I nodded, thinking. "And Morehouse asked me if I thought Fitzgerald brought Pebbles here."

"He did? You didn't say that." He eyed me with something akin to suspicion.

"I didn't think of it." I pointed to my list. "That makes me wonder if Mr. Fitzgerald knew Moira Peebles well."

"Okay, why don't you start there, and we can talk tomorrow afternoon. But Jolie, we have to…"

"Share," we said together.

He grunted and stood.

"George…" I wasn't sure what to say.

"I know, I know. Look, if we're going to work on this together, we can't be hemming and hawing all the time. Just pretend you're as pissed at me as you used to get before we dated."

I grinned. "At least I'll know how to act."

Chapter Nineteen

THREE WEEKS HAD PASSED since I'd found the jewelry. I had a feeling that if word got out someone would come forward to claim it. Whether it was theirs or not, it could tell me something. Ramona was probably my best bet to get the word out.

Friday morning I was at the Purple Cow almost as soon as it opened. The white board was inside the door, probably because it was so cool. It said, "Holding onto anger is like drinking poison and expecting the other person to die." This was attributed to Buddha, and I took Ramona's choice of quote as a hopeful sign.

I looked around. Ramona was probably in the back room. Roland finished bagging something for a customer and turned to me. "What are the odds that you're buying?" he asked, mostly good naturedly.

"I wish that's all that was on my mind." I told him about being at the fire where Clive Dorner's body was found. The paper had just said that several people noted the fire at about the same time. It did mention that the house had been for sale.

"Good Lord. I didn't know him. I'm glad you weren't hurt." He gave me an odd look and walked to the back room to get Ramona for me.

I looked out the store's front window for a couple moments, not letting myself think of anything related to murders. It was all just too much.

Ramona walked out with Roland, and I looked at her. Her expression was cool, but the way to Ramona's heart is through news she can pass on, so she wanted to know what I knew.

Roland repeated what I'd told him, and neither Ramona or I let on that she already knew I'd been at the fire.

Ramona finally spoke. "Do they…know how it started?" She had a lightweight shawl draped around her shoulders and knotted in the front, and she drew it closer.

"I don't know. My guess is it wasn't from careless smoking. The house was supposed to be empty."

Roland's mobile phone rang and he walked away from us.

"I'm sorry I was a jerk," I said to Ramona.

Her lips twitched slightly. "I know you weren't trying. I just have a hard time with all this."

"Me, too."

"But I'm not helping you," she said, very firmly.

This was too bad, but I wasn't going to urge her. It wouldn't be worth losing her as a friend just to get her to give me ideas. Plus, she'd probably still pass on what she heard.

"I promise I won't ask."

She rolled her eyes and walked to a nearby shelf to straighten a couple of items that a customer had probably recently moved.

"I'm thinking even more of telling some people about the jewelry. Someone might be able to identify it and…"

"And come to relieve you of it?" she asked. "Are you sure you didn't bump your head when you fell off that stoop at the fire?"

"I landed on my tailbone and rolled. I'd find a way to make sure that people knew I didn't have it in the house. If we know who the original owner was we may know about when Fitzgerald took it."

"So?" She turned her back on me and walked toward the front window.

She's still really annoyed with me.

My eyes followed her back, but I stayed near the cash register. "If it was as long ago as I think it was, then it could mean he stole a lot more over the years, and a lot of people were really mad at him. Plus, I bet Father Teehan's remarks at the funeral combined with Elmira's mouth have people wondering if he paid them all he should have after an auction."

"So what?" She didn't look at me as she straightened something in the front display window.

"If there is a broader suspect pool, the police have more to investigate. They might catch the killer, and I can stop looking over my shoulder."

Ramona faced me, face flushing. "Suspect pool? It's not TV. You live *alone.*"

I registered her emphasis on my single status.

She literally shook a finger at me. "Any more publicity means someone who got rooked knows to come to your house and look for more, or finds you in a vacant house when you're working and makes you take them to the jewelry."

"A lot of the houses I appraise have people in them." I waited until she looked at me directly. "You could mention what I found to a few customers and…"

Roland's voice was calm, but firm. "Enough, Jolie."

"Oh, uh, hi, Roland," I said.

"What you and Ramona decide to do on your own time is up to you. But when Ramona is at work I don't want her talking about possible jewelry thefts or saying anything that would disparage someone like the late Mr. Fitzgerald."

My mouth was dry. "Sometimes I get carried away."

Roland gave me a kind of knowing smile and turned to walk back to his office in the stock room. "You can say that again."

Ramona and I watched his back until Roland was out of the sales area, and then Ramona took a spray bottle of glass cleaner from under the counter. She used a paper towel to wipe at fingerprints on the display case next to the cash register.

"I'm sorry. It was dumb to ask."

She stopped cleaning and looked at me "There aren't too many rowdy women in my yoga class. I'll wear the bracelets there."

I grinned. "You said you weren't going to help."

SINCE MY PART OF the duties George and I were dividing started with my house, I went to the library to look at Moira Peebles' obituary. Then I was going to visit Virginia Mulligan to ask if she'd had Pebbles over the winter.

The first line of Mrs. Peebles' obituary told me a lot. Moira (Bridler) Peebles' late husband was Horace Peebles, and her parents were John Bridler and Annie Fitzgerald. The name Bridler sounded familiar, but I couldn't think why.

I had no idea how Annie Fitzgerald was related to my auctioneer Fitzgerald and I was already confused by names and generations. I pulled a notebook from my purse and started tracing families, working backwards from current obituaries to the parents mentioned in them.

I already knew Norman Fitzgerald's parents were Mary Donnelly and Lawrence Fitzgerald, and his sister was Norma and he had two brothers, Michael and Paul. They all died before Norman.

Lawrence Fitzgerald's father was Peter, but Moira's mother Annie had a different father, a man named Hugh Fitzgerald. I finally figured out that Moira Peebles and Norman Fitzgerald shared a great grandfather, which I thought made them third cousins.

A lot of people wouldn't know their third cousins if they met them on the street, but in a town the size of Ocean Alley, Norman and Moira probably knew they were related somehow, even if they weren't sure what kind of cousins they were.

Did their relationship matter? Maybe yes, maybe no. It could just be a coincidence that Norman's mother's cousin lived there years ago and Moira owned it later, but I doubted it. However, it didn't mean there was anything sinister about selling a house to someone who's a distant cousin. I didn't even bother trying to figure out how Moira and Norman's mother's cousin were related.

"Wait a minute." I glanced around the library. It's never good for people to see you talking to yourself.

Bridler, I thought. Norman Fitzgerald's mother's cousin was Naomi Bridler, and that was Moira's maiden name. So, Moira might have been a first cousin to the woman she bought the house from.

The precise relationship didn't really matter, but it was a further indication that Norman Fitzgerald knew he would have access to my house for many years. He could get at things he hid there. Until I bought it.

I couldn't figure out why he waited until after it was in my possession to look for what he had hidden. The only thing that made sense was the timing. Everyone's lives were crazy for the months after Sandy. Fitzgerald probably didn't even know Moira's house was going to be in the tax auction. I would probably have to be content with not knowing why he hadn't tried to get the jewelry before I bought the house. I didn't like that at all.

I called Sergeant Morehouse. "You asked me if Norman Fitzgerald had brought Pebbles to my house. Why did you think he would?"

There were a couple of seconds of silence. "I thought I told you to stay outta this, Jolie."

"I am." I crossed my fingers. "I was just buying some food for Pebbles and it reminded me that you asked me that."

"Him and Moira were some kind of shirttail cousins. They knew each other a little, I don't think much."

"Well enough that you thought Norman had her skunk."

"I didn't think he had her skunk! That's why I asked you." When I didn't say anything, Morehouse said, "Everybody knew Moira Peebles hated to leave that skunk, but her daughter wasn't having anything to do with it. I thought there was maybe an off chance that Norman took it."

"Oh."

"That's all you got to say is *oh?* You think I don't know how to do my job?"

He's definitely grouchy today. "I'm sure you do, I just…"

"Good-bye, Jolie."

I looked at my now quiet mobile phone. "Huh. He said good-bye."

VIRGINIA MULLIGAN did not look too pleased to see me, but she did ask me to come in. I suppose she was afraid I would trade fart jokes with her grandson, whom I gathered was playing a video game in a back bedroom.

As we sat in her cheerfully decorated living room, I said, "I hear I might have you to thank for Pebbles."

"Oh dear. Who told you?" She looked apprehensive.

"A couple of people commented that skunks don't have much of a homing instinct, and then your grandson said he fed her when

Mrs. Peebles was in the hospital." I had decided not to give away Mrs. Murphy as the person who suggested Mrs. Mulligan as the Pebbles-keeper. "I guessed."

"When the hurricane was coming, I got so worried about her. I knew she wouldn't survive it. I took some of that smelly Skunkie Delight out to the wildlife area, and it didn't take her ten minutes to smell it and find me."

"Where do you get that stuff, anyway? Harry Steele gave me some and I keep meaning to ask him where he got it."

"Moira got it by mail order, I'm not sure from where. I helped her pack, and I can't tell you why I kept what she had left." She looked at me as if she was a kid who'd been caught with a spitball. "I suppose you want me to take her back. I let her out hoping you'd like her because my grandson was coming for spring break. I knew I could never give her away once he saw her here."

I smiled. "You're in luck. My cat likes her, and she was really lonely without Aunt Madge's dogs."

She smiled broadly. "Thank goodness. She uses more litter than three cats."

"I noticed," I said, dryly.

She sighed. "Moira was such a good friend. I miss her a lot. We'd wave at each other from our windows when it was raining. I still look over there expecting to see her."

"You can visit Pebbles anytime." I was about to go when I thought of something. "Did you know Norman Fitzgerald very well?"

"Not especially. He and Moira were some kind of distant cousin, and sometimes she'd see him at bingo at St. Anthony's."

"So, uh, you can't think of any reason why he'd have been on my porch that night, can you?"

She looked surprised. "I just assumed you knew him well. Didn't he help you move in?"

"No. Why would you think that?"

"I saw him over there the day you moved in. I thought," she looked confused, "that he had a key to your back door. Or maybe it was open."

"My back door?" I asked. "You mean he went in the house?"

"Why yes, he did. He came back out after a couple of minutes. You don't know him well?" Virginia looked uneasy.

"No, but I did buy some furniture from his auction just before that." I thought fast. I didn't want to give Virginia any reason to talk a lot about this. "In fact, afterwards he brought over a drawer to the chest of drawers I bought. Maybe he was just making sure it fit okay."

Her worried expression changed. "That would be like him."

After a quick hello to Nicholas, who was absorbed in his game, I left. *Norman Fitzgerald had a key to the back door. Did he go in the night he died, or did he give the key to someone else?*

I paused next to my car. "Who has that damn key now?"

Chapter Twenty

I WENT DIRECTLY to the hardware store and bought one of those locks that are hard metal and make it impossible to open the door from the outside if it's locked from the inside. Much better than a chain lock, and I had no idea how to install a deadbolt. Aunt Madge or Harry would. In fact, I thought George and Scoobie put one on Aunt Madge's basement door for her. But I wasn't sure if I wanted them to know about Fitzgerald having had a key.

Then I remembered I was supposed to share information with George. "Crud."

I had to share. It was the only way he'd tell me what he found, and I kind of liked having a reason to talk to him. I had begun to tell myself that whether George and I got back together was okay either way. We hadn't dated that long. I'd had a life before that. *A lot of it spent being angry with George…*

I pushed that thought aside. It had been two weeks since I had taken a fast walk or jog, and I ached from painting above my head and packing and unpacking boxes. Heck, there was enough boardwalk reconstructed that I could walk on it. That would be a treat. When I finished I'd find George.

MY WALKS AND JOGS provide good opportunities for clear thinking. However, when my thoughts were as muddled as they were now, clarity was elusive. I moved quickly down the boardwalk, not running but walking with my arms pumping at my sides, taking deep breaths of the salty smell of the ocean.

Every now and then I glanced in a store that was being readied for the first post-Sandy summer season. The Hurricane had damaged a number of boardwalk businesses, with most having a lot more damage than broken windows. A couple of smaller hotels fronted the boardwalk, and they had fared the best. They were newer construction. Even so, their lowest floor had taken water from the storm surge.

All of the boardwalk stores were painted in bright colors, and most of them either had been or were being repainted. Wind had blown sand so hard that it was as if the frame buildings had been sandblasted.

I forced myself to stop looking at boardwalk activity and focus. As far as I knew, no one had seen Clive Dorner and Norman Fitzgerald together in the few days before Norman's death. There was no reason to think that they had been constant buddies, but since Clive was Norman's executor, Clive must have been closer to his uncle than some of the other nieces and nephews. *So what?*

I assumed that the jewelry behind the wall in my house had been placed there by Mr. Fitzgerald. He was the thieving auctioneer related to the woman who owned the house when it seemed the wall had been redone.

Though it would be hard to get at the diamonds, if he didn't plan to sell them right away (and maybe he couldn't because they would be recognized), the wall was perfect. Maybe his cousin even knew what he was doing. Maybe he stole the stuff he put in my house early in his criminal career and had forgotten it.

So why not remove the jewelry before Naomi Bridler moved? It occurred to me that I didn't know if the elderly cousin had died somewhat suddenly, making it hard to get at the diamonds. Mr. Fitzgerald must have been pleased that another relative had bought it. And why not get the jewelry when Moira Peebles lived there?

Of course, if he had one of the back door keys, what did it matter who lived there? I supposed it would be hard to explain if you were caught cutting into the wall board, whether you had a key or not. Again I wondered if he had forgotten he hid jewelry there long ago.

And then there was Clive Dorner. Why call me to look around Ocean Alley? He must have learned that the jewels were hidden in the house. And only Norman Fitzgerald could have told him that.

"Jolie! Jolie!"

I slowed and turned to see Max hurrying down the boardwalk toward me.

"Hi, Jolie. Do you like your house? Your house?" he asked, breathless.

"I do. Thanks for helping me move in."

He stopped a few feet in front of me and looked around. "The boardwalk's really different. Really different." He looked sad.

"It is, but I think it will be as nice as it ever was, once everything is finished."

"There's holes," he said, very seriously.

"Holes? Oh, where a couple of the stores were torn down. I think there will be more stores, just not all for this summer." Technically, all of the buildings probably could have been repaired, but some were so old that the owners were glad to be able to take them down and build a more modern facility.

I gestured to one of the benches that had only recently been installed on the boardwalk. They were the kind with large concrete legs, with wooden seats and backs. The benches were fastened so well there was no moving them. Apparently the city council hoped they would be sturdier should we get another major hurricane. *Not if, when.*

As we sat I remembered what I wanted to ask Max. "You said a friend of mine came to the house before I got there with the truck, on moving day."

"I said that, yes I did."

"Did you know him?" I asked. At the time it did not seem he did.

"I do now. He was in the paper." He frowned. "I don't want to sit on your porch swing again. Not again."

"So it was Mr. Fitzgerald?" I asked, quietly.

He frowned and nodded. "You should throw it away."

"You're probably right. But I have to wait a bit. It'll be kind of expensive to get another swing."

His expression brightened. "The VA gives me money." He frowned. "But I can't spend it all."

I realized that he probably had some kind of financial guardian. "Do you, uh, get what you need?"

He nodded emphatically. "I have a nice house. Nice house. You can visit. Scoobie comes."

Scoobie is full of surprises. "Good for him. I'll come sometime."

He got up quickly. "I'm walking. Walking."

I watched him move down the boardwalk, toward Java Jolt. Joe sometimes gave him day-old muffins.

When I lived at the Cozy Corner it was an easy walk to the boardwalk, but my house was not as close, so I had driven. I stood slowly and began to walk to my car.

All my conversation with Max had done was confirm what Virginia Mulligan had told me. Norman Fitzgerald had been in my house the day I moved in.

I needed to call George. With a small pang of guilt–very small–I realized I should tell Sergeant Morehouse as well. *He wouldn't tell you. True, but he can toss you in jail, and you can't toss him anywhere.*

GEORGE DIDN'T ANSWER my phone call, which meant he was working on a story or in his editor's office. Or ignoring me.

I was in Harry's office trolling the Internet looking for banks or mortgage companies Harry and I had not previously contacted. I wanted to make sure every one of them knew Steele Appraisals would appraise any house, any time.

Now that Harry mostly lived at the Cozy Corner, his house had a kind of forlorn feel. He comes to the office, of course, and he was still doing some renovation work upstairs. But there was no longer the smell of coffee in the morning and there was a layer of dust on the file cabinet in the office. *I should dust them.*

My phone chirped. "Find anything?" George asked, before I could say hello.

"Would finding out that Mr. Fitzgerald apparently had a key to the back door of my house be anything?"

"You're kidding. You're not kidding?"

"The day we moved in Max said a friend of mine had stopped by, and I didn't think anything of it. This morning Virginia Mulligan said she thought Fitzgerald helped me move in because she saw him go in the back door the day we brought all my stuff over there."

"Damn," he said, softly. "Maybe looking for the jewelry, you think?"

"Maybe. But he knew I'd taken the walls down to studs." I paused. "It's not so important for that day, but it tells me he may have had other hiding places. And that he could have been in there the night he died, or maybe…"

"Maybe someone knew he had a key and killed him for it," George said.

"I guess I should tell Morehouse."

"Are you nuts? He'd tell us, you, to lay off."

"Like I care. Besides, it's murder, George."

I was going to tell Sergeant Morehouse, I just hadn't decided when.

Chapter Twenty-One

CLIVE DORNER'S FUNERAL was in Ocean Grove on Saturday, but I did not plan to attend. I hadn't known him well, and while that in and of itself was not a reason to stay home, there was the Sergeant Morehouse reason. He or someone else from the Ocean Alley Police Department would go to the funeral, and I'd be reminded that I was to stay away from anything to do with Norman Fitzgerald or Clive Dorner.

Since no one had said to stay away from people Dorner knew, I decided to find Fiona Henderson. She wasn't in the phone book. Scoobie had said he thought he'd seen her around town, but he didn't seem to know much about her. Since Scoobie thought I should butt out, he might not tell me how to find her even if he did know.

That left Aunt Madge, and all I'd get from her was more advice to mind my own business. *You could ask George.* Yes, I could, but I opted for Java Jolt first, since I had seen Fiona in there with Dorner. I had not counted on Lester being there.

"Hey, kid. Lemme know when you want to look for a bigger place." He was busily pouring multiple packs of sugar into his coffee.

Joe gave me an amused grin and slight shake of his head.

"Lester." I waited for him to look at me. "I like my little house."

"Sure, sure." He patted the table. "Come over after you get your cuppa joe."

I ordered a mocha latte and waited for Joe to turn on the milk scalding machine before I asked, quietly, "Did you know the woman Clive Dorner was with the other day? I mean, I know her name is Fiona Henderson, but I wanted to talk to her. Does she live in town?"

"I figured you'd know her. She's one of the Murphy girls. Lives with her sister and a bunch of kids."

It took me a few seconds to work it out. "Her mom is the Mrs. Murphy who lives in the assisted living place?"

"Bingo. I take it you're going to bug her?"

"Bug who?" Lester asked.

My back was to Lester, and Joe could see my expression, which surely looked as frustrated as I felt. Joe smirked. I smoothed my expression and turned toward Lester.

"Bug Fiona Henderson. You know her, right?" I sat next to Lester.

He frowned lightly. "If she's who I think, she's Francis and Mary Murphy's daughter."

"I saw her in here with Clive Dorner one day."

"Jerk God rest his soul." He said this in one fast sentence.

"Do you have a phone number for her, or know her address? I couldn't find her in the phone book."

"Cause she had a restraining order on her ex," Lester slurped as he took a drink of his coffee. "You're better off stopping by her place." He gave me the address, which was not far from First Prez.

"Thanks." I jotted it in my small notebook.

"Um…" I started to tell him about Betty Fowler and decided against it. If Lester thought Dorner was a jerk for being in a vacant house without his agent, I could only imagine what he'd say if he learned Dorner had probably been looking with another agent. It occurred to me that maybe Betty knew something more about Dorner, but that would have to wait.

"Um what?" Lester asked.

"Um, I can't remember what I was going to say. Too much going on, I guess."

"Yeah," Lester said, seeming to be sympathetic. "You know what would distract you? I gotta house on Conch that…"

He ducked as I hurled a sugar packet at him.

FIONA HENDERSON look embarrassed as she offered me a seat in the family room of the large frame house she shared with her sister and all of their kids. "You probably wonder why I didn't mention who my mom was the first time we met."

"Not really." I smiled. "I have actually been known to deny who my mother is, but she's a special case."

That seemed to relax her. "I wasn't embarrassed. Patricia had a kind of new boyfriend, Arman, so I didn't want to keep us standing there talking about mom. You said you thought I could help you with something." She gestured to an upholstered chair that had seen better days, and took a plastic truck off its mate and sat across from me.

"You can imagine what a shock it was to find Norman Fitzgerald on my front porch."

"I'm sure it was very hard for you." She hesitated. "You talked to my mom, so you know he was in business with my father."

"And I have heard he may not have been a very scrupulous business partner."

"When we were little he always gave us peppermint candies." She shook her head slightly, with a frown. "The stealing wouldn't have been so bad, except my mother has to live on very limited resources. Assisted living costs a lot, and even with watching every penny, she'll be out of money in about eighteen months."

"And she might not be in that situation if the proceeds had been split evenly?"

"You never know how retirement investments are going to work out, but my parents were very frugal. Anytime they had something extra they socked it away. Some of the things Norman Fitzgerald kept for himself were quite valuable."

"And," I wanted to be sure I understood here, "if your parents had had that money twenty or more years ago, then the investment would have grown quite a bit."

She shrugged. "Grown, and maybe my dad would have been comfortable buying a riskier mutual fund or something that would have grown even more. Or it all could have gone down the drain, I guess."

"But you don't think so."

She shook her head firmly. "Like I said, my parents saved and invested well."

"So, how does all that put you with Clive Dorner?" I asked.

A look of what I guessed to be frustration or dislike crossed her face. "You already know he was Fitzgerald's nephew. He called me, maybe three weeks before you saw me with him. He said he knew his uncle had "rooked" my father, those were his words, and while he could not change that, he could help me make some money for my kids and me. And Patricia's, but she didn't want anything to do with him."

"Make some money?"

"He said he was really good at buying houses that needed just a little bit of work, like paint and such, and then selling them for a lot more. He said he could make me a partner for a couple of the houses." She shrugged. "Sounded good."

The words that went through my mind were *too good to be true*. "How much did you have to put up?"

"He said only three thousand dollars, to cover some of the closing costs. I took it out of my 401(k)." She guessed my skepticism from my expression. "I know, sounds pretty generous, since he said he'd give me half of the profits."

Generous? Not likely. "Did he explain that, uh, generosity?"

"He said he spent a lot of time in Ocean Alley when he was little, with Norman and his wife. You know she died a long time ago, right?"

I nodded.

"Apparently Norman used to do some nice things for him then, and later, like send him money when he was in college. He said he felt kind of guilty because some of that money should probably have been my parents', or ours. Patricia's and mine."

I sat back in my chair and just looked at her. "You know, I only talked to Clive a few times. I guess this doesn't sound very charitable, but he never struck me as being too concerned with anyone but himself."

"That's what Patricia said. And mom. I dunno, maybe I shouldn't have agreed to meet him at Java Jolt that day. It's just," she waved her hand around the room, "divorce doesn't leave you with a lot to raise your kids with."

I knew about divorce cleaning your clock, but I couldn't imagine having to raise kids without a partner's income. From what little I knew, even if a high-wage earning spouse paid child support, it's nothing like having another wage earner under the same roof.

"Did you ever see any of your $3,000 again?"

"I had only just given it to him. He had me wait until he found something that would be really good. He wanted me to see it before we, I guess I should say he, actually invested the money." She sighed. "He had left me a message a couple of days before he died. He said he'd found a good one and would call back when I could look at it. Then he died. I know I should feel really bad for him, and of course I do, but it would have been so nice to have something saved for the kids' college."

"Do you have any way to get your money back?"

"Peter, my boyfriend, said he would find out who is handling Dorner's estate. I have my canceled check."

"I bet that'll work." *If you're really, really lucky.* After another second, I asked, "Did you know that I was at the house where he died?"

Her eyes widened, her mouth opened in a small oh, and she almost stammered. "You mean at the same time? That wasn't in the paper."

"Jennifer Stenner and I were both there. The paper played it down, just said a few people saw the fire at the same time."

"That's really weird." She looked at me with an odd expression. I figured she was wondering if it had been a smart thing to let me into her house.

"I don't really think anyone knew we'd be there then. It was just a house to appraise, and I didn't have a schedule."

"Still…you are either very lucky yourself or very unlucky for other people."

"I've heard that before. I guess because I was around both of them right after they died I'm more than just interested."

"Are you helping the police?" she asked.

"They would definitely say no."

Fiona didn't say anything, but she radiated *what do you care?*

"I just…didn't like finding Mr. Fitzgerald like that."

We spoke for another couple of minutes about her three children, ages five, seven and nine, and as she walked me to the door, Fiona said she was really glad I wasn't hurt at the house fire.

I had my hand on the doorknob when it was pushed open, very fast, and I stepped back a couple of steps rather than get bowled over. I recognized the man as one of the two who had been with Fiona and her sister at the auction. He didn't look pleased to see me, but recovered quickly.

"Gosh, I'm sorry. With the kids at soccer, I didn't think anyone would be here except Fiona." He pulled the screen door shut and left the main door open as he held out a hand. "Peter McManus. We saw each other at the auction where you beat out the girls."

He had an air of self-confidence that seemed to go with his kind of rugged good looks. Piercing blue eyes stared into mine as I took his hand, which he had extended in a forthright shake. "I remember. I think you were the one who said the drawers would be too shallow. I have to agree."

He laughed. "Damn, I love to say I told you so." He leaned over and gave Fiona a kiss on the cheek. "Do you have time for coffee before the kids get home from soccer?"

Fiona nodded and smiled at him, and then me. "Peter has the independent insurance agency next to Mr. Markle's grocery store."

"I'll have to remember that." I put my hand on the screen door's knob.

"Hang on." Peter took out a card and handed it to me. "Never let it be said that a good sales agent is shy."

As I drove away, I thought about Fiona and Patricia and their children. I figured some of the money from the jewelry hidden behind my walls should be theirs, maybe all of it. But before I raised their hopes, I thought I should do more digging. What if it had been Moira Peebles' jewelry, or another prior owner's? A premature assumption could lead to a court fight and a lot of disappointment.

Chapter Twenty-Two

WHEN I'M TRYING to decide whether to tell Sergeant Morehouse something, my primary criterion is whether he could hear it from someone else first. The business with the key to my house was probably a toss-up in terms of him finding out, but I decided I was better off telling him about it, even if George disagreed. I debated whether to tell him what Fiona had told me about Clive offering to make her a partner in a couple of rehabbed houses.

I was not sure if Morehouse would be in on a Saturday, but the young officer at the desk said he was, and this time he did not ask why I was there.

Morehouse waved me into his office and I sat across from him. "And?"

"There's something I need to tell you," I began.

"It damn well better be something like what you feed that skunk," he growled.

"She likes beans better than cauliflower, but no, it's more like I think Mr. Fitzgerald had a key to my back door."

"What?! And you didn't tell me this? Where's the key?"

"First, I'm not one hundred percent positive, but Virginia Mulligan said that on the day I moved in she saw him go in the back door, which would have been before I got there."

"That was Sunday a week ago. You shoulda told me right away." He pulled his notebook to him and scribbled something.

"She just told me. She assumed I'd given it to him so she didn't think it was odd. If I hadn't gone over to her place to see if she'd had Pebbles over the winter, we wouldn't have even talked."

"She had the damn skunk?"

I nodded.

He stared at me for a couple of seconds, then put both hands behind his head and stared at the ceiling for at least fifteen seconds. Finally, he looked at me. "This could mean a couple of important things. Or nothing."

"But more likely important, don't you think? It means he could have gone in there the night he was murdered, or the killer did, too."

"Which begs the question, what were they looking for?"

Morehouse said "the jewelry" and I said, "Stuff that Mr. Fitzgerald took from the auctions."

He shook a finger at me. "What makes you say that? Who have you been talking to?"

I gave him what I hoped was a cool stare. "I read in Mr. Fitzgerald's obit that his partner was Francis Murphy, and I know his wife."

"You mean your aunt knows his wife. You don't."

"Excuse me, I know who I know. I met her at Ruth Riordan's funeral, and she's funny. I visited her a couple of times."

His expression was almost amused. "People you visit end up dead sometimes." Then he got serious again. "But you must have talked to her about your jewelry or something like that."

"I did tell her what I found, yes."

He massaged his temples as he spoke. "It's not likely she goes around killing people, though she could have told someone that there might be valuables hidden in your house."

"Her daughters, maybe, but they both work and have young children. Even if they wished the guy dead I doubt they could find the time to do it. Anyway, I didn't talk to her until after Fitzgerald died."

"It was a strong blow to the head. A strong woman could have done it, of course, but more likely a man. Besides," he hesitated, then said, "Even if you told her before he died, I've known her girls all their lives. They'd be near the bottom of any list of suspects I had."

"If you had one."

"Don't you have to be somewhere?"

I DID HAVE PLACES TO GO. But first I wanted to know if Clive Dorner had bought houses in Ocean Alley. From Lester, I knew that Dorner had signed contracts to buy a couple, but the contracts hadn't gone through yet. He could have bought through Betty or another agent.

If he had been a more up-front person, Dorner would have worked with only one local agent, and I could ask that person. Since Dorner was apparently pitting agents against one another, and I had no idea how many he used, I thought about the title company.

Title companies search the past owners of a property to make sure the current owner has the right to sell it and there are no liens on a property. They often know who has made recent offers on properties. True, they may not be brought into the process until after a potential buyer makes an offer, but in a town like Ocean Alley they generally know the status of properties on the market. Banks might, too, but no banker would talk to me about a client, dead or alive.

I pulled into the parking lot for Ocean Ally Title Search, glad it was before noon. They weren't open Saturday afternoon. A married couple owned it, Cassie and Glenn Stetson. I always remembered their name because Glenn wore the large hat of the same name and liked to pretend he was from Texas. I happened to know he was from Hoboken.

The door tinkled as I entered. There were two doors off the main room, and a narrow hallway that I assumed led to rest rooms or a small kitchenette. A counter separated the entry area from all of this. I stood on the public side of the counter.

Cassie looked up from a desk on the far side of the office. "Jolie. Goodness. You found Norman Fitzgerald." Cassie was about fifty, with hips that showed that she had had several children. She wasn't heavy, but had the air of someone who was comfortable with a middle-aged body. Which I doubted I would be. *Not that I have immediate plans for kidlets.*

"I did. It was not a good day for either of us." *Lame.*

Cassie walked to the counter and stood across from me, elbows resting on the counter. "He was a good man. We'd known each other for at least twenty years."

I nodded. It seemed safer than commenting on what I had learned about the 'good man' in the last few days. "I'm actually here about his nephew, Clive Dorner. I wondered if you would be comfortable giving me some information."

She frowned. "Gosh. I didn't realize Mr. Dorner was Norman's nephew."

Aha. She's been working with Dorner.

"He wasn't from here, though he grew up in Ocean Grove, so he was apparently here a lot as a kid."

"Dorner spoke at his uncle's funeral." Glenn Stetson spoke from the doorway of one of the two offices.

"Oh, he did?" Cassie looked at me. "We need to keep the office open, so usually only one of us goes to funerals or meetings."

"I believe I saw you at Norman's funeral." Glenn's tone was not as welcoming as Cassie's had been. "Kind of odd that his nephew died so soon after he did."

"I thought so, too," I said.

"What was your business with Clive Dorner?" Glenn asked.

Cassie stepped back to the desk, apparently having decided that her husband had a reason for being somewhat distant with me.

"He called me a couple of weeks ago. I guess he thought I was still working in real estate rather than just doing appraisals, because he wanted me to show him around town…"

"He was working with Betty Fowler," Glenn said.

"And, at my recommendation, with Lester Argrow."

"Lester!" Cassie and Glenn looked at each other as they said this together.

"He said he wanted bargains, and Lester is pretty good at sniffing those out. I didn't know he'd been working with Betty, of course."

"I bet Betty doesn't know that," Cassie said. "I can only imagine the fight over commissions."

"And it's not really our business," her husband said. He kind of implied it might not be mine.

"Clive also talked to me a couple of times about how I might fix up the little house I just bought." *Okay, a slight exaggeration.* "And he talked to a friend of mine about investing with him." *Friend? A bigger exaggeration.* "It seemed as if he was…into a lot at once. I suppose I'm just being plain nosy, wondering if he ever closed a deal."

Cassie looked as if she might understand my interest, but Glenn did not seem to share that view. "And you don't want to talk to Betty or Lester?"

I raised an eyebrow at him. "How far away do you think I'd have to stand from either of them if they found out Dorner was using two agents? And that I might have had something to do with that."

At that Glenn relaxed. "Good point." He glanced at his wife, who shrugged. "We had just begun a couple of title searches. I don't think it would be right to tell you which properties. They'll probably go right back on the market."

"I appreciate you telling me that. I had been about to appraise the house Clive was found in and…"

"He put in a contract on it?" Glenn asked.

"Uh, no. I was appraising it on behalf of a bank."

Glenn frowned. "I supposed the bank was about to sell it. We were doing a title search on it, but not with him as the buyer."

"I wonder what he was doing there?" I mused.

"That might be a question better left to the police," Glenn said.

That was when I knew I had made a mistake coming to their office.

Chapter Twenty-Three

I DIDN'T RETURN Sergeant Morehouse's phone call Sunday morning. I figured he was calling me about the visit to the Stetson's rather than about something I needed to know. He didn't call me back.

As I made a second cup of instant coffee, something furry nudged my ankle. "What are you looking at?" I asked Pebbles.

She nudged again, harder. "I know you didn't nudge Mrs. Peebles that hard. She probably would have fallen over."

The skunk turned and waddled toward the bathroom. Since she usually only bugs me when she wants food, which is often, I finished stirring my coffee and followed her. Jazz sat on the bathroom sink, swatting at something in it.

"Tattle tale." I peered into the sink.

"Ugh!" The cicada was at least two inches long. With its translucent wings and colorful orange and black back it looked like something that should be in an exhibit in a science class. Certainly it had no place in my house.

"Where did that come from?"

Jazz, intent on her pastime, did not respond.

I picked up a washcloth and laid it over the cicada. Jazz double-swatted my hand as I began to lift it out of the sink. "It isn't yours."

She thought differently and tried to climb up my arm. Even as small as she is, when a cat tries to claw its way up one of your appendages, it hurts.

"Cut it out." I jiggled my arm and she jumped to the floor. That put her nose to nose with Pebbles, and for a moment I thought they'd go after each other, but they just sniffed. Jazz walked around Pebbles, with her tail in the air.

I looked back at the washcloth, which was moving slightly. I didn't want to kill the damn cicada, just let it outside. I didn't want to pick it up. I'm not overly afraid of bugs, but it was as long as my pinky.

Someone pounded on my front door, and I jumped. I walked into the living room, careful not to show myself, and peered out of the window. Sergeant Morehouse stood on the front porch.

"Nuts." I opened the door. Before he could say anything, I said, "Could you get the cicada out of my bathroom sink, please?"

"You're kiddin' right?" He walked in.

"Nope." I pointed to the small hallway that led to the bathroom and two bedrooms.

He shook his head as he walked in and looked at the washcloth in the sink. "You're saying it's under here?"

"Yep. I didn't want to kill it, but I want it outside."

He picked up the washcloth, carefully cupping the cicada in it. He walked to the door, shook the bug outside, and threw the washcloth at me.

I caught it. "Isn't it early for them?" I gestured to the rocking chair.

"I didn't come over here to talk cicadas with you." He sat. "But it's April so the first crop is out. What in the hell were you doing talking to the Stetsons about Dorner's real estate dealings?"

"Why would they call you about that? They know me." I countered.

"Which is probably why they called. What were you doin'?"

"Two people died near me in the last few days. I want to know why." I held his gaze, which was intense.

Morehouse spoke slowly. "I'm here rather than screaming at you on the phone because I'm trying to figure what makes you tick before I arrest you for interfering with a police investigation."

I started to tell him Dorner probably rooked Fiona Henderson out of $3,000, but that was her business and she likely had not told this to Morehouse. "I want to know…" I began.

"No, you want to meddle. Jolie, these deaths are likely related, and the person who killed these two men could just as easily add one more notch to his murder belt."

"So, Dorner didn't die because of smoke or fire? Do you know if they were both killed by the same person?" I asked.

"Damn it to hell, listen to me! Lay off. Don't get involved. Mind your own beeswax. Can I be any clearer?"

"Do you know if Dorner spent a lot of time with his uncle?"

He briefly put his head in his hands, then stood. "I'm not kiddin' about arresting you if you interfere." He pointed at me. "And then I'll ask the judge to recognize that you're a danger to yourself so you can only get out on bail if you stay with Madge and Harry."

"Why punish them?"

Morehouse slammed the door on his way out.

BECAUSE PLANNING the so-called Harvest for All birthday party took a lot of time, I decided to wait a couple of days before I looked into Dorner's death any more. Neither he or I was going anywhere, and the diamonds and two of the gold bracelets were secure in the jewelry store's safe.

Ramona had worn the other gold bracelet several times. While she'd had several compliments about it, no one mentioned that it looked familiar.

We wanted the birthday party to be held before the full tourist season began on Memorial Day weekend. That meant we had to hustle, so I spent part of Tuesday collecting door prizes and asking businesses to donate cake and ice cream and such.

Aunt Madge, who would never admit that the party idea was hers, had suggested asking businesses to donate cakes that said, "Happy Birthday from" and then named the business. Jennifer coordinated this. She's active in the Chamber and knows everyone, plus she's good at sucking up.

I was glad she agreed to find the cakes. She had been even more rattled by the fire than I had, and I thought she might want to stay away from me. She probably did, but she's good to Harvest for All.

I worked on donations for door prizes. They cost us nothing and people are generally willing to spend one dollar for each chance to win. We did have one prize that people could register to win without making a donation. Charlotte Evans said she would donate a basket full of, as she said, anything that a person could use on the beach—sun screen, towel, bug spray, a visor cap, inflatable beach ball, and more.

Lester wanted us to raffle a one-percent discount off of his commission if he sold a house, but I told him it was blatant self-advertising and people would rather have a tangible prize, even if it was a gift certificate or something. He said he would donate two cases of the liquid string and a bunch of long handled scrub brushes to clean up the soapy string foam.

At Java Jolt one day he said, "I'm thinkin' I can ask Ramona to put my business name and phone number on the scrub brush handles." He said this with a certainty I did not share. Ramona had her hands full organizing her supplies to do the caricatures she does for a donation to Harvest for All.

Scoobie had two big tests coming up, but he managed to convince the two local radio stations to do public service announcements, and said he would personally record them. I didn't think I would want to hear them in advance, and when he asked why, I simply said that way I didn't have to share the blame. He saw my point.

George was not focusing on the birthday party. I remembered that he wiggled out of doing a lot at last year's hotdog eating contest. Now he was working on an article that tied together the so-called pilfering at the auctions to Mr. Fitzgerald's recently evident wealth. It would not be a popular article, and his editor was demanding "rock solid proof."

"Does that mean you don't always have proof?" I asked. "I can think of some examples."

He bristled. "I always think what I print is true."

He, Scoobie, Ramona, Jennifer and I were at Newhart's. The diner is an Ocean Alley institution. Its walls host dozens of photos of local people and events, including one of Uncle Gordon.

We talked about the business contributions Jennifer garnered. I pressed George again about how he would get rock solid proof. Jennifer and Ramona were at the salad bar, and Scoobie had ordered his favorite, a grilled cheese on wheat, and he followed the conversation George and I were having, his eyes traveling between us.

George glowered. "Are you kidding? I don't get you. After you told Morehouse about Fitzgerald having a key, I'm not sharing much with you."

I frowned. "I've told you what I know. I just thought the police should know about the key."

"Plus, Morehouse would kill her if he found out later," Scoobie said.

Scoobie gets me more than George does.

"What key?" Jennifer asked. She placed her salad bowl on the table and swung into the booth.

"Nuts," George said.

"Nuts what?" she asked. She was carefully slicing lettuce in her salad and did not see him wince.

This ought to be good.

His tone implied a warning. "You can't tell anyone this."

I cleared my throat and he looked at me.

"Whose house is it we're talking about?" I asked.

"Oh, right." It was clear he had not considered this.

I looked at Jennifer. "You know Mrs. Mulligan?" Jennifer nodded. "She thought Mr. Fitzgerald had a key to my house. I don't know that he did." *Oh yes I do.*

"That's interesting." She popped a cherry tomato in her mouth and chewed for a few seconds. "He could have had keys to a lot of places, you know?"

George choked and dribbled water down his chin.

Ramona handed him a napkin. "What makes you think that?"

Jennifer shrugged. "I don't know, but a lot of people gave him keys so he could take stuff out of houses. You know, to take things to an auction. Or even if they had the auction at their house, it might be that the people who lived there had died or gone into a nursing home. Norman's people would go through everything."

"So, he could have made copies," I said.

"If he did," Scoobie said, "there could be a bunch of them in his house."

"In his house? Why would he keep them?" Jennifer asked.

I chose my words carefully. "Some people wonder how he accumulated the kind of wealth he must have had to make all those donations. Especially the one to the hospital for the new pediatrics wing."

Jennifer's eyes widened. "Oh! You mean he took things from houses? Like a cat burglar?"

George had recovered his voice. "A cat burglar breaks into a house, usually when people aren't home. There is some question about whether Mr. Fitzgerald took some things he was supposed to auction."

"She waved a hand as she picked up her iced tea. "Only Elmira." She took a drink and set it down. "We need to get to work."

I was happy to get off the topic. Newhart's was not crowded, and we were not yelling, but it still seemed better to keep a conversation like this private. Plus, I had to think about how to get into Norman Fitzgerald's house to see if there were extra keys.

ON WEDNESDAY I went to visit Mrs. Murphy again, in part because I wanted to and in part to keep George from doing it. He wanted quotes from Elmira Washington and Mrs. Murphy about how Fitzgerald may have swindled them.

Elmira was all for it, and it was to the point that he had stopped returning her phone calls. She demanded to know when the article would be printed.

Mrs. Murphy very politely told George she would think about it, and that she would call him if she wanted to talk to him.

However, when I visited her she was very interested in hearing that others might think Fitzgerald did not get all his money honestly. "Have you heard of anyone other than Elmira?"

"Not yet. One issue is that a lot of the items were part of estate sales, so the people who best knew the merchandise were not there to see if anything was missing."

"I won't mind saying something publicly at some time," she said, "but right now Peter, that's Fiona's boyfriend, is working with the lawyer handling Norman's estate. I don't want to create hard feelings. Not yet, anyway."

I knew that a local attorney had become executor after Clive's death. Apparently sensing it could be a dangerous job, none of his cousins wanted to do it.

"Is the attorney someone you know?" All I knew was that the name was Charles Jessup. I didn't know him.

"No. Very young, I hear." As I settled on one of her overstuffed armchairs, she continued. "Peter is sharp. Fitzgerald's surviving nieces and nephews have banded together and they want a fifty-fifty split from the sale of the business. That's me getting half. Peter thinks that if we can show that Norman stole items and it reduced Francis' income, I might be able to get more."

"How can you prove that?"

"In the basement of the house the girls share there are a lot of files for auctions. I had forgotten about them. They were in my basement, and I wanted to throw them away when I sold our house and moved in here."

"But your daughters kept them? Did they suspect Mr. Fitzgerald of any thefts?"

"They say no, that it just seemed someone should go through the files before they were tossed, and they kept meaning to do it." She gave a smile of pride. "My girls are so responsible."

"Thank goodness for busy lives." A light finally lit in my distracted brain. "So Peter and Fiona, and maybe Patricia and her boyfriend are going to go through the files? Maybe I could help."

She laughed and then grimaced with her chronic back pain. "I knew you'd say that. Have a peek at a few of the files that are on the stack on my dresser. That will show you what we're dealing with."

She pointed to a room on the right, and I walked into it. "Yikes." The stack of brown accordion folders, the kind that could hold several manila folders, was almost one foot high. I looked at a few tabs, most of which were names of individuals who'd had property auctioned. A couple were businesses, and I spotted the name of a small drug store that had gone out of business when two chains had opened large pharmacies in the area.

I took two files from the top of the pile and settled in across from Mrs. Murphy. The first item in each folder was an inventory sheet. It listed the items and assigned them individual inventory numbers, gave the suggested opening bid, and then listed the actual selling price. The final column listed the bid number of the person who bought the item.

Next in the folder was a list of people who signed up to bid. They had to show ID, so there was an address next to each name. Each person had a unique bidder number, and a look at the inventory list showed me that some people bought a number of items.

The final piece of paperwork was the original contract to conduct the auction. It was almost amusingly short. I supposed that Francis Murphy and Norman Fitzgerald generally dealt with people they knew. *Plus, a lot of them were dead.*

The reason each auction had its own accordion folder was the receipt books. Each was about six by three inches, and they contained a carbon of every receipt from auction purchases. I glanced at one. Each of the receipts had a name and the person's auction number, and then the inventory item numbers for what they bought. You could not tell what they paid for each item, just the total paid. *That would take forever to cross reference.*

A few items on the inventory list were crossed off. "Does the line through an item on the inventory sheet mean it didn't sell?" I asked.

"It means the item was removed from the auction," Mrs. Murphy said.

"Was that common?"

She put a hand in front of her, palm down and at about heart height, and wiggled it. "Maybe yes, maybe no. The person who contracted for the auction got to see the list of inventoried items before the sale, and they signed off agreeing that that's what was to be sold. If it was their parents' house, they might not have realized what all was in it. Occasionally they would see something they didn't want to sell."

She took a drink from the small glass of iced tea I had poured for her. "There are some auctioneers who say once you turn a batch of items over to them to inventory you can't remove something without some kind of fee, but Francis and Norman never did that."

I thought for a moment. "How would you know if something never made it to the inventory list?"

"It could have happened anytime. We didn't have two people work together at all times. Of course, we knew the employees well. We never saw missing items as an issue until Francis spotted that the Cartier watch hadn't been specifically mentioned on an inventory list."

"And there would have been no way to go back to see what else had been stolen before it was inventoried."

"Not really," she said. "Only if an owner or an estate lawyer spotted that something in the house wasn't on the list, or perhaps a close friend hoped to bid on a particular item and couldn't find it at the auction. That would have been unusual."

I walked back into the room that had the stack of folders and this time looked at all the names on the folders. I was astounded to see a folder marked Gordon Richards. Aunt Madge had never mentioned that any of Uncle Gordon's belongings had been auctioned. I pulled the folder and sat across from Mrs. Murphy.

"I asked Peter to see if his file was still there." She nodded to herself. "Madge had his things as part of a larger auction, but of course each person's goods were inventoried separately. Madge might take a look at that."

I studied the inventory list. I had been only five when Uncle Gordon died and had few memories of any of his things except his pocket watch. Most of my childhood memories were at the Cozy Corner, after Aunt Madge sold their bungalow and opened the B&B.

I understood why she had participated in an auction as I reviewed the list. There were several hunting rifles and bows, a lot of fishing equipment, a fertilizer spreader, baseball bats, a pipe holder, oars—in short, things Aunt Madge would not use. I glanced at the total amount she had earned—eight hundred forty dollars. That would have been a meaningful amount. At prices of the time, she could have bought an entire room of B&B furniture at another auction.

Aunt Madge bought most of the furniture at the B&B after Uncle Gordon died. They had a two-bedroom bungalow, and the

B&B has eight guest rooms, even though she rarely rents all of them. In fact, one is now a den for Harry.

"If I know Aunt Madge, she has a list of everything she gave them to auction."

"More than twenty years ago?" Mrs. Murphy asked.

"If it pertained to Uncle Gordon, she's got it. Hunting and sports stuff aside."

"OH MY. I'D FORGOTTEN about most of this. Wait a sec." Aunt Madge walked back into the bedroom she and Harry now share and came out with one of those small photo albums you used to get when pictures were actually developed at the drug store.

"I don't remember that album."

"It's new. Harry and I each did one about our late spouses, kind of a life story. I especially wanted to learn about his Agnes, since his children and grandchildren talk about her a lot."

As she flipped back a couple of pages all I could think of was how…grounded she and Harry were. I could barely imagine such a secure relationship.

"Here it is." We both sat on the love seat and she handed me the album.

I started to laugh. Uncle Gordon held a very large bow and a quiver with maybe a dozen arrows. He had posed for the photo next to a large target that sat on a bale of hay. On the ground next to him, reaching for the bow, was a two-year old who was definitely me.

"Your father and Gordon thought that was so funny. Your mother and Renée were shopping for her Easter dress. When she saw the picture, your mother didn't see the humor."

"Yeah, well." *No surprise there.* "Can I look at more?"

She handed it to me and I flipped through slowly. "Oh, here's one with his bootlegger boat."

"Rum runner. Remember the difference?"

I did, and nodded. A bootlegger made the illicit liquor during Prohibition, a rum runner merely delivered it. Uncle Gordon was a lot older than Aunt Madge, and he would help his uncle bring in booze delivered to the beach, at night. They sold it to a local speakeasy.

I handed her back the album. "Very nice to have these in one place."

"Yes, they're kind of biographies of the people we most loved." She had a matter-of-fact tone as she put the album on the coffee table and picked up the inventory list. "I didn't look at this much at the time. I needed the money to start to furnish this place, and it was hard to part with some of his things."

"Couldn't my parents…?" I began.

"Your father said ask anytime if I needed money, but I knew I could make it work. And now this place almost runs itself. Hmmm." She flipped through the three-page list quickly.

"Hmmm what?" I asked.

"He had an antique rifle that belonged to his grandfather. The story was that he brought it home from the Civil War, but Gordon didn't think it was that old." She ran her finger down each page of the list. "I know I gave it to Norman."

We looked at each other. "That was almost twenty-five years ago."

Aunt Madge frowned. "No wonder he had so much money."

Chapter Twenty-Four

FIONA'S BOYFRIEND BEAT me to the proverbial punch by calling on Thursday to suggest we get together, and said we could use his insurance office. His conference room table bore three piles of folders. Each pile was about twelve inches high.

I surveyed the folders.

"Sorry you're here?" he asked

"No, just…overwhelmed, maybe."

"Me, too, and I know the girls are having a hard time with all this. Mrs. Murphy said you might have some good ideas, and we could use the help going through these files."

Within a few minutes we had developed a system. We would make notes of any items that appeared to have been removed from the inventory list. That was the easy part. If we could find a family member we could learn whether they removed the item from the inventory or if they thought the item had been sold.

The hard part was to go through the items that were sold to see if there were some items that stayed on the inventory list but were not in the receipt book. That could indicate that an item didn't sell. But, supposedly everything sold unless an owner said that a specific item couldn't go for less than a specific amount. That should have been noted, so those things should be easy to spot.

After about twenty minutes, a buzz sounded as someone had apparently come in the front door. Peter excused himself.

I stood, stretched, and walked around the conference room looking at various insurance licenses and membership certificates on the walls. It occurred to me that he had accomplished a lot for a guy in his mid-thirties, and that Fiona would be lucky if she married him.

He stuck his head back in the room. "I have to develop some quotes. You mind being in here alone?"

"Not at all." He went back to the main part of the office and I sat down and pulled the stack of folders to me. I had just realized that it made sense to try to first find an auction for which there were still family members in the area. Maybe someone else would be like Aunt Madge and remember something that seemed not to have been sold.

I vaguely recognized a couple of names and was almost sorry to see Rebecca Washington Estate as the title of one folder. Probably Elmira's mother. I opened the folder and saw that the contract to conduct the auction had been signed by Elmira. I put it aside. Surely there would be someone else.

My eyes fell on the name Gerald Stenner, and I eagerly opened that folder. Then I realized it was Jennifer's grandfather's estate of twenty-eight years ago. Jennifer's father died when she and I were in college. If Jennifer's dad were alive he would have been familiar with her grandfather's things. It wasn't likely Jennifer would know as much. It was also a huge auction, meaning there would be a lot more paperwork to go through.

I sighed and pulled Elmira's mother's folder to me. I scanned it and saw that there was only one set of candlesticks. Having a starting point made the process easier.

The brass candlesticks were on the inventory and were never crossed off as having been removed from the sale. I went through the book that had carbons of receipts for items sold. The inventory number assigned to the candlesticks did not appear on any receipt. Since there were only about one-hundred receipts I went through again, this time more slowly. Still no record of a candlestick sale.

Should I check every one of Mrs. Washington's inventory items?

With a sigh I began going through the individual sales. For each inventory item on a receipt I put a check mark next to the item on the original inventory list. Peter came back in and worked for ten minutes before having to help another client. Apparently his business was not profitable enough for a full-time receptionist or secretary.

Finally, I had gone through every one of the receipts for Elmira's mother's auction. There was one other item that appeared not to have sold. An amethyst bracelet. That was smart. It wasn't too valuable, so no one would look to see what it sold for as they might for a sapphire and diamond bracelet.

The results of the auction of her mother's possessions netted Elmira a tidy sum. She probably didn't look at what each item was sold for, so hadn't noticed the candlesticks were not sold until she saw them in the pawn shop.

I decided there was no reason to discuss this with Elmira. If we came up with a pattern of thefts, it seemed that talking to her would be Sergeant Morehouse's duty. I smiled, envisioning a so-called blue flu that had the entire police force calling in sick to avoid having to talk with Elmira.

At three-forty five, I was almost cross-eyed, and glanced at Peter, who had been working steadily across from me for twenty minutes. "So far, only one folder appears to have had items not auctioned, two items total in it."

"You think this is worth doing?" he asked.

I thought for a moment. "We aren't trying to document everything, just find a pattern. I mean, all you really want is for Mrs. Murphy to be able to show she and her husband were cheated, right?"

He nodded.

"We do have Aunt Madge, who thinks Uncle Gordon's antique gun never made it to an inventory list. Let's give it a bit longer. I can come by again."

As I pulled my purse toward me, he said, "Uh, Jolie. Could we talk about what you found already?"

"Sure." I should have expected this. "What would you like to know?"

"Do you think it's worth a lot? Can you tell whose it was?"

"The first I'm not sure. Sergeant Morehouse asked that jeweler, Mark Foster, to look at it, and Mark thought a couple items could net a nice amount. Second, not at all. And I'm not trying to keep it," I said hastily.

"You're not?" Peter looked surprised, and definitely happy.

"It makes sense to me to see if owners can be found. If they can't then I guess it's mine. I'll have to think about how to divvy it up."

He hesitated, and then said, "I'm not sure that Mr. Fitzgerald's heirs would have any right to it."

"I agree. I'll have to get it back and…"

"You don't have it?" he asked.

"Nope. The jeweler is keeping it in his safe." I realized that I was glad to tell Peter that I didn't have the stuff. He didn't seem like someone who would come after it, but how could I be sure of anything?

I DROVE BY Norman Fitzgerald's house a couple of times. I had a street map on the front seat of my Toyota. If anyone from the Police Department spotted me driving up and down his street, I planned to say I wanted to get to know some of the smaller streets better. A good appraiser would do that.

I had not thought there were any streets I did not know in Ocean Alley, but Mr. Fitzgerald's had only three houses. Behind it a concrete creek carried excess rain water into a small filtration plant. The plant cleaned it and dumped it in the ocean. I used to think that was ridiculous, but Ramona had explained that the rain runoff often had fertilizer and stuff in it, which was bad for marine life. *Who knew?*

I parked in front of the house next to Mr. Fitzgerald's and stared at the late auctioneer's home. I had half expected there to be police tape, since two people who lived or stayed there had been murdered. Apparently the police had gotten what they wanted from the house, because there was no tape and the house had a forlorn look about it.

It was a two-story home that had likely had the second story added. Nothing about it seemed special. In fact, the trim needed paint and there was no storm door on the main entry. If you judged his bank account by his house, you would have come to the wrong conclusion about Mr. Fitzgerald's finances.

No cars graced any of the three driveways on the street. People were probably at work. Given that it was daylight and I had a clip board and camera, anyone who saw me would think I was working. I pulled into the driveway. No sense giving people the idea I'm up to something.

I walked around the house and took a couple of photos in the front and in the back. I walked onto the back porch. It was about ten by five feet and had a couple of canvas chairs and a small metal table. More important, two windows faced the porch, so I wouldn't have to stand on my toes to look in.

The window closest to the back door looked into the kitchen, the other one to a small bedroom that Mr. Fitzgerald seemed to have used as an office. I almost drooled. The office had a couple of file cabinets. A pile of white storage boxes stood along one wall. *I bet there're all kinds of stuff in there that good old Norman wouldn't want me to see. Didn't the man own a shredder?*

The desk was not large. On it were a can that held pencils, a pencil sharpener, and a phone. I doubted Mr. Fitzgerald had been that neat. Probably the police had taken any papers that had been on the desk.

The kitchen appeared to be where he had done some of his work. The large Formica-topped table had an old adding machine and a couple of manila folders. *I'd love to get into those folders.*

What interested me more was a line of hooks that were on the wall next to the refrigerator. A couple had single keys, and others had potholders or dish towels. However, the pot holders sort of bulged, as if there were a ring of keys behind them. How could I…?

"Jolie?"

"Holy crap!" I turned to face Dana Johnson. My heart pounded so hard I could hear it in my ears. "I was, um…"

"You were snooping." She appeared to be trying to hide a smile.

"Oh, okay. I was. How did you know I was here?"

Dana walked up the two steps onto the porch and sat in one of the canvas chairs and pointed to the other.

"I don't know who called. Someone just said there might be a prowler here. As soon as I heard the address I knew it was you."

I sat. "Do you have to tell on me?"

"It's a murder investigation, not first grade," she said, but her tone was not harsh. "What are you looking for?"

I paused. "It's probably going to sound odd…"

"I'll consider the source."

"Some of us were talking the other day, about how Mr. Fitzgerald might have had keys to a lot of houses."

"Kind of like a real estate appraiser?" She had a definite smirk.

"In a way, yes. We'd both be given a key to get into the house if the owner wasn't going to be there, and we would both be supposed to return the key to the owner or whoever gave it to us."

Now she looked interested. "And maybe Fitzgerald didn't return them?"

"Or made a copy. There's a bulge behind the potholders on those hooks by the fridge."

Dana adopted a patient tone. "Jolie, when he's finished working at a house, it's usually empty. Why would he want a key?"

I thought fast. "They inventory the stuff in a house. But who's to know if he goes by alone one day, before a sale, and helps himself to some small items? Before they're inventoried, I mean." I saw her skeptical expression and continued. "Or maybe he hides stuff in an attic and goes back for it. Or, get this, he sticks stuff behind the walls."

She didn't address my ideas, but simply said, "We didn't have any complaints. His reputation was for giving, not taking."

"But where did he get all that money to give?"

She met my eyes and looked away. When she glanced back at me she gave a small sigh. "People are talking about that, but he did a lot of his business with cash. People might write a check at an auction, but he was known for selling some things directly to individuals."

I had my business hat on. "But large cash deposits have to be reported." I knew this was one way Uncle Sam tried to ferret out money being laundered for the drug trade.

She shook her head. "Only if greater than about ten thousand dollars. He made a lot of deposits for amounts under that, and then he did make some good investments."

I looked at her. "Why are you telling me this?"

"Because I hear you and George still aren't a couple again, so you won't tell him. And sometimes you have good ideas."

I smiled. "You'll get in trouble."

"It's not likely I'll say you were here. Don't do it again." She stood.

"Why don't you say you saw me in the grocery store and I asked about the key idea?"

"Because I like my job." She saw the disappointment on my face. "I'll think of a way to look into it." She glanced at the window. "Behind the potholders. Where do you come up with this stuff?"

Since she wasn't expecting an answer I didn't offer one and we walked back to our cars without speaking.

Jennifer would be fried if I told anyone the keys were her idea.

THE DOOR TO NEWHART'S Diner was almost slammed open. Betty Fowler looked as if she was in a foul mood. Aunt Madge was at the salad bar, but Betty saw Harry and me and came straight to our table.

She stopped and pointed a finger at me. "Jolie Gentil. I just heard you were undermining me by referring Clive Dorner to Lester Argrow."

"Nope." I said this calmly.

Harry started to say something but I gave him a quick wink, so he didn't.

"You referred Clive to him." Gone was the big smile and she sure wasn't calling me sugar.

"I did."

"How is that not stealing sales from me?" She asked this in as close to a snarl as I've seen anyone do.

"It would be if I had had even the faintest idea that you were working with Clive. I didn't know that until the day I saw you talk to him in Java Jolt."

"That rat bastard!"

"Betty," Harry said, quite coolly. "The man is dead."

"Ahem." Aunt Madge had come up behind Betty.

"Oh, Madge." Betty calmed down about ninety percent. "Of course, I would not have used that term if *you* had been here."

"And yet you use it in front of my husband and niece." Aunt Madge slid into the booth next to Harry. She only glanced at Betty, but it was a quelling look.

Betty stiffened and flushed. "Good day." She turned and left, high heels clicking on the old tile floor.

Harry looked at me. "You told Lester that he and Betty were both working with Clive?"

"Nope. I was hoping neither of them would figure it out. I wonder how Betty would take it if she found out that Clive initially asked me to show him around town?"

"I wonder how she found out?" Aunt Madge mused.

I shrugged. "Lester runs his mouth at Java Jolt and Burger King. I doubt Betty goes to Burger King, but I know she goes to Java Jolt. I don't really see how she can be mad at me about it."

Chapter Twenty-Five

AS IF IN ANSWER to my assumption, Betty called on my mobile phone promptly at eight o'clock Friday morning. "Jolie, I am really, really sorry about yesterday. The last six months have been so upsetting, and my income's gone down so much…" her voice trailed off.

I actually wasn't mad at her. As a citizen of New Jersey or the world, I can refer anyone to any agent I want, but it would be really rude for someone connected with the real estate industry to deliberately try to steer business away from an agent who was already working with a client.

"I know how it is, Betty. So many fewer sales since Sandy. Don't worry about it."

"Let me buy you coffee and a muffin at Java Jolt." Her tone was almost pleading.

I was half amused. Betty no doubt regretted her public display of temper, but a lot of that regret would be because she had no idea who had seen her in Newhart's last night. She wanted to be seen being nice to me so she wasn't the fodder for as much gossip. So, while I didn't really care to have coffee with her, I agreed to meet her. As one who has embarrassed herself on many occasions, I didn't mind helping her save face.

Java Jolt was crowded when I walked in. Betty sat at a table near the back of the small shop with a chocolate chip muffin and an extra mug of coffee in front of the vacant chair next to her.

"I asked Joe what you like." She still had her penitent air.

"Thanks Betty. Honest, I'm not mad. If I'd been you I'd have been furious with me if I'd tried to steer Clive away from you."

She relaxed a bit. "I worked so hard with that SOB."

I laughed. "If you talked directly to Lester he probably told you he had, too."

She rolled her eyes. "He doesn't know I worked with Clive. Lester was boring Joe with his woes about working with a client who was going to buy several properties and passed away. Of course Lester said kicked the bucket."

"Of course."

"All of a sudden it hit me that Lester was talking about Clive. I didn't say anything. I was so mad I was afraid I'd throw coffee on someone. I went back later and Joe said he thought you referred Clive to Lester."

I frowned. "Joe…should maybe talk to me before he throws my name around." Since we were in Java Jolt, I said this quietly.

"He was quick to say he doubted you knew I'd worked with Clive. I just didn't believe him."

"Ah." I wasn't sure what to say. "This will be a chance for us to get to know each other. I don't think we've appraised one of your sales, have we?"

She shook her head. "My firm is solidly in Stenner Appraisals' corner, I'm afraid."

"It's a good firm. Jennifer and I are friends." I smiled. "We are a bit less expensive, though."

Her eyebrows shot up. "I'll remember that." She paused. "So, did you know Clive well?"

I shook my head. "He tried to get to know me. He called one day and then stopped by at the office another. He wanted to give me pointers about fixing up the bungalow I bought."

Betty and I chatted about my house and what I'd done to get it ready to move into.

Out of the corner of my eye I saw someone with red hair and it reminded me of Fiona. "Did Clive actually buy anything with you?"

Her eyes looked shrewd, but just for a moment. "He was close, but we were still negotiating some offers."

"I just wondered. A friend of mine said he had approached her to invest with him."

"What?" Betty's question was harsh, and I stared at her.

She flushed. "I'm sorry. He never let me know he had co-investors. That could have helped or hindered financing."

"That's true. He was a wheeler dealer. Who knows if any of his contracts would have even made it through financing?" I was kind of asking her this, and watched her expression.

"He led me to believe his finances were strong." I picked my purse off the floor as Betty asked, "Did you know that Clive Dorner was Norman Fitzgerald's nephew? Awfully sad for one family to lose two people in such a short time."

I nodded. "I went to Mr. Fitzgerald's funeral. You know where he died, right?"

She nodded. "I didn't want to bring that up."

Yes you did. That's why you asked if I knew they were related. Everyone was curious about a murder.

I THOUGHT I'D PULLED one over on the Harvest for All Committee at our Saturday meeting. No doubt they expected me to participate in the scavenger hunt as a contestant rather than as a spot that had something game players needed to find. If Monica had not been the one keeping track of suggested locations and clues to find them, Dr. Welby would have learned what I wanted to do. He probably would have overruled me, since he was the chief party planner.

Scoobie certainly would have pestered me until I changed my mind. He and George had planned to do the hunt in teams of Ramona and George and Scoobie and me. Until they found out that Bill had asked Ramona to work with him.

Serves them right, making assumptions. I figured they'd either team up together or con Jennifer into working with them.

"My house is already in the list of scavenger sites," I said, to an annoyed Dr. Welby and the others at our last meeting before the event. "And we're getting it ready to go to the printer." This was not one hundred percent true. There were a lot of clues left to write.

"What is it, find something smelly and come away with a treat?" Lance asked.

"You'll find out."

"Are you giving away Pebbles to the first person who knocks on your door?" Scoobie asked.

"I wish. Jazz sleeps with her."

Sylvia looked at me. "Pebbles and Jazz…?"

"My skunk and my cat."

Sylvia looked to the heavens.

"Are you giving anything away?" Megan asked.

"I'm not telling." I planned to give any scavenger hunter who came to the house a photo of Pebbles and Jazz sitting in her cat bed, plus a package of black licorice. The back of the photo would be the clue for another item on the scavenger trail, and some information about Harvest for All.

"Do you think committee members should actually go on the hunt?" Aretha's question more or less implied she didn't think so.

"Just the birthday members," Scoobie said, with an engaging smile that took in everyone at the meeting. "We won't be part of the group that comes up with the scavenger hunt clues."

Dr. Welby cleared his throat, which meant the rest of us stopped talking. "Scoobie, I was counting on you to develop some of the clues."

"Yes, I'm not sure our minds are devious enough," Megan said.

Scoobie looked at Sylvia, and Dr. Welby interrupted. "What if each of the birthday people is the answer to one of the clues? You, Ramona, Bill, Daphne and Jennifer?"

Lance gave me a little head bow, "That's basically what Jolie wants to do."

"Yeah," Scoobie did an exaggerated sigh. "We'll do it Jolie's way. But we can't tell each other what our clue is. And the committee has to vote on which one of us had the best riddle to lead to us."

Lance kind of groaned. "You're setting us up."

"I'll vote," Sylvia said. She gave Scoobie an and-it-won't-be-you look.

"So, if the birthday kids only work on their own clues, who will finish getting all of the clues together?" Lance asked.

Megan snapped her fingers. "Alicia and her friends. But everyone has to feed them ideas."

This met with immediate agreement, probably because it meant less work for everyone on the committee.

"OKAY, JOLIE AND SCOOBIE, you have to act like adults." This from fifteen-year-old Alicia, who was sitting on the counter at the food pantry looking down on us as we sat on the floor, laughing.

It was just before one of our monthly Sunday-afternoon food distribution times. I had written a press release and Scoobie had drafted a public service announcement for radio stations and the paper.

Come to the Harvest for All birthday party and scavenger hunt at the Ocean Alley Tennis Club on Saturday. Individual and team play will improve your eye-hand coordination and critical thinking skills as you scavenge for clues and aim lightweight foam at one another.

Please bring a nonperishable food item or cash donation and wear very casual clothes.

A sense of humor and a change of clothes would also be good.

Games and refreshments at 1 p.m.

Scavenger hunt begins at 2:30

"Prizes," Alicia said. "More people will come if you say you have prizes."

"Good point." I wiped my eyes. "Jennifer's going to have to tell us what some of them are."

"You can put a lot of detail in your Craig's List ad," she offered.

The chime above the door dinged and Megan walked in. "Where is Jolie?" Alicia pointed to the floor on the other side of the counter and hopped down to begin unloading a bunch of canned food from a Girl Scout drive.

Megan leaned over the counter. "Like it down there?"

"Jolie does," Scoobie said. "I'm just keeping her company."

I started to stand and Scoobie said, "What if we said people should bring cans of food and leave their half-baked ideas at home?"

I had to sit back on the floor to laugh. After the tension of moving and adding a skunk to my household—to say nothing of finding a dead man on my porch and opening a door to find a fire—it felt good to be silly.

Megan had walked behind the counter and put on an apron as she nodded to Alicia. "I thought you and your friends were coming up with some of the scavenger clues."

"We are, but they're coming after Jolie and Scoobie leave, or we won't get anything done."

As Alicia said this, Scoobie saluted her, and stood. "I gotta get to the library to study. You're on your own, Jolie."

"Just in time for the pantry to open," Megan said.

I scrambled to my feet. "Okay, but look at our list of scavenger sites." I put my list on the counter and Megan and Alicia read it.

- Burger King with Lester
- Park behind Mr. Markle's store, with Bill and Ramona
- George and Scoobie, at the paper
- Library, with Daphne and Jennifer
- Harry's house, with him
- Final spot. Jolie's house, with info on the food pantry

My spot in the lineup, as Dr. Welby had decreed, was to be last, to emphasize the food pantry.

"What's so special about the park?" Alicia asked.

"That's the one with a huge crab painted on the wall of the picnic shelter. We thought that might be good for clues. Plus, it gives Mr. Markle's store some attention. He's always good to us." *Bless his sour face.*

"Okay. We can think of stuff," she said. "Especially for Lester."

"For that one, I think you'll need three clues. Everybody will be starting out at once, and we want it to look as if they're going to different places. And we don't want Lester writing clues."

"Why?" she asked.

"We thought if they were all the same they'd all just follow one person."

"I meant why not Lester?" Alicia asked.

I gave her a raised eyebrow look, and she laughed. "They would be funny."

"Yes, but this is a family event."

The bell chimed as our first customers for the afternoon arrived. We let people pick a small box, in which case they can come twice per month, or a large box, meaning they can only come once. I spent the next half hour scurrying among the shelves to get the items on each person's grocery list. We can't always get them everything that they need, but we try to come close.

At the end of the first hour Max came in and insisted he could help me. It added a lot of time to my tasks, but people are very patient with him.

ON SUNDAY EVENING I had the TV on and a to-do list for the fundraiser on my lap. I was propped up on pillows on the couch and Jazz was supposedly sitting in my lap. In reality, she kept trying to attack my pencil every minute or so.

"I can't play until I'm done with this list, and you're making it take longer." She moved up to my collar bone and tried to take a swipe at my nose, claws in of course.

"Okay, you're on the floor." I gave her a small push on the backside and she walked away very nonchalantly. I figured her little mind thought that if she acted as if getting down was her idea she could impress Pebbles, who was sitting outside the door to the bathroom, staring at us.

"Play with her so she won't bother me, okay?" Pebbles appeared nonplussed.

I glanced at the clock. I had promised myself I would stop for the eleven o'clock news. I got a shawl from the foot of my bed and turned out all the lights except the bathroom and got back on the couch.

I set the TV timer to go off at midnight in case I fell asleep. The announcer had just finished a story describing which beach towns seemed more ready for Memorial Day Weekend when I began to doze. I woke up at about one in the morning and stretched, causing Jazz to jump from her spot by my head to the floor.

I pushed the shawl off me, sat up, and yawned. I was about to go into the bathroom to brush my teeth when there was a tapping sound from the back porch. "What was that?" I whispered.

The light tapping sound became a louder one and I realized someone was tapping on the window glass in the kitchen. *Someone's trying to get in here*! I heard Jazz hiss from the vicinity of the kitchen. *Not someone I know!*

I rolled off the couch and crawled to where my house phone sat on a small table near the rocking chair. I pushed the button for the dial tone. The line was dead. That meant someone had cut my Internet cable, because it provided my phone service.

I cursed and looked around my living room, feeling more frantic by the second. The coat closet was a place to hide, but it was in the hall. To get to it I'd have to cross the hall and could be seen from the kitchen.

My cell phone was on the counter in the kitchen. I debated going out the front door. But maybe someone else would be out there, a lookout or something. I felt cold all over. *Think, think.* At about one o'clock in the morning and scared out of my wits, thinking was at a premium.

My sofa sat against one wall, but it didn't touch the wall. If I turned sideways I thought I could scoot behind it. I half crawled and half slithered behind it, and flattened my back against the wall so my face was stuffed into the upholstery.

I held my breath and was just letting it out when Jazz stuck her head under the couch. I was pretty sure her expression said, "That's my spot." I wanted to laugh. I wiggled a finger to her, but instead of walking to me she pulled her head back and disappeared.

What if they hurt Jazz? I was moving from panic to mad.

After several seconds of silence I thought I heard whoever it was trying to get the sash up so they could come in the window. I was about to scream when I heard a police siren, and it was very close. I held my breath, wishing it to come to my house. About ten seconds later, it sounded as if it stopped at the curb in front of my house.

Whoever was at the kitchen window apparently heard the car, too. He or she ran down the couple of back porch steps. It sounded as if the person ran toward Virginia Mulligan's house.

I jumped from behind the couch and pulled open the front door as a very young police officer stepped onto my front porch. "Someone's in the back. I think they…" Before I could say more, the officer pointed to the right and ran that way, and a second officer ran toward the left side of the house.

"Lights, I need more lights." I walked through my little house flipping on every light I could find. Then I sat in my rocker and shivered.

Someone shouted, "Over there!" I hoped it was a cop.

There was the sound of several people running, and then the noise grew fainter. Suddenly a loud voice yelled, "Police. Stop!"

The voices were close, but not quite close enough for me to hear what they were saying, and I wasn't moving out of my rocker. Then they got closer and I heard a man say, "It weren't me! I'm the one who called you."

I stood up and walked to the front door. The officer who had come to the door first was walking a handcuffed man toward the police car. A second officer started to come up my short walkway.

The man now in the back seat of the car saw me and yelled. "You know me. You know me." He was perhaps in his late thirties, a bit unkempt, with a shock of bright red hair and wire rim glasses.

The second officer I recognized as Edgar Quinn, and I opened the screen door. "I think maybe the man in the car comes to Harvest for All."

"So, he knows you?" Officer Quinn asked.

"Sort of."

"It weren't me! All in black, they was," the red-haired man yelled.

The police car with the apparent would-be thief pulled away as another car drove up. Lights were coming on in the houses around me.

I gestured that Officer Quinn should sit down, but he said, "Better if I look around."

"The tapping was on the kitchen window," I said.

He pulled some latex gloves out of a pocket and walked back into the kitchen. Using only two fingers he flipped my lock, opened the back door, and walked out on the back porch. He looked at the window, then peered closely and said, "Take a look at this." Apparently another officer walked toward him, because Quinn said something to him and then came back in.

"It looks as if someone scored it." At my blank look, he added, "They were using a glass cutter to make a rectangle on the glass. It makes it easier to break, and there would usually be less noise. Then they could reach in and unlock the window. You're lucky something scared them off."

I must have looked the way I felt, which was very light-headed. He grabbed my upper arm and steered me to my dinette table and held out a chair with his other hand. "Sit, and put your head on the table." He walked back into the kitchen and I could hear him running water. He came back to me and placed a glass of water and a couple of paper towels on the table. "Can you dampen these and wipe your face?"

He didn't wait for an answer, but pulled what I knew to be a radio phone from his belt and pushed a button. "Dennison probably told you, but we're clear here. Need someone to dust." He listened for a second and then pushed a button to end the call. Then he sat in the other dinette chair and smiled at me. "You look a little better."

I nodded. "Thanks. Do you know that man?"

"He lives at the rooming house on F Street, and he's been around town for years. Never knew of him to be in trouble." He gave a brief smile. "It's not remotely funny, of course, but Sergeant Morehouse will have something to say about the guy's first brush with the law being here."

He lives where Scoobie lives. I felt calmer, but more puzzled than ever. "Why do you suppose he was here?"

"Hard to say. Word's going around that you have some expensive jewelry here."

I put my head back on the table.

Chapter Twenty-Six

AT LEAST MY UNWELCOME VISITOR had arrived too late to be in the Monday *Ocean Alley Press*.

Since I knew she would hear about the person on my back porch from someone, I called Aunt Madge and Harry early in the morning. The part of the morning when you're supposed to be up. I downplayed the event, trying to present it as someone who could have just come to the wrong porch. *Yeah, right.*

"It had to be the jewelry. And on top of the murders! Maybe you should come here until they figure out who killed those men." Aunt Madge's voice was almost strident.

"Pebbles and Jazz will keep an eye on me." I kept my tone light.

"I'll call Virginia Mulligan and Charlotte Evans. They can be more aware of goings-on at your house."

"They're going to be really sorry I moved here."

"Only when they get to know you better." She hung up.

I stared at the phone. Aunt Madge was sounding more like Scoobie. *That can't be good.*

I SHOWED UP AT the police station at nine-thirty. The time had been agreed to by Officer Quinn and whoever was in charge at the station last night. I think Quinn convinced the person in charge that I looked like I needed sleep.

Which did not come easily, of course. I had finally fallen asleep at about two-thirty.

I sat on one of the hard plastic chairs in the reception area at the police station and thought. It seemed awfully risky for someone to try to break into my house. It was such a small house, surely they would know I'd hear them. It probably did look as if I was asleep, with all lights out except the bathroom. Maybe when the timer turned off the television set, the burglar, assuming that was the goal, thought I was asleep.

Since early this morning I'd considered whether someone could really be looking for the jewelry I'd found. It was possible they had simply noticed that my bungalow had had work done lately and a new person had moved in. Fresh bait for a chronic burglar.

The locked door that led to the area where officers sit opened and Sergeant Morehouse motioned for me to come in. As I got closer, he said, "Get a good night's sleep?"

"You're as funny as sand crabs."

He grunted.

I followed him down the hall. "What's the guy's name?"

"I keep tellin' you, I ask the questions." He gestured to his office. "Reuben Harris."

"Right." I thought for a couple of seconds. "I've seen his name on our list of people who come to Harvest for All. He never says much, as I recall."

Morehouse sat behind his desk and I sat across from him. "The thing is," he said, "he's not someone who's been in trouble here before, and it would take more skill than I thought he had to disconnect your Internet from that spot under your back porch."

"Skill how?"

"I guess not real technical skill, but Internet doesn't come into every house the same way, like a telephone line does."

"And they wanted to be sure my phone didn't work." I shivered. "They meant business."

"We're checking to see if Harris has a history somewhere else. Has he ever threatened you, or said anything even mildly unusual?"

I shook my head. "I've seen him in the pantry, but he mostly deals with Megan or one of the regular volunteers."

Morehouse made a note. "Hmm. Okay, tell me about last night." He opened his notebook.

I pulled a piece of paper from my purse. "I made notes. I was so rattled I was afraid I'd forget something."

After listening to me for a couple of minutes, he asked, "Where was Pebbles in all of this?" Probably my exasperation showed, because he smiled and added, "Maybe you can get guard-dog training for her."

I relaxed a bit. "Under the bed. That's her spot when anyone else is in the house."

"Even Scoobie?" he asked.

"She'll come to the door of my bedroom. She sees Jazz sitting on him, so she's getting the idea that he's not too dangerous."

When I mentioned that the person who jumped off the porch sounded as if he was running toward Virginia Mulligan's house, he stopped me. "That's not where we found him."

"Maybe he runs really fast. Where was he when your guys caught up to him?"

"By the Evans' place."

"What? That's the opposite direction."

"It is, and it doesn't…"

"Sergeant." Dana Johnson appeared at the door and she held what appeared to be several pieces of something that had come in on a fax. "You'll want to see this." She leaned across his desk and handed them to him, and then looked at me. "You okay?"

"Sort of."

"At least this guy was alive," she offered.

"You're taking after him." I nodded to Sergeant Morehouse.

"Well, I'll be damned," he said. "We may have our Peeping Tom."

"That's what I thought," Dana nodded.

"You're kidding," I said. Morehouse kept reading, and I looked at Dana. "That's all there was for him? Peeping Tom history?"

Sergeant Morehouse cleared his throat and I looked at him. "I'm not asking inappropriate questions. Dana brought it in while I was here."

"You're here a lot," he said.

"Not by my doing," I snapped.

He ignored me and looked at Dana. "It does kind of match what he said."

"What did he say?" I asked.

Morehouse looked at me. "You aren't telling this to your buddy George, are you?"

"Of course not."

"He said he was standing near a house across the street. That house with the red trim."

I knew the house. I used to baby-sit there the year I lived in Ocean Alley in high school.

"He said," Morehouse continued, "that he saw the person on your porch and used his cell phone to call us."

"I wonder why he hung around?" I asked.

"He says to be sure you were all right. Says he knew the 'food lady' lived there, so he never went near your windows."

I wasn't sure whether to laugh or cry. I might be in danger from a burglar, but the Peeping Tom was leaving me alone. "Now what?" I asked.

"Now we see if there's any clear indication that the person who was at your window maybe did run toward Virginia's house. If that's the case, Reuben Harris may be telling the truth."

"You want me to check out footprints or whatever over there?" Dana asked. When Morehouse nodded she walked out.

A voice from the hallway asked, "Sergeant, you wanna talk to the guy from the *Press*? He's on the phone."

"Tell him I'll call him back in five minutes."

I smiled. "To hear George tell it, you never call him back."

"I don't want him makin' stuff up."

THE *OCEAN ALLEY PRESS* headline on Tuesday was, "Rumored Treasure Trove at Fixer-Upper."

The article noted that "the homeowner was asleep when an unknown burglar attempted to gain entry through a back window." It then said, while identifying the house by the block rather than the specific number, that a new owner had discovered some items a prior owner had left behind. The article did not mention that the suspected Peeping Tom had alerted the police to the burglar.

In the Purple Cow Tuesday morning, I fumed in Ramona's direction. "My house is the only one in that block that's turned over lately. The headline is like advertising that there's stuff to steal in it!"

"I thought so, too," Ramona said. She tried not to smile. "At least this time you didn't end up in the hospital for anything. And you and George are still speaking."

"Says you," I said, but quietly. "Anyway, he's staying out of my way."

"Why don't you call him?"

"Because I'm at Aunt Madge's for a couple of days and she doesn't like that much cussing."

My sister had invited me to Lakewood for a few days, but I said I had too much going on. I was mostly staying at the Cozy Corner for a time to make my parents feel better. If I hadn't agreed to stay out of my house "until everyone knew I didn't have magnificent jewelry," as my father said, my parents were going to come up from Florida. I didn't need that.

"I think Madge has heard all the words before," Ramona said.

I STOPPED AT Mr. Markle's grocery to be sure that our order of liquid string (God help me) was going to arrive before the so-called birthday party.

"You know this stuff makes quite a mess, don't you?" He had his usual dour expression, but I detected a slight glint in his eyes.

"It was Scoobie's idea, so I'm prepared."

That out of the way, I stopped by the office to see if there were any faxes or phone messages. The doorbell rang as I was reviewing a fax from Lester. It suggested that Harry take off his blinders and revise an appraisal that Lester thought was too low. Since I had done the appraisal, Lester didn't use some of his choicer language.

I peered from a window to the side of the door and saw George, who held a bouquet of daffodils. I didn't want to let him in, but since my car was parked on the street he knew I was in the office.

I opened the door. "If you've come to lead an expedition to tear my house apart looking for treasure, you can go over there and wait on the porch."

He walked in. "I'm not sitting on the swing."

I winced, and then took the flowers he held out. "Thanks."

He walked to the sofa. "I didn't say you found a lot of diamonds."

"And I appreciate that." I sat next to him and placed the flowers, which were well wrapped, between us. "But you and Scoobie can't be there all the time, and I figure your article will encourage other burglars."

"So, I'm buying you a present."

"Second amendment aside, I'm not going to keep a gun."

"Right. I'd give you a gun when you're still mad at me."

I smiled and gestured to the flowers. "Very nice."

"Those are a peace offering. The present is a security system." He looked at the floor.

"I bought window locks and deadbolts."

"The guys from Ocean Alley Security are coming this afternoon. If you can't be there, Madge said she'll hang out while they put in the sensors and the alarm box."

"You talked to Aunt Madge?"

"Yeah. She found me, actually." He gave a kind of awkward grin. "Well, me and my editor. I didn't know she could get that mad."

"She didn't mention that you'd talked."

"I mostly listened. Then I had the security system idea, and she calmed down a lot. Plus, I think she figured out everyone in the news room was staring at her for telling off the boss."

This was starting to seem funny. "Didn't your editor give her a lecture on freedom of the press?"

"There wasn't much of a chance to actually *talk* to her. Look," he gave me an almost pleading look, "I had to write the story the way I would have written it for anybody else. There were valuables hidden in your house when you tore down that wall. It's newsworthy."

He looked pitiful. "Okay, I get it. Mostly it was the headline. Did you have to call it a treasure trove?"

"That was my editor," he said, quickly.

"I guess if you can mollify Aunt Madge I'll get over it."

His pained expression vanished. "So, you want help looking for more stuff?"

"Nope. If there's more there, it's staying put." As he started to say something, I added, "Really staying put."

"Okay." He glanced at the flowers and then back at me. "How about a movie?"

A few weeks ago I would have been thrilled. Now, having George as a boyfriend didn't seem to matter. I didn't want to worry about whether something I did made him mad at me.

"I…don't know, George. It seems like we've struck a kind of happy medium. I think I like it."

"I shouldn't have broken up with you," he said. "I'm sorry."

"You had every right to be angry. We'd agreed we'd share information, and I didn't share."

"Yeah, but you weren't any different than you usually were. I was the one who wanted you to be different," he said.

I smiled. "Talked about this at an AA meeting, did you?"

I could see a retort forming, and he stopped himself. "I didn't go to a meeting to talk about that, but I…I've been trying to learn, for a long time, that the only person's actions I can control are my own."

I nodded, and said, softly, "I know the concept. I think you're a bit farther along that path than I am."

He grinned. "Tell me about it." He watched the expression on my face and his smile faded.

I drew a breath. "I'm glad, really glad, that we're friends again. And not just because I'm tired of it being so awkward."

"But you aren't ready for anything else," he said.

"For a while I thought I was. I guess it's me."

"That's the standard line when people break up, you know."

I laughed. "That day in the library, you told me to act like I felt before we dated."

"My words always come back to haunt me," he groaned.

"Especially the ones in the paper. Seriously, that felt…normal. I mean, I'm not always mad at you."

"Okay." He stood. "I don't want to grovel."

"I might pay to see that." I stood.

He leaned over and kissed me on the cheek. "Leave 'em wanting more." He headed for the door.

THOUGH HARRY WANTED to be with me when the security people arrived, I had tried to discourage him. However, he and Aunt Madge were both on edge about me being home alone, so I had graciously given in. At least, given in with more good grace than I felt.

I pulled in front of my bungalow at the same time that an Ocean Alley Security Systems truck parked across the street. Two guys stayed in the front seat comparing notes on a clipboard, so I walked onto the front porch, which I had decided to use again. Aunt Madge was behind the honeysuckle bush, on the porch swing.

I dropped my keys. "Jeez! You couldn't sit anywhere else?"

She stood. "Put out some of those canvas chairs."

I picked up my keys and we walked in. Aunt Madge walked into my kitchen and turned a burner on under my tea kettle. Then she peered in it and decided to add water. "Thank you for letting us be with you when they installed the security system."

"George told me it calmed you down."

She simply gave me a raised-eyebrow glance and looked around the kitchen. "It's a really cute little house. Pretty soon you'll forget everything that happened."

"I'm going to try…" Someone pounded on the front door.

The two guys from the security company stared at me. "You still got the skunk?" This from the taller of the two. For all his beefcake physique his expression looked kind of like that of a little kid.

"She's here, but her scent glands were taken out a long time ago." I opened the door and they walked in.

"And she doesn't bite?" The man who asked this was shorter and what might be called pudgy. His brown hair hung to his eyebrows, making him look about fourteen. I pegged both of them at about twenty-five.

"You'll never see her. She hides under the bed." I moved aside so the men could walk in.

A honk at the curb heralded Harry, and for the next hour he talked to the security guys as they stunk up the place with the glue they used to affix sensors. I retreated to the kitchen and mixed a bowl of brownies and felt like some kind of stereotype. However, there wasn't a need for two sets of eyes watching the installation, and everybody likes brownies.

Aunt Madge hadn't stayed long. She wanted to get home to make the afternoon loaves of bread for B&B guests.

I took the brownies out of the oven as the taller of the two security guys stuck his head in the kitchen. "I need to test the alarm. Don't jump outta your skin."

"Fair enough. Brownies'll be ready in a minute."

I was glad I was using a Teflon spatula to cut them, because the booming alarm made me jump and push the spatula along the bottom of the pan.

"Too loud?" yelled the guy.

"Yes!"

Harry and I said this together as he walked into the kitchen. "Smells good. I'm taking some brownies home. I'm not a huge fan of her cheddar bread."

"Does she know?"

"Are you kidding?"

The next alarm sound was lower, so Harry and I could hear each other as we said goodbye. I put a few brownies on a paper plate when the two men came back into the kitchen. Their names were Dale and Chuck, but I couldn't remember who was which. "All done?" I asked.

"Pretty much. We'll show you how to set a security code and we can walk you through the instructions on how to use it."

"I think it's the same system Aunt Madge has. I'll take a quick look and call you if I have questions."

After they took too long explaining the system and thanked me for the brownies, they left. I sank onto my couch and flipped my legs up to lie down. Less than two minutes later, the doorbell rang. I figured the security guys had left something and was surprised to find Patricia and her boyfriend on the porch. "Come in."

Patricia looked very nervous. "I'm not sure you've formally met Arman."

"How do you do?" I gestured that they should come in.

Arman walked in first. His chin jutted forward like a guy posturing when someone else threatened to throw a punch.

"Jolie," Patricia began.

"You doing some repairs or something?" Arman asked, sniffing the air.

"Getting a security system put in," I said. "They just left, so you came at the perfect time." *As if.*

"Been looking for more stuff behind your walls?" Arman asked.

Patricia looked more nervous.

"No, and I don't plan…" I began.

"We want to talk to you about how you're going to divide up what you found," Arman said, in an aggressive tone.

"Those aren't going to be totally my decisions," I began. "Peter and I are going through…"

Arman waved a hand. "I know what you're doing with him. You two are looking at how to give away what you found."

I didn't like his tone. "Not looking to give…"

"It should come to Mrs. Murphy, to give to her family," Arman said.

"Arman, please," Patricia said. She seemed almost cowed by his behavior.

"Don't give me that. This Fitzgerald cheated your father out of a lot of money. Money we could use for all those kids of yours. I don't want to spend all my money on them!"

"We should go," Patricia murmured, blushing deeply.

I looked at both of them, my gaze resting on Arman. "And before he held out on Mr. Murphy he cheated the people who gave goods to be auctioned. Those people have a right…"

He swore and moved a step closer. "They're probably all dead."

It took all my nerve not to step back a foot. "That could be. And then I think there is a strong case to be made for any income from the items going to Mrs. Murphy. We can't simply decide on our own…"

"I want to see it," Arman said, standing.

"It's not here. The police have most of it."

He moved another step closer to where I was standing next to the rocking chair. "So get it back. It was in your house, it's yours. You can give it to us. Patricia's losing her summer job. You said the building wasn't worth much, so they're selling the place."

I caught the pronoun, and figured he expected some of any find or money from its sale to come not just to Patricia, but to him. I was less than one foot from him. "I'm sorry about the job. I get your anger and…"

"No you don't!" He was yelling now. Patricia touched his elbow and he jerked his arm from her. "Every month Patricia and Fiona give their mother money for that place she lives in. We need…she needs that money."

"Do you want me to call Sergeant Morehouse and ask him to bring over some of the items?"

"No, I don't want you to *call Sergeant Morehouse*." He said these last words in a kind of simpering tone. "If it's not here, you figure out where else Fitzgerald hid stuff and hand it over."

"Arman," Patricia almost whispered.

"Shut up." He turned to me. "Where haven't you looked?"

I couldn't imagine Arman would hurt me, but why find out? "The only place anything's been found was behind that living room wall," I nodded toward it.

"So tear down the rest of the damn wall."

"We did. That's how Scoobie and I found it. We took down all the walls in this room except that one." I nodded to the plaster wall.

"So, get a tire iron or something to use on that wall," he shouted.

Patricia started to cry.

The front door opened, and Scoobie walked in. He glanced at all of us, finally staring at Arman. "Sounds as if you want something." He said this to Arman in a very calm tone.

"You can help her tear down that wall," Arman said.

"It's not Berlin," Scoobie said.

"What are you talking about?" Arman was becoming even angrier.

"You know," Scoobie said. "When President Reagan told Gorbachev to 'tear down that wall.'"

I knew what Scoobie was doing. He wanted to distract Arman, maybe get him to realize how ridiculously he was behaving. And leave it to Scoobie to remember a more than thirty-year-old quote.

"I don't care one bit about some stupid wall in Berlin," Arman said, but in a slightly calmer tone. "Just look for more stuff."

"Sure. But I wouldn't start there." Scoobie nodded at the wall. "I watched her peel three layers of wallpaper off there. There weren't any patched areas. If it was me I'd start with the walls under the sinks. Plaster under there is always torn up, from leaks, you know. Good place to hide stuff. "

Possibly it was Scoobie's tone of reason, or maybe just because he wasn't me, Arman seemed to like this idea. "You got some tools?" Arman asked.

"Jolie doesn't keep much here, but she's got a tool box." He looked at me. "In the linen closet, isn't it?"

How does he know that's where the security guys put the alarm pad?

"Yep. I'll get it." It wasn't as if Arman was pointing a gun at us, but I sensed that we were not supposed to do anything that would irritate him.

There was no chit chat in the living room as I walked into the bathroom. The linen closet was behind the door. I pushed the silent alarm button on the console. The security company would call and I would not answer the phone. They'd send someone over.

I walked out of the bathroom, empty-handed. "I'm sorry. Harry probably put it under the kitchen sink. That's where he keeps his."

Arman glared at me but didn't say anything.

I walked into the kitchen, bent down, picked up the tool box, and carried it to the living room. Arman took it from me. He placed it on the small dining table and opened it. "There's nothing in here we can use."

Scoobie looked over his shoulder. "Grab that really long screwdriver. We can bang on the plaster under the sinks to see if it's hollow anywhere."

He handed the screwdriver to Scoobie. "You do it."

"Sure." Scoobie said this as the phone rang. He ignored it and went into the kitchen, and Arman and Patricia looked at me.

Without looking, I said, "It's probably Lester. He calls me for coffee, and he'll keep me on the phone trying to talk me into meeting him at Java Jolt."

"That airbag," Arman muttered. Scoobie started digging at the wall under the sink.

Scoobie's voice was a bit muffled since his head was under the sink. "Do you know the size of whatever it is you're looking for?"

"How in the hell would I know?" Arman said.

A car came to an abrupt halt at the curb and two doors slammed. The phone started ringing again. I picked up the handset to look at the caller ID. It said "Ocean Alley." I figured this was the security company, so I said, "Lester again."

Arman ignored me and walked to the screen door. "Crap!" He pushed the wooden door to shut it but a firm hand slapped the door just before it closed.

"Let me in, Arman." It was Peter.

"Let us in!" Fiona's tone was frantic.

I wasn't sure whether Fiona and Peter were here to add their demands to Arman's, but I thought not.

Patricia began to cry again. "I called them. Let them in."

"Hey, I found something!" Scoobie yelled.

Arman stopped trying to keep the door closed and dashed to the kitchen. Peter almost fell into the living room.

"Where? What is it?" Arman called.

"It's one of those phony soup cans where people hide valuables," Scoobie said.

Apparently Arman took it from Scoobie, because he said, "Gee, it feels like soup."

"That's because it is, you damn bully," Scoobie said.

"What...?"

Peter had moved quickly to the kitchen doorway and I peered around him. Fiona pulled me back, but not before I saw Arman in between Scoobie and Peter. He looked from one to the other and after a second, his shoulders sagged.

A police car came to a fast halt in front of the house and car doors slammed. *At least I know the alarm company calls the cops.*

Fiona beat me the few steps to the front door and pushed open the screen. "I guess you should come in," she said.

Dana Johnson and Edgar Quinn came in, and they both looked to me and then to the kitchen door, where Arman, with Peter's hand on his upper arm, was walking into the living room.

"You don't want me," he sneered to the police. He nodded to Peter. "He's the murderer."

Chapter Twenty-Seven

"WHAT DO YOU MEAN?" Fiona and I asked the same question, but while my tone was demanding hers was almost sobbed.

"Jolie." Dana's voice was firm as she stood by Peter and Arman, one hand on her gun. "What's going on?"

"Arman wanted me to look for more hidden stuff," I said.

"Did you invite him here?" Edgar asked.

I shook my head.

Dana pulled her handcuffs from her belt. "We're going for a short ride."

Arman let himself be handcuffed. I would have been willing to have him get a lecture and be sent home, but the word murderer kind of changed the tone in the room.

Arman rode in the police car and Fiona and Patricia rode to the police station with Peter. Patricia was still crying when they pulled away.

Scoobie and I were silent for the first minute of our drive. Then I asked, "Did you know the alarm panel was in the linen closet?"

"Harry saw me get off the bus a few blocks from here and gave me a ride over. He told me to keep my fingers in my ears if the security guys were still testing. I thought it might be there, but all you needed was a reason to get to it, wherever it was."

"Smart. You think he would have hurt us?"

He shrugged. "Doubt it. Didn't want to find out."

We parked on the street instead of in the small police lot, and followed Peter and the sisters into the police station. Dana and Edgar must have taken Arman in a back way.

I glanced at Peter as the five of us stood in the small waiting area. He wore a grim expression and looked nervous. Fiona had her arm around Patricia, whose sobs had turned to sniffles.

The door to the secure part of the police station opened and Sergeant Morehouse looked at all of us. "You five, sit in the captain's office." The officer on duty at the front desk held open the door and we followed Morehouse down the hall. I heard Dana's voice from the small conference room, whose door was closed.

Captain Edwards, whom I barely knew, was not in his office. Morehouse gestured to chairs around a conference table, and as we sat he gave me a grim look. No teasing about me getting in trouble.

"All right. What the hell is this guy talking about when he says one of you killed Clive Dorner?" He looked at all of us briefly, one by one.

"It was an accident," Peter said, softly.

"My God." Fiona touched his shoulder.

Patricia put her head on the table and bawled, "Arman said I couldn't tell you!"

Morehouse used his small notebook to hit the table and no one said anything. He pointed at Peter. "Explain."

Peter took a breath. "I was meeting Fiona at her house, and she was late. I thought the blinking light on the answering machine might be her, so I pushed play. It was that ass…jerk, Dorner. He had left this long message about how he's going to make Fiona's money turn to gold or some…stuff like that. And he says he's found a perfect house and tells her when to meet him there."

"This is the day he died?" Morehouse asked.

Peter nodded. "I erased the message and called Arman, and we went to the address on Ferry. I forget the number. I just wanted to tell him to leave Fiona alone."

Morehouse nodded.

"Dorner was really angry that we came instead of Fiona. He didn't want to tell us what he meant about Fiona's money, but I got in his face and he said she'd given him three thousand dollars.

Three thousand dollars! The bastard said he was going to at least double her money. Like he was betting on horses."

He looked at Fiona, who seemed about to cry. "I took it out of my 401(k)," she whispered.

"We both, Arman and me, started yelling at Dorner. He starts telling us you need to spend money to make money, and he wants to move past me to leave. I stood in his way. He shoved me and I shoved back. We did a couple more shoves, and he falls backward, and hits his head on the kitchen counter." Peter put his fist to his mouth. "Then he just…fell."

"And what, you don't know how to call 9-1-1?" Morehouse asked, his voice rising.

"There was no…you could tell he was dead. I checked for a pulse in his neck, on his wrists. His eyes just…stared."

I couldn't help myself. "So you set a fire?"

"Quiet, Jolie!" Morehouse said.

"We talked about what to do. I wanted to call, Arman didn't, but it's my fault. I didn't need him to make up my mind. But he kept talking about prison." Peter looked at Fiona. "We were going to get married. And then I thought of those other fires that no one can figure out…" his voice trailed off and he put his elbows on the table and hands over his face.

"It was an accident," she said softly.

"Not the fire," Morehouse said, abruptly. "I'm reading you your rights, Peter. At this point, you're under arrest for arson. You have the right to remain silent, anything you say can and will be used against you…" He finished the standard litany.

I'd never heard it said other than on television. I felt numb, and from the look on Fiona's face, she did, too.

Lieutenant Tortino had apparently heard Morehouse, and he walked into the chief's office. "What the…?"

"Dorner," Morehouse said. "Death could have been accidental, fire wasn't." He looked at Scoobie and me. "You know about this?"

We both shook our heads without saying anything.

"Go sit in the waiting room. You two know?" He looked at Fiona and Patricia.

"Fiona didn't," Patricia said, sitting up straighter.

"Waiting room," Tortino said to Fiona.

"I'd like to stay with…" she began.

"Maybe later," Morehouse said.

Fiona stood. "I'm calling her a lawyer. And Peter."

"Excellent idea," Tortino said.

"THIS IS ONE OF those times you're glad you have a word like surreal in your vocabulary," Scoobie said.

We were still in the uncomfortable outer waiting room an hour later. Fiona had walked back to the secure area with the two lawyers. This meant we didn't have to make small talk or comfort her. She'd grown more upset by the minute, certain that Peter would never have hurt anyone if he didn't see himself as somehow defending her.

"Would you ever have guessed?" I asked.

"Nah," Scoobie said. "Peter is a Mister-Chamber-of-Commerce type."

I smiled slightly. Scoobie rarely trusts anyone he views as part of the establishment. I have debated telling him he will be part of it when he graduates from college.

"It was an accident," I said.

"The death, maybe, not his decisions about disposal of the body."

I grimaced just as Dana walked out of the office area and motioned that Scoobie and I should go to the counter.

"Fiona wants you to go tell her mother what's going on. She says you'll know how to do it."

"Oh boy." I thought for a moment. "Sure. Tell her we'll uh, be gentle."

"Not really any sugar coating this," Dana said.

MRS. MURPHY'S EXPRESSION was wary when we entered her apartment. "Elmira Washington says my girls are at the police station." She said this before we were all seated.

Damn that woman. She must pay people to feed her gossip. "They're fine, really."

Scoobie rolled his eyes at me, but Mrs. Murphy wasn't looking at him.

I stood next to Mrs. Murphy as she settled in her chair. No sense in her falling over if she was nervous.

I sat across from her. "It's not really about them. It's more about Clive Dorner."

"That bastard," she said.

I almost fell onto the floor instead of parking myself in a chair facing her. "I'm sure you aren't the first to…" I stopped, remembering an earlier conversation with her. "I thought you said you didn't know him. When I was here before."

Mrs. Murphy looked at me and looked away. Then she met my gaze again. "I only met him a few times, when he was a little boy. He was always wheedling something out of Norman. Ice cream, a toy from an auction table. Norman said he bought them for him, of course." Her tone was bitter.

"What difference did it make?" I asked, my tone becoming angry. "Why did you lie to me?"

"Jolie," Scoobie said, gently. "Pretend she's Aunt Madge."

Mrs. Murphy smiled at him. "You'd be good for her." She nodded at me.

Scoobie's expression didn't change, and Mrs. Murphy turned back to me. "I'd already talked to him before you came by that day. I told him his uncle's estate owed me money. The next thing I knew, he had called my daughters with some lame-brained idea of investing with him. Same brat behavior as when he was a kid."

"Couldn't you let them know what he was like?" I asked.

"Patricia listened, Fiona saw dollar signs. And then the girls said they had all those old files, and Peter said that we could probably prove that Fitzgerald stole those things. I told him that was fine, but not to take too long. I figured that moocher Clive would steal or sell anything of value he could find in Fitzgerald's house."

Mrs. Murphy leaned back in her chair as if all this was as exhausting as walking a mile with her walker.

"It seems that Fiona may have invested a small sum with Dorner." I watched her carefully as I said this.

Her shoulders almost sagged. "Fiona didn't tell me, but after Dorner died she told Patricia, and Patricia told me."

I hated to tell her something else that would upset her, but better from me than a reporter or nosy resident in her place.

"There is an issue regarding Clive Dorner's death."

Her tone was sharp. "What kind of issue?"

Apparently Peter and Arman were with him in the house, and…"

When I hesitated, Scoobie picked up. "There was a shouting match, and it didn't end well for Dorner."

Mrs. Murphy looked from Scoobie to me. "Do you mean those two boys had something to do with Clive Dorner's death?"

"It appears so, but I don't think they meant to kill him," I said.

"That man should burn in hell. But I'm sorry if he got a head start on it if it means Peter and Arman are in trouble."

Chapter Twenty-Eight

I STARED AT THE CEILING for a full minute when I woke up on Wednesday. Part of me felt really bad for Peter. He was trying to help Fiona. He hadn't meant to kill Dorner.

The rest of me knew that cover-ups never work, and even if they did, he should have done the right thing and called an ambulance and the police.

So, Fiona's boyfriend was looking out for her and Patricia's boyfriend seemed to have been looking out for himself. I could see Fiona and Peter getting through all this and staying together. But if Patricia was smart she'd dump Arman. On the surface it might seem as if he was looking out for her financial future, but Scoobie was right. Arman was a bully. She couldn't possibly want him around her kids.

I showered and dressed and walked down the back stairs to Aunt Madge's kitchen. I was determined to move back to my own house today. It must have been Arman on my back porch, and he wasn't going to try to get in my windows anytime soon. Besides, Pebbles didn't like being locked in the bathroom overnight when I was gone that long. If she was going to be Jazz's full-time companion, I needed to keep her happy.

I could hear Aunt Madge in the breakfast room talking to her guests. I didn't see Jazz, who had run downstairs when I opened the bedroom door a few minutes ago. A closer look around the room showed she was sitting in between Mister Rogers and Miss Piggy, who were on their rug by the sliding glass door. She cocked her head at me, probably daring me to pick her up to take her back to my house.

The *Ocean Alley Press* was on the table with the headline clearly visible. "Local Murder Solved." I scanned it quickly. The focus was on the reason that Peter and Arman met Clive Dorner in the house on Ferry Street, and that both men maintained that Dorner's death was an accident. The fire marshal discussed the fire and the medical examiner said that Dorner was dead before the fire started. It was not clear how they started the fire, but it wouldn't have been hard to get the old house to burn.

After giving background information on Clive Dorner and noting that he was the nephew of the murdered Norman Fitzgerald, the article mentioned that the two men were brought to the police station from a home on Bay Street.

I groaned as I kept reading. The rest of the article rehashed the "attempted burglary at the same house on Bay Street" and said that the burglar was thwarted by Reuben Harris, whom the article identified as "the Peeping Tom who had troubled Ocean Alley neighborhoods for months." Not mentioned was that he had been across the street when he called the police about the burglary.

My cell phone chirped. I answered it without looking at caller ID, and was sorry I had not checked.

"So," Lester said, "did the Peeping Tom see much?"

"He was across the street."

"Yeah, but maybe he'd been at your place first." There was a definite chuckle in his voice.

"Lester, I don't need this."

"I'm just sayin'…" he began.

"I'll catch you later." I hung up.

I CAPTURED JAZZ to take back to my house by tricking her with canned tuna. Pebbles seemed glad to see her, and I left them sitting next to each other in front of the couch. Fortunately, Pebbles was a bit too hefty to jump on it in the deft manner Jazz did when she thought I wasn't looking.

The house I had to appraise was large and I spent an hour and a half taking measurements and trying to avoid talking to a very chatty homeowner. When I pulled up to Harry's house so I could enter data into the appraisal software, I wished I had stayed away longer.

Elmira Washington sat on the top step of Harry's porch. She stood as I parked my car and waited until I was at the bottom of the steps before she spoke.

Elmira is a kind of squat woman whose stiff, short gray hair makes her look like an aging drill sergeant. "Now what? If Fitzgerald is dead and Mary Murphy's son-in-law is in jail, who's going to prove those auctioneers stole from me?"

I walked up and did not stop next to her as I took out the keys and put them into the lock. "I think Norman Fitzgerald was the only thief."

She followed me into the house. "Maybe, but somebody owes me money."

"I suppose Mrs. Murphy will still make an effort to be awarded money from the sale of the business. Maybe you can talk to the lawyer who represents the Dorner cousins. Ask that you be reimbursed from their portion of the sale revenue." I kept my back to her as I turned on my computer.

"That lawyer's a young pipsqueak," she said.

I did not tell Elmira she was an old complainer. "That may be, but there's not one thing I can do to help you."

She sat in Harry's office chair. "People all over town are saying that you found some jewelry in that house. Where did it come from?"

I sat in my desk chair and swiveled to face her. "There was some hidden in the house. I don't think it's worth a huge amount. Peter and I were going through auction files to see if we could identify who it belonged to." This was not exactly our purpose, but she didn't need to know we were looking for evidence of other Fitzgerald thefts. And of course Peter hoped we would not find any prior owners.

"What files?"

I gave myself a mental head slap. "Mrs. Murphy had a few old records. They weren't for all the auctions."

"I need to see those right now." Elmira stood and picked up her purse from where she had placed it on Harry's desk.

"Elmira, to see those you'd probably need to work with an attorney. Stuff brings almost nothing at an auction. Is it really worth a lot of legal fees to get maybe twenty-five dollars?"

She looked at me. "They were worth a lot more than that."

"Maybe. But at an auction people try to pay less than something is worth. I just bought an antique chest of drawers for not much more than one hundred dollars. It was probably worth two to three times that."

"I still want my money." She had a very stubborn expression.

"Suit yourself. I have work to do." I gestured to my computer and did not get up to escort her to the front door.

I HAD SPENT ALL of Thursday and this morning planning for tomorrow's fundraiser. Part of this entailed telling Scoobie there was no need for a practice session with the liquid string.

The article about the fundraiser that was in the Friday morning paper led to a lot of calls with questions about the upcoming party. One woman who couldn't come wanted to donate a box of canned goods, so I was waiting for her at the pantry. It was good that I stopped by. Even though it wasn't a distribution day, there were several bags of donations at the door. I lugged them in and started stocking shelves.

When Reverend Jamison first talked me into running the food pantry about sixteen months ago, I hated the idea. Since then I'd worked it into my schedule pretty well and learned about a side of Ocean Alley I didn't know much about. There were many people who couldn't buy fries on the boardwalk whenever they wanted to, people whose food stamps didn't stretch to the end of the month.

There was a knock on the door and George peered in. "I saw your car."

I opened the door and stepped aside to let him in.

"Did my article get you a lot of food?"

"It did. I didn't think about that."

He glanced around the room and picked up a bag of food to sort. "I've been thinking about Fitzgerald. With Dorner dead, I bet we never find out who killed the old guy."

"You really think Dorner did it? He seemed to really like the guy."

"Yeah, but he was a sleaze.""

I smiled. "Plenty of those around."

"Yeah, yeah. But he needed money."

I thought about that. "It just doesn't make sense that he'd kill him on my porch. He'd have lots of less obvious places to do it. What about Arman?"

"Nah." George looked at a can of Brussels sprouts and made a face.

"You don't think he's that big a bully?"

"I don't think he knew enough about Fitzgerald's thefts to try to badger the old guy. Plus, I did my own badgering. Morehouse told me that Peter and Arman have good alibis for that night."

"So, we may never know who killed a man on my porch."

I hated that thought.

Chapter Twenty-Nine

AS DOCTOR WELBY had predicted, the weather was gorgeous, and the mid-May temperature of about sixty-five degrees gave us a perfect Saturday.

The sign in front of the Ocean Alley Tennis Club said "Harvest for All Birthday Party and Scavenger Hunt." Roland and a local printer had donated it.

The club is a rambling one-story building not far from downtown, since it was built long before Ocean Alley was as populated as it is now. Today colorful triangle flags flew on long strips of string. It reminded me of a car dealership promoting a sale.

The manager also had information about tennis club membership on a table near the entrance to the parking lots. I added brochures on the food pantry to his table when he wasn't looking.

We had two hours to use the club. Plus some advance set-up time and post clean-up time. Saturdays mornings are for lessons and team play, and early evening for doubles and singles matches for members. We had the hot time of the day, when there are no scheduled events and not too many people want to play. We weren't going to be on the courts, but would probably hog the rest rooms.

I wanted to keep the local teens invested in Harvest for All beyond the scavenger clues, so I had asked Alicia to get a bunch of them to keep track of the canned and boxed food donations people brought. Sylvia would collect money from those who paid an entry fee or made a donation, though neither Lance or Scoobie could talk her into wearing one of the half-aprons with pockets that the hardware store lends us for every fundraiser.

Monica had her bake sale, with Aunt Madge and Harry helping, and Aretha oversaw Scoobie, Bill, and George as they unpacked the liquid string. This was necessary because Scoobie and George had opened a case last night. They had picked it up at Mr. Markle's grocery store, ostensibly to have it ready to bring to the tennis club today.

I did not hear all of the conversation this morning, but enough to gather that it was a good thing the *Ocean Alley Press* editor relied heavily on George before the two of them emptied a couple of cans of the stuff in the newsroom yesterday evening. *You'd think they were sixteen sometimes.*

I could see Ramona and Jennifer on the far side of the parking lot. Ramona did caricatures for a small donation and Jennifer collected those donations. She was willing to wear an apron.

I had the scavenger hunt instructions to pass out when that started. We didn't want anyone to get a head start to figure out the clues for the first location. Lance and Doctor Welby guided delivery people from the bakery as Harry and Megan placed six large sheet cakes on a row of tables.

What could possibly go wrong?

"LADIES AND GENTLEMEN." It doesn't matter what our event is, Doctor Welby opens it with his booming voice.

"We'll take about twenty minutes for those of you who want to change into bathing suits or older clothes to do that before we start the, uh, string spraying contest. When that's over, we'll get a chance to eat some cake before the scavenger hunt." He beamed at the crowd, which already boasted more than one hundred people. "We're going to have a grand time today."

With the scavenger hunt instructions safe in my fanny pack, I walked around the tennis club parking lot greeting people. With likely visions of lawsuits in his head, the club manager had borrowed ten large canvas tarps from various building and painting contractors around town, and the tarps covered a large part of the parking lot. Probably this would be less slippery than asphalt once all the soapy foam had been sprayed.

"Now, kids," I heard Dr. Welby say to Alicia and her friends, "I really appreciate that you're going to hose down the tarps and parking lot when the contest is over. Can I count on you to limit the amount you spray on people?"

As if.

Alicia caught my eye and gave me a huge grin. Her friend Clark had an equally devious expression. I'm still not sure if they are officially dating. Alicia with her long, dark hair and huge brown eyes, would probably snare interest based on her looks alone, but she's also funny and kind. I've watched Clark try to become more than a friend for months, and he actually has Megan's approval, though she is smart enough not to say that to anyone except me.

I was still trying to figure out how to be on the far side of the parking lot when the liquid string activity started. In theory, people were to do things like see who could shoot it the farthest, and who could draw a recognizable picture with just one can. In reality, we would all get sprayed in various colors.

I had on a Harvest for All tee shirt and denim shorts. Aunt Madge said that she and Monica were staying behind the bake-sale table, which had a sign that said, "No Liquid String Near the Food." I thought Monica might want to be drawn into the activity because her cardigan was not buttoned up to her neck.

Aretha said Sylvia was going to hide in the women's rest room. I figured if Scoobie had heard this he would have asked the club manager if he could go in after her.

"Jolie!"

I turned to see Annie Milner, who went to high school with us and is the county's prosecuting attorney. With a sinking feeling I realized we should have made her one of the birthday honorees as well. I hoped I hadn't hurt her feelings. She also knew a lot of attorneys who might have joined the party and donated money. *Oh well, next time.*

"Annie, thanks so much for coming."

"Wouldn't have missed it." She lowered her voice. "Thanks for not asking me to be one of the birthday people. With this job, I can't make myself look too silly."

I looked at her lovely cream-colored top and light green knit cardigan that had the same cream color in a strip down the sides next to the buttons and button holes. "You, uh, might want to stay off the tarps when the liquid string game starts," I said to her.

"Surely they'll know I'm not playing."

I raised an eyebrow at her. "Have you forgotten my best bud Scoobie?"

Before she could answer I heard a whoop of laughter from Aunt Madge and turned toward her. People had started to assemble on the tarps. Many had on large black trash bags in which they had put a hole for their head. We were providing those for a $5 donation, unless someone said they could not afford one, in which case they were free.

The laughter was largely aimed at George, Bill, and Scoobie, who had on bathing suits and scuba-diving goggles complete with a snorkel in each of their mouths. They also had on swim fins, so they kind of walked like ducks, only in a bit less of a side-to-side motion.

I grinned at Annie. "It looks as if the fun is about to begin."

I walked over to Dr. Welby. There were six cases of the liquid string behind him, on the grass near the closest tennis court. "You didn't get your armed guards." I nodded at the boxes.

"George and Bill said that if anyone tried to get one early they would tackle them," he said.

I almost snorted. "You realize they would tackle them so they could get to the cans first, right?"

Lance had heard me. "I think the swim fins will keep them calmer than I would have anticipated." He handed me a small sign that said birthday girl. It was in a plastic name badge holders and had a kind of elastic band that I could put around my neck.

"We put the pictures on these so you guys can't get someone else to wear them," Lance said.

Ramona and Jennifer walked up. Jennifer had on a beautiful bathing suit and cover-up combo. Her hair, piled on top of her head, was held there with a couple of large combs that were the same color as her suit. She kept looking over her shoulder.

Ramona, who usually has on kind of gauzy calf-length skirts, was in cut-offs and a tee shirt that read, Ask me about the Purple Cow.

I looked at the two of them. "Do you know something I don't?" I asked. Lance handed them their name badges. I thought he smirked, and Dr. Welby grinned.

Uh oh.

"There is a rumor…" Lance began.

Dr. Welby seemed to deliberately cut him off by calling out, "Okay folks, almost time to get started. Can you gather over here?"

Lance moved toward the bake sale table. "Chicken," I called after him. I turned to Ramona. "What rumor?"

"I'm not sure," she said, "but I heard that the birthday honorees might be targets of more of the stuff than the others."

I groaned and Jennifer gave me a stiff smile. "Do you suppose the dye in that string washes out?"

"It would have to," Ramona said. "The makers would get the daylights sued out of them if it didn't."

Jennifer looked reassured and I looked back at Dr. Welby, who was speaking again. "Each person gets one can at a time…"

"Two!" This came from the back of the group of about one-hundred-fifty that now stood on the tarps. "One for each hand."

Scoobie walked over, or rather, clomped, and took the snorkel tube out of his mouth. "I think that'll work, Doc. It'll save you having to keep passing them out. Could be quite a stampede."

"Ah, never be let it said we are not flexible. Two." The rules were listed on two pieces of poster board tied to the tree branch behind Dr. Welby, but he still went over them. He was so serious it was hard not to laugh.

Dr. Welby explained that Reverend Jamison, Father Teehan, and the minister from the Unitarian Church, Isaac Gibson, would judge the longest string shots. He and Lance would judge the string drawings on the tarps, but only after all people were finished using the liquid string.

After a final caution to not spray directly at people, especially the eyes, he said that after everyone had two cans he would do a countdown from five to begin the activity.

Who is he kidding?

The high school group passed out the cans. They had recruited more students than usually helped at our can drives or in the pantry, which was a good thing. It was a big job to hand out cans to so many people. I noted that the boys all had cans of string sticking out of their pockets.

"Should we help?" I asked Ramona and Jennifer.

"Are you kidding?" Ramona asked. "As soon as we get near the guys we're toast."

"Maybe I should help with the bake sale," Jennifer said, clearly nervous.

"I think Bill is assigned to get you," Ramona said. "That's better than Scoobie or George."

Jennifer looked almost panic-stricken.

"How do you know they divided up their targets?" I asked.

"I heard Scoobie and George arguing over who got you." She smiled as she took two cans from Alicia.

"Thanks," I said to Alicia. "Where's your mom?"

"Hiding," she said, cheerfully. "But I know where."

"Where is she?" Jennifer asked, and stayed with Alicia, apparently to pry the information out of her.

"Who got me?" I asked Ramona.

"Not telling," she said.

"Come on, Ramona."

"I don't actually know. They were still arguing when they left the store yesterday."

"You must have a clue…" I began.

"Okay, it looks as if everyone has their string," Dr. Welby said. "Remember to play nice on the countdown from five. Five. Four. Three. Two…"

He didn't get to one. Or if he did, I didn't hear him. The shrieks and calls of "got you," were loud and continuing. I ducked as Ramona aimed at me, but not fast enough.

"Gotcha!" she hollered, and took off.

The cans emptied quickly. Apparently, this had been anticipated, because Aretha and two of her friends each had a case in front of them and they were passing out additional cans faster than I thought they could move.

I hadn't sprayed yet, but they wouldn't know mine weren't empty, so I tucked the ones I had under one arm and sprinted the few yards and grabbed two more.

"Cheater, cheater!" Scoobie yelled, and I was immediately covered in a combination of purple and yellow string. "Easter colors. Father Teehan's idea!"

I barely got him. He had discarded the swim fins in favor of sneakers, and moved away fast.

I could hear Jennifer squealing, and had a quick view of Bill dousing her, two-handed, before she shot back and seemed to get him in the mouth, because he started spitting.

The nape of my tee shirt was pulled back and I felt a can of string cascade down my back.

"Eeek!" I ducked and didn't bother looking before I sprayed. I had no idea it would be Harry. I got him in the ear before he slid away. "Careful!" I said this just before George got me with two cans, one on my shirt and one in my hair.

"Arrgh!" I aimed a can, but barely got him in the shoulder before he was gone, laughing like a maniac.

It was over in less than five minutes, but only because the cans empty quickly. People sat on the ground laughing, and a couple of kids slid on the slippery tarps, as if they were an icy pond.

Dr. Welby and Reverend Jamison were covered in several colors, but Lance had stood just off the tarps and no one had gotten him. Since he looks his age of close to mid-nineties, he must have been exempt in everyone's minds. I scooped up some nearly melted string from the tarp and walked over and put it on his shoulder.

"Thank you so much." He grinned broadly.

Dr. Welby was trying to regain some control. "Uh, Reverends, do we have any contest results?"

There was a great deal of laughter. No one had aimed at anything except other people.

"It's okay, Jennifer." I turned around. Bill's tone was close to consoling. "Come on, I'll walk you to the showers." He put his hand on her shoulder and turned her to face the club house. She was quite covered. It had to be more than Bill's cans.

I couldn't see Ramona. "I'll get her later," I muttered.

"Would you like a paper towel, dear?" Aunt Madge called this from behind the bake sale table.

"Only if you come over here to give it to me." I gave her a sweet smile. She wisely chose to stay where she was.

Alicia and her crew walked over to the two rolls of hoses that were just behind the tree that had the rules. If any had been obeyed I would be amazed. "Careful now," Dr. Welby said, not too loudly.

"We will," Clark promised. "Alicia's mom made us promise."

I looked around. Megan was at the bake sale table and had blue foam in her hair. Aunt Madge, Sylvia, and Monica had none. Harry was setting up an additional table to hold the paper goods for the birthday cakes. He didn't have much. He must have just darted out to get me.

The hosing of the tarps began, with many people wanting a scoop of water to use to get the foam off. It was soap, after all. A number of people started for the showers. There were two outdoor ones, like the ones at the beach, and kids used those.

I figured we owed the tennis club manager a case of beer or a couple of good bottles of wine.

I HAD HASTILY rinsed my hair under the outdoor shower and most of the cake had been served. I caught Aunt Madge's eye. "I'm heading to my location as soon as we pass out the first clues." I gestured at my clothes.

She nodded and went back to cutting cake.

The hosts for the scavenger sites were supposed to leave about now. There were three initial clues, to be passed out randomly. They all led to Lester at Burger King. He was giving out free Whopper Junior coupons as he gave contestants the second clue. Scoobie told me that Lester had stapled his business card to the back of the clue.

Each stop on the scavenger hunt would yield a clue for the next location, with my house being the last one. I would distribute prize coupons to the first five arriving players. To prevent people from claiming a prize in the contest by simply going to my house, they had to show me all the clues they had picked up along the way.

I would give each person a thank you card and the licorice. Ramona had talked me into black and red, and suggested that Pebbles be left in the bathroom.

The initial clues were folded in half and stapled, so everyone could open them at the same time. Dr. Welby was about to announce distribution of the clues and the few ground rules, most of which were because he was a doctor and included things like no running and be sure to look both ways before crossing the street.

Sergeant Morehouse had said that, barring some criminal outbreak, there would be police officers greeting the crowd on several corners. He had thought he was quite funny when he said, "And since you won't be on the loose, it'll probably be calm."

I had a single piece of paper that had all the clues on it, in very small print, and I glanced at them. Despite Alicia's efforts, the ones that led to Burger King were largely Lester's concoction, with guidance from Harry to make sure they weren't raunchy. The three Burger King clues were:

In its crowning glory
Lies a royal story
If you're at all on the ball
You'll know it, large or small,
Finding it is a worthy feat,
Either way, it's good grub to eat.

A place without fried
No tiara will you need
For this we provide
Your nose you must heed
If you want this clue to succeed

If you're ready for a drink
And under 18, don't even think
You can get one without getting caught.
Look around if you would

And you'll see something good.
King or queen you may be,
Just enter what you see.

I thought the first clue was as good as telling the scavenger hunters the name of the place, but it was supposed to be an easy game. The third clue let the hunters know Burger King was across from the Sandpiper Bar and Grill, a favorite haunt of Ocean Alley's seamier residents. And any high school kid who wanted to try to be served before they were twenty-one.

I liked the clue for my house. It had taken me a long time to write, even with Scoobie's so-called help.

When Sandy paid a call
Ocean Alley had some luck.
There was damage last fall
But not the huge piles of muck
With which further south was stuck.
Still, lots of houses needed repair.
Go to this one if you dare.
You'll find our fearless chair.
But watch out or she'll call
And you'll help at Harvest for All.

When I gave them the licorice they'd also get a blue three by five card that said thank you on one side and had the food pantry's address and hours, and a phone number to call if anyone wanted to volunteer. This was Reverend Jamison's idea. I should have thought of it.

I CLEANED UP QUICKLY. I didn't think anyone would be at my house too early, since they had to get through the other locations before they got to me. Then I spent about ten minutes trying to get Pebbles to come out from under my bed so I could put her in the bathroom. Since I occasionally did this with Jazz at the B&B, my cat is onto me. I was tempted to think she had ratted me out to Pebbles and that was why the skunk stayed just out of my reach.

Finally, I gave up. Anytime anyone came over Pebbles scooted under my bed. She'd never go to the door. Lance had talked me out of handing out a picture of Jazz and Pebbles. He thought it would be an advertisement that I owned a skunk and someone might try to take her. I should be so lucky.

I was beginning to wonder if Harry had decided not to pass out my clue, but finally there were footsteps on the porch.

"Jolie. Jolie. I beat them all. Beat them all." Max had a huge smile.

I opened the door to let him in. "Wow. How did you do it?" I'd seen him at the tennis club, but he had seemed very unsure of himself and mostly hung out at the bake sale table. He's not big on dealing with people he doesn't know. And he knows Aunt Madge will give him free chocolate brownies or cookies.

He laughed and whispered. "I didn't really. I went with Scoobie and George." He held out a piece of paper. Scoobie said to give you this. Can I read it, too?"

The brief rhyme was written in two handwritings, so I figured they had both worked on it. I scanned it, hoping it was something I could share with Max.

If you're looking for trouble
Come to this house on the double.
Some would say the lady's nosy
But the atmosphere is cozy.
Be careful dealing with her pets
For odder animals you won't have met.
When all's said and done she's a barrel of fun.
Having said this, we're on the run.

"Where are they running?" Max asked.

"They're being funny. They mean they're going away from me because they think I won't like the poem."

"They laughed really hard when they wrote it," he offered.

"I'm not surprised." As I said this more footsteps clambered up the porch.

"Slow down, guys!" Two boys about ten ran onto the porch. They were very out of breath and their faces were red. "We ran the whole time," the tallest one said. I looked behind them and saw two of the women who worked at the salt water taffy store on the boardwalk. They waved at me.

"I bet you did. There's a nice prize for you back at the tennis club." I took two of the blue cards from the top of the pile. Each one said prize winner. "You saw that table of prizes, right? You can each pick one."

They did a sort of victory dance and each raised one fist in the air.

"I told my mom we'd win," said one boy.

"No, I told my mom we'd win," said the other.

"Would the grown-ups like a bottle of water?" I asked.

The women said yes and walked onto the porch to begin a brief discussion on teamwork and how both boys were right. I smiled and walked to the kitchen, glad I had bought a new case of water this week.

The next hour passed quickly. Max stayed for a good part of it, but he got bored and left to find Scoobie. "Or I might get more cake."

When fifteen minutes had passed with no more hunters, I closed the front door and walked to my bedroom and flopped on the bed. "It's safe, guys." Jazz pounced on the bed and then on me in two quick leaps.

I stroked her and she gave me a look that said she was tired of company. Or I thought that's what she said, anyway. "I know. Let me rest for five minutes and then I have to go back to the tennis club to see if there's more clean-up work."

I shut my eyes and was immediately asleep. After some period of time my eyes opened and I listened carefully. It sounded as if someone had come in the front door. "Scoobie? George?" Jazz dove under the bed.

"No," said a kind of squeaky woman's voice.

I swung my legs over the side of the bed and stood as someone wearing a stocking mask and dark, long-sleeved clothing pointed a small gun at me and walked into the room.

It was very quiet and I felt my heart beating very fast. "What do you want?" I tried to say this calmly, but didn't manage that.

The woman, I was sure it was a woman, gestured with the gun, pointing toward the closet.

"I really don't want to go in there."

She held up a note. "Take off the last board, at the back, on the right."

Oddly, I felt myself relax. This was someone who knew about the jewelry, or whatever else Fitzgerald had hidden here. She wanted that, not me. "Okay." I raised my hands like a robber who'd been caught. I wanted her to know I had every intention of doing what she said. I backed toward the closet and bumped into the corner of the chest of drawers. "Ow!"

She gave a sharp jab in the air with her gun. Clearly, I was not to delay. I turned to face the closet. The closets in my house were small and this one was packed full of my clothes. I moved them to the left side. It still didn't leave much room.

The closet was not deep. I kind of backed against the clothes and put my hands on the back panels on the right side of the cedar closet. *At least I'll smell good.*

"Now what?" I asked.

The squeaky voice replied. "Screwdriver on the floor. Pry off the last board."

"Jeez! How many people have keys to my house?" My anger felt better than scared. I stooped, picked up the long-handled screwdriver, and stood back up. I couldn't imagine how I would be able to wiggle the board loose.

"Down lower," she squeaked.

I squatted and peered at the bottom of the closet wall. Even in limited light I could see that at the very bottom on the right, the long cedar board had a piece about six inches tall that must have been sawed off the board before it was fitted. Someone had apparently then hammered the six-inch piece into place below the rest of the board. I had never noticed this, but since I hadn't had to paint this closet I hadn't been on the floor previously.

The piece of board wiggled easily. I forced the screwdriver into the small space at the corner and applied some force. It moved more and I jammed the screwdriver into the space and then angled it to try to pop the board off. To my surprise, it flipped off. Fitzgerald must have used much smaller nails to fit the bottom piece in place.

The woman didn't need to tell me what to do. I reached into the vacant space and pulled out—surprise—another canvas sack, this one folded in half to fit into the space. I felt it and thought it was full of jewels and coins. Unless the small round cylinders were marbles, which I doubted.

"Here!" she squeaked.

I jumped. Intent on my task, I didn't realize she had almost come into the closet. I handed her the bag and made to stand. She didn't look at the sack, but pointed the gun toward me and I sat back on the floor. Panic hit me for the first time. *Maybe she'll shoot me and leave me in the closet.*

I kept my eyes on her hands. The one without the gun held the sack and she fingered it, as if trying to gauge its contents. Her right hand still held the gun.

After a few seconds she stuck the bag in the pocket of her jacket and gestured at me with the gun. I was pretty sure she was telling me to stay in the closet.

I yelled, "Point that somewhere else!" I head butted her in the knee and she stumbled backwards a couple of steps.

Her gun discharged as she stumbled back and then she sat down, hard, on the edge of my bed. It was a tiny gun, probably a twenty-two if I remembered from TV detective shows. It was still really loud in my small bedroom.

I crawled out of the closet and half-crouched. I wasn't sure what she would do next, and she was still holding the gun. Plus, her knee was a very hard place to head butt, and I was dizzy.

"Bitch!" she yelled, and rose awkwardly to her feet.

Apparently Pebbles likes gunshots even less than strange people, and she darted out from under the bed almost at the intruder's feet. The woman shrieked and raised a foot to kick her. Faster than I could keep track of her, Jazz launched herself at the robber's ankle. Pebbles swung around and raised her tail at the woman.

"Get away! Get away!" she screamed.

She raised the gun, but she was really off balance, trying to shake Jazz off her foot. As I had seen her do many times, Jazz sank her claws into skin and began to climb.

I launched myself at the gun and grabbed it with both hands, making it point to the ceiling. The woman started to fall backwards onto the bed, but not before she had grabbed a chunk of my hair. I fell onto the bed beside her and inhaled her sweet-smelling perfume.

"Let go!" I yelled.

I wanted to pull her hand off my hair, but wasn't willing to take both hands off of the gun. I might not have claws, but I moved one hand down a bit and dug my fingernails into the little bit of wrist that showed between the long sleeves and a cotton glove. She let go of my hair and hit me in the side of the head. I kept hold of the gun, but my ears rang and I felt my hands start to slide off the gun.

The woman reached her free hand up to grab at the gun, which was still pointing at the ceiling. She fired it again, and my head throbbed with the sound.

I thought the second shot surprised her, and her grip on the gun loosened. Or maybe it was the smell that caught her off guard. Being this close to her gun I got a good whiff of the sort of acrid burning odor of what I assumed was gunpowder.

In the back of my mind I heard footsteps pounding up my porch and people calling my name. I fastened my hand on the wrist of the hand holding the gun, wanting to get her finger off the trigger.

Suddenly someone grabbed me by the collar to pull me off the robber, and a man's hand covered mine over the gun. Whoever it was slugged the woman in the head with his other hand just as I let go of the gun and the other rescuer pulled me off the woman.

She sank onto the bed, moaning. "Don't shoot me." The squeaky voice was gone, replaced by one that sounded a bit familiar.

George had hit her and now had the gun. He held it at his side and said, "Stay down there, do not move!"

I looked to my left and saw a white-faced Scoobie.

He gave me a quick look and let go of me, and then looked toward the floor. "Damn. That is one pissed off cat." Only then did Jazz let go of her prey. She had made it up to the woman's knee.

Pebbles was back under the bed even before George pulled the ski mask off the woman.

All three of us said, "Betty!" at the same time.

"It was supposed to be mine! It was my payback!" she screamed at us. Her expression was truly crazed.

"I KNOW THIS ONE WASN'T your fault," Morehouse said, "but you shoulda told me about that second sack of stuff." He had handcuffed a crying Betty and two officers had taken her outside to put her in a police car.

"Like I knew." I sat in my rocker with my head leaning against its back. George paced the living room and Scoobie sat, silently, on the couch. Morehouse sat next to him and opened his notebook.

"Where was it?" George asked, stopping for a moment.

"George, shut up. Where was it?" Morehouse asked.

In the back of the cedar closet in my bedroom. You'll see a hole at the bottom."

Dana had just come in the front door, catching the end of my comment.

"Stick your head in that closet for a minute, would you?" Morehouse asked.

"Sure." She walked into the bedroom.

"One of the back boards. It was sawed at the bottom and the piece put back in place. The sack was behind it." I closed my eyes.

"You gonna be okay? You didn't get hit in the head or anything, did you?"

"You know," I said slowly, "I believe she did try, but she mostly missed."

Dana walked back into the living room. "Small piece of board on the bottom pulled out. I think I've spotted both bullets." She pulled a small camera out of her pocket and returned to the bedroom.

There was an exchange of words on the porch. "Get out of my way or I'll throw you off this porch!"

"Madge." It was Harry's voice now.

"She can come in," Morehouse yelled.

The screen yanked open and I stood halfway up and then sat down again. I felt kind of weak. Aunt Madge then pulled at me, half in a hug and half I don't know what.

"You're all right. Virginia said there was gunfire."

I patted her on the back, and again tried to stand, but she kind of pushed me back into the chair. "It was a little gun."

"Little, schmittle." Harry said. "Who was it?"

"Betty Fowler," George said.

"What?!" This was from Aunt Madge and Harry.

"Madge." Morehouse had stood. "Sit on the couch. You need to let me talk to her."

She stared at him and sat next to Scoobie. Harry squeezed my shoulder and went to sit next to her. George took the two dinette chairs and swung them toward the rocker and couch, and Morehouse sat in one. I thought George might sit, but he didn't.

"Okay," Morehouse said. "Start at the beginning."

I stared at him without smiling. "That's kind of like TV."

He grunted, and I took a breath. "She came in after the last scavenger person left. Or about fifteen minutes after that." I glanced at Scoobie. "What time is it?"

"Almost four. That's why we walked over."

"Oh, that's later than I thought. I went in to lie down for a minute, but I fell asleep. She must have come in then. I didn't lock the door."

"Swell," George said. "You have a security system but you don't lock the door."

"Shut up, George," Morehouse said.

I told them that Betty had held up the sign telling me where to go, and that there had been a screwdriver on the floor. This caused a brief discussion between Harry and George about how it could have gotten there, and Morehouse told them both to "pipe down or leave."

I finished telling the chain of events, including that I wasn't sure she meant to fire the gun. "It was a good thing, though. If Pebbles hadn't come out from under the bed when Betty fired it, I don't think she would have been distracted enough for me to try to grab the gun."

"Did Pebbles go after her?" Scoobie asked.

Probably because it was the question he was about to ask, Morehouse did not tell him to shut up.

"She raised her tail to spray. When Sam came the day I found her, he said that was instinct when they were threatened, even if their scent glands had been removed." I thought for a second. "Betty was freaked out by Pebbles. And then Jazz latched onto her foot or ankle, or whatever it was."

Morehouse shook his head. "Saved by a skunk."

I saw George's face light up and quickly become serious again. He was thinking of headlines, I was sure.

"Betty ain't poor," Morehouse said. "Why in the hell would she do this?"

"She said something…" I paused.

"She said it was supposed to be hers. Something about payback," Scoobie said.

I sat up straighter. "I bet Dorner got her to give him some money for an investment property and told her he'd pay her back with money from the jewelry. He talked big, but his house was in foreclosure in Philly, remember?"

Morehouse nodded at me and then looked at his notes.

"Norman must have told him it was here," Aunt Madge said, softly.

Morehouse ignored her and spoke to me. "Dorner ask you for money?"

I shook my head. "No, but remember, he got three thousand dollars from Fiona Henderson."

"No wonder Betty called him a rat bastard," Harry said, almost to himself.

I let Harry and Aunt Madge describe the encounter in Newhart's and I added that Betty had apologized and treated me at Java Jolt.

When Morehouse had gotten as much information as he apparently thought he could wring out of me and asked me if I needed to go to the hospital—I most definitely did not—he left, taking George and Scoobie with him.

I realized I still had no idea what was in the bag.

Chapter Thirty

ON SUNDAY the *Ocean Alley Press* only had a two-inch article because Morehouse kept George at the police station answering questions until late. Morehouse said it was because George had handled the gun. Scoobie got to leave a little earlier, which he said was a good thing because he had had it with people for the day.

After assuring my parents, sister, and Ramona that I was okay, I slept half of Sunday.

The Monday *Press* annoyed me. I wished George had focused more on Pebbles than on me. I read the article three times. It did not link Betty to either Fitzgerald's or Dorner's deaths, but said she recently learned about the jewelry that had been hidden behind the walls for "probably decades."

Jewelry Thief Finds Prize

Betty Fowler, an Ocean Alley realtor, was arrested last night for an attempted robbery of the Bay Street home of Jolie Gentil, a local appraiser. Fowler had learned that the late Clive Dorner believed that his uncle, the late Norman Fitzgerald, had hidden some items in the house when it was owned by distant Fitzgerald cousins.

Because Dorner had an outstanding debt with her when he died, Fowler believed that she was entitled to at least a portion of the value of any hidden items she might find. Fowler had made at least one prior attempt to enter the home, and was frightened off by a passing citizen. She maintains that both times she tried to gain illegal entry she believed that Gentil was not at home.

Fowler forced Gentil to look for stolen items behind a panel in a closet. Police will only say that there were items of value in the sack Gentil retrieved.

The rest of the story described what Betty said was her "unintentional use" of her small handgun and said that she was cooperating with local police.

This did not answer all my questions, not even half, but Morehouse had said he would call me. I impatiently waited to hear from him. At about noon, Morehouse actually invited me to his office to learn what he knew about the death of Norman Fitzgerald.

"IT FEELS FUNNY TO be sitting here when you aren't trying to tell me to stay out of something."

"Don't push your luck," Morehouse said.

He explained that Betty told the police that she had given Dorner money for down payments on houses he was buying for investment. This came about because Dorner had taken Betty to dinner and worked into the conversation that he knew of a couple of great bargains, but as he was in the middle of flipping three other homes, he was having a temporary cash flow issue. He asked if she was interested in partnering with him.

This woman is a realtor and doesn't know how to do a credit check?

The bottom line, according to Betty's version, was that Dorner said that he would repay Betty by selling some of Fitzgerald's diamonds, which he claimed were stones his uncle had bought from some of the estates he auctioned. Stones that Fitzgerald planned to give to his favorite nephew. Stones that Dorner did not mention were not in his or his uncle's possession.

Fitzgerald and Dorner probably figured that they could not get to the jewelry that Scoobie and I had found. However, Fitzgerald had told his nephew that additional jewelry was in the cedar closet in my house, and Dorner confided this to Betty.

Betty's rose-colored glasses had turned clear by this time. She pressured Dorner to give her back the thousands of dollars she had lent him, even if he had to break into my house to get the money.

But, when Fitzgerald, at Dorner's urging, went to get the diamonds from the cedar closet the day I moved into the house, he was interrupted by the arrival of my friends and furniture. He left the large screwdriver behind, in his haste.

"That maybe accounts for why Norman Fitzgerald was at my house on move-in day, but it doesn't tell us why he died on my porch."

Morehouse drummed his fingers on his desk. "Again, we only know what Betty Fowler said, but she's tripping over her words to tell us what she knows."

In the Betty version, Fitzgerald told Dorner that he had a key that would let them get into the house, but he was getting more afraid of getting caught. Dorner agreed to meet his uncle at my house for what he called moral support. The day Dorner killed Fitzgerald, the auctioneer had begun to say that he wanted to use some of the money from the sale of the diamonds for charity.

Supposedly, Dorner and Fitzgerald went in through the back door of my house. Fitzgerald was on the floor of my closet, trying to loosen the board with the long screwdriver. When he got insistent about giving away some of the money and Dorner was equally committed to lining his pockets, Fitzgerald stormed out.

Dorner grabbed him as he started down the porch steps and pulled him back onto the porch. When Fitzgerald tried again to leave, Dorner grabbed a small flower pot from the edge of my porch and hit his uncle with it. He characterized this action to Betty as "a thoughtless act."

Gee, you think?

"Do you know what flower pot he was taking about?" Morehouse asked.

I shook my head. "There were some gardening things on the porch. They were inside the house when I bought it and I stuck them out there." I felt queasy. If I had stored the stuff in the tiny shed in the back yard Dorner wouldn't have had a ready murder weapon.

Morehouse sighed. "We'll never find the flower pot or whatever he killed Fitzgerald with. The autopsy showed it was a rounded object, so probably one of those little ceramic pots."

"I think the couple of pots had dirt in them. That would make them kind of heavy."

"Huh. Doesn't really matter at this point. Dorner likely tossed it somewhere far from your house."

Morehouse paused for a moment, as if debating whether to tell me something. "Her story is plausible. After Dorner died we took his prints. They matched some unidentified prints that were on your porch and the swing."

"You didn't tell me that!"

"You do remember it was a police investigation, right? Anyway, he had never been arrested, so his prints weren't in the system until after he died."

I started to retort, but thought of something else. "Hey, Dorner told Betty he killed his uncle and she kept it to herself?"

He gave a mirthless smile. "Betty said that Dorner was frantic. He told her he ran down the porch steps and stayed out of sight for a day and a half. Said he was mourning his uncle."

"Yeah, right. More like working on an alibi."

"He was never a suspect. When he said he had driven back to Philly earlier in the day, and that's where we found him, we didn't even check."

I raised my eyebrows and Morehouse looked at me and looked away.

"So, he told Betty what he did," I mused.

"And Betty tells us that when she heard this story she urged Dorner to turn himself in to us."

"And you believed her?" I asked Morehouse.

"No one believes her, but since anyone who could contradict her is pushing up daisies, there's no one to challenge her version. And her fingerprints were nowhere on your porch or in your house. Maybe accessory after the fact." He shrugged. "That's for the prosecuting attorney to decide."

"Too bad Virginia didn't see Betty at my place with Dorner or Fitzgerald."

He shrugged. "I don't think she was with him that night. Betty probably didn't know where anything was until Dorner had to explain the delay in him getting the jewelry. Where he thought he'd sell it, that's what's nuts."

I sighed. "Thanks to Geo…the *Ocean Alley Press*, I bet there will be other people looking for treasure."

Morehouse shook his head. "I talked to the editor this morning. He knows I know he can print what he wants, but that headline… Anyway, in a day or two a story will say there's no reason to believe there's more of the crap in your house."

"Damn George," I said, almost to myself.

"You don't think there's more, do you?" Morehouse asked.

I shook my head. "I would bet that there's none. And I'm not doing any remodeling soon, so if diamonds or anything else are there, they're staying where they are."

"And you've already proved your security system works." He had the hint of a smile.

"Yes…hey, when do I get to see what was in the bag? All I know is it was more jewelry."

Morehouse looked surprised. "I guess I figured you woulda looked at it. I only took a quick look before it was locked up. More diamonds, one in a setting, a couple colored stones of some kind, and a bunch of really old silver dollars. You can look at the evidence list. We'll try not to keep it too long."

"When can I have it?"

"You gonna keep it at your place or in a bank box?"

"Bank box. I'm going to make George run an article saying that some items that were in my house may have been stolen decades ago, and if someone can describe them well I'll consider giving them back."

"Every nut job in town will call you. Hell, every one of 'em on the east coast."

I shrugged. "The article can say my attorney is holding them."

Morehouse gave me a questioning look. "Who's your attorney?"

"I'm not paying an attorney. Whatever's not claimed I'll split with Mrs. Murphy."

I had originally planned not to keep any of the bounty, but I figured I had a boatload of trouble because of the stuff behind my walls, so I'd earned it. I'd probably give a chunk of anything that came to me to Harvest for All.

"Don't forget Shop with a Cop at Christmas." He stood.

I gave him a small bow and left. I walked out of the police station figuring that Betty would probably only be charged with crimes related to breaking into my house. Given her use of a gun, I figured she'd get at least some punishment beyond community service. She was lucky she didn't end up like Mr. Fitzgerald. *And so am I.*

ON TUESDAY, I FOCUSED ON trying to get my life back to some semblance of order. I longed to be concerned only with feeding my pets, hanging out at Java Jolt, and appraising houses.

And Harvest for All. Betty's invasion of my space had overshadowed the results of the birthday fundraiser. Lance called Tuesday morning to tell me how much money we had raised.

"The thing is, Jolie, it's still coming in. That article about Betty shooting up your house said it was just after the scavenger hunt. It was good publicity."

"I'm glad it was good for something. George hasn't had the nerve to find me."

Lance gave a grunt that could pass for a stifled laugh. "We should celebrate. When's our next Harvest for All meeting?"

I wasn't in the mood to have a meeting, but one thing I've learned is that volunteers stay motivated when they have a purpose. I told him I'd get back with him.

Before I went to the office I called Reverend Jamieson's secretary to see if we could use the First Prez conference room Thursday evening. She must have thought my brush with Betty was punishment enough for the week, because she wasn't her usual rude self and even volunteered to let the other committee members know about the meeting.

MY CELL PHONE CHIRPED as I left Harry's house to grab some lunch.

Dana Johnson said, "If you behave yourself, you can come to Fitzgerald's house with me."

"Inside you mean?" Despite swearing myself to normalcy, I felt a keen interest. Everything pointed to Fitzgerald as a thief, but there was nothing solid. Even Uncle Gordon's missing rifle didn't prove it was Fitzgerald who took it.

"Yep. I told Tortino I plan to study for the sergeant's exam, and I wanted to look at a crime scene for myself. He agreed."

"And he said you could take me?"

She laughed. "Get real."

"No wonder I like you so much."

I forgot about lunch and drove the half-mile to Norman Fitzgerald's forlorn-looking house. Dana pulled up a minute later.

As she unlocked the front door, she said, "I'm supposed to practice lifting prints to compare to Fitzgerald's and Dorner's."

"But they should be all over."

"Which is why it's practice. We have guys who specialize in crime scene stuff, but anybody sergeant and above has to know how to lift prints."

We stood in the small entry foyer and looked around. The house had the kind of musty smell of one that had been closed up for days.

"I guess we should start with what you think are keys behind the pot holders on those hooks," Dana said.

We walked to the kitchen and I noticed that the floor that had looked like vinyl when I peered in the window was actually linoleum and it was cracked around the fridge and stove. Dana took two pot holders off their hooks near the fridge. Behind each was a ring of keys, with maybe ten or twelve keys on each.

I started to reach for one and Dana held my wrist. "I suppose you shouldn't touch anything. No one should dust again, but just in case…"

I grinned. "I could get myself up on a murder charge."

She put on latex gloves and took down the two rings. "Only if Sergeant Morehouse has anything to do with it."

Dana placed the key rings on the table and spread out the keys. Some had tiny labels taped to them, but they weren't words that looked like family names.

I started saying the label names as she flipped through them. "Toby, Fluffy, Pete, Princess…"

"Nicknames I guess," she said.

"Sammie, Pebbles!"

We stared at each other and said at the same time, "Pet names."

I squinted at the one with Pebbles' name. It was longer than most of the other keys and not quite round at the head.

"I had all the locks rekeyed except the back door. I thought it was a unique key."

"So you think this is the key he used to get in your back door?"

"Probably. I'll check it again to be sure. It's an old fashioned lock. It has a brass plate around it, and the locksmith said that she couldn't rekey it. We figured there was probably only the key I got at settlement."

"So it looks as if he had an easy way in that day your neighbor saw him go in the back door."

"Guess so." I looked at the other keys on the table. "So, we know he kept keys to houses. We'll never know who had pets with these names."

"Ask your aunt."

"Oh, and Lance."

"And maybe a couple of vets," Dana said.

My mind tried to think of how to link the keys to auction files. I figured we'd have to develop lists of pet names and owners and compare them to the names on the folders. *This is going to be a lot of work.* Then I remembered probably no one on the police force would let me help, and for a change that felt good.

Dana took a folded black, canvas-like sack from the small bag she had slung over her shoulder. "This place was printed after Fitzgerald died, and Dorner must have cleaned up the goop. I'm going to try some door jambs and areas that might not have been checked before."

"Okay if I walk around?"

"That's why I brought you. You think differently than most people. But if you want something opened, call me."

"I'll keep my hands in my pocket, mom."

"Smart aleck," she murmured as she unzipped the bag.

There were two floors, but each had only about six-hundred square feet. I glanced at the boxes in Fitzgerald's office, but didn't want to ask Dana to interrupt her fingerprint lifting. I headed for the stairs. Not that I knew what I was looking for.

There were two bedrooms and a large, old-fashioned bathroom. It even had a claw-foot tub. I stooped to look at it. It was not fastened to the floor. He probably got it at an auction and replaced the tub that had been there. I glanced at the faucet. It was built into the wall, but the tile surrounding it was probably less than ten years old. Maybe another hiding place.

One bedroom appeared to have been Fitzgerald's. A wooden butler stand atop the dresser had an inexpensive watch, a few coins, and a pair of cuff links. The closet had the kind of clothing I'd seen Fitzgerald wear, including a brown cardigan sweater he had worn the day he returned the drawer to my chest.

A chair with an ottoman in front of it and a floor lamp beside it sat in front of the room's lone window. On the chair was a dog-eared paperback. An Earl Stanley Gardner book. So, he liked detective stories.

There were few personal touches to the room. There were two photos on his dresser. One was fairly recent, and showed Fitzgerald with several of the nieces and nephews who had attended his funeral.

The other was probably fifty years old. It was a head and shoulder shot, like a Kindergarten school photo, except the girl was only two or three years old. She had on a dress with the kind of smocked stitching that you saw in the 1950s, and her sweet face had a big smile. I'd have to ask Dana if she knew who she was.

The second bedroom seemed to be where Clive Dorner had slept. An open suitcase of men's clothes was on the floor in the corner and the single bed was unmade. Two bottles of expensive men's cologne were on a small bedside table.

"Jolie?"

I walked to the head of the stairs. "How's the practice?"

"Done. Anything interesting up there?"

"Couple things, maybe."

Dana walked up and followed me into Fitzgerald's bedroom.

"It doesn't matter, I guess, but who is the little girl? I thought his obit said his only child died as an infant."

Dana shook her head. "Whoever gave the paper the information was wrong. The little girl died sixty years ago or so, and Fitzgerald's nieces and nephews were born years after that."

"So she was his daughter?

"Elizabeth, I think someone said. We wondered why he gave to so many children's charities, so we looked into it."

I stared at the photo. "How did she die?"

"Meningitis. It was initially misdiagnosed. Hours count with that, especially for such a young child."

We both looked at the photo for another few seconds. Losing a child was no excuse for stealing from others to make donations to children's groups, but at least I thought I understood Fitzgerald's motives.

"What else?" Dana asked.

"Could you poke through Dorner's suitcase?" I asked.

She started down the hall. "If you tell anyone I touched his underwear you're toast."

"I'm not George."

Dana stood in the doorway and took in the room. "Kind of sparse if he was living here."

"He had a house in foreclosure in Philly. I guess most of his stuff was there."

She stooped next to the suitcase and gently lifted clothes, patting them to see if there was anything in the pockets. "Expensive shirts."

"He dressed better than his bank account, apparently," I said.

Dana flipped the lid down and put her hands in the zipper pockets on the front of the soft-side suitcase. She pulled out a wad of cotton swabs and a couple of the hotel shampoo packets that are thin plastic rather than bottles. She replaced it all and stood. "Nothing special that I can see."

"Is there one of those thin pockets in the back of the suitcase? That's where I always lose earrings."

She opened the main part of the suitcase again. "I didn't notice one…oh, there is one. It's only a couple of inches tall." She ran her hand through it and grinned as she pulled out something and held it up.

It was a camera memory card and it was the same brand that was missing from my camera.

MOREHOUSE CALLED WEDNESDAY morning to say my camera's memory card had been found in Dorner's suitcase. They were sure it was my card because it had the photos I'd taken of the jewelry. I feigned surprise and delight.

"You can thank Dana. She wanted to go through Fitzgerald's house again on her own. Oh, there's also a key we want you to check to see if it goes to your back door."

"Sure." I thought for a moment. "So, we know who the purse snatcher was, and he must have looked at the photos on the card."

"Yeah." I could hear Morehouse tapping his pencil on his desk or phone. "But it's funny that he would even know to look in your purse."

I had thought about this a lot since we found the camera card. "I'll bet Fitzgerald told him I took down that wall, and he and Dorner wanted to know if I'd found his bag of goodies behind it."

"I gotta admit, I thought that purse thing was random."

There was no point in irritating him, so I didn't tell him it never seemed random to me. "Whatever happened to Reuben Harris?"

"Your Peeping Tom friend is out on his own recognizance, provided he stays in his rooming house or goes to the grocery store or the hole-in-the-wall where he rents videos. Or a church, but I don't imagine he goes."

"Oh, swell. He can still rent porn to feed his lewd habit?"

"It's the family video place just off the boardwalk. Did you ever thank him?"

With a guilty jolt I realized I should have. Who knew if Betty had a gun that night?

"I take it that's a no," Morehouse said. "We don't think he's dangerous."

"How can…?"

"Talk to him. In a public place, if it makes you more comfortable."

BECAUSE A POLICE SERGEANT told me I wouldn't be in danger, Rueben Harris was sitting in the back pew of First Prez telling me the story of his life — a sad one. Three foster homes between ages ten and eighteen because his mother died and he had no idea who his father was. Kids made fun of him at school and there was no money for college or even to rent an apartment when he turned eighteen.

Reuben was a downtrodden-looking man in his mid-twenties who rarely looked at me directly. His tone was almost pleading. "See, I wasn't trying to see anything bad. I just like to look at families." He emphasized the last word.

I wasn't sure what to say, but I took a stab. "If you tried making some friends, maybe they'd invite you to meet their families."

His expression was glum. "I'm no good at making friends."

"What if…"

"And I'm not supposed to talk to anyone unless I'm in the grocery store or something."

I nodded slowly. "It may be harder for you now that people know what you did, but you're the only one who can take the first step."

He kept his gaze on the floor. "You harvest people should have some dinners for people with no friends." He looked at me with something bordering on interest. "The Knights of Columbus Hall has a fireplace. It's almost like a house in the winter."

"It's a thought," I didn't want to commit us to something specific. I stood. "Come on, we'll go to the food pantry. You can get there through the community room area."

"I can go there?" he asked.

"It's part of the church, and it's kind of like a grocery store."

We filled one of the large donation boxes and I drove him back to the boarding house on F Street. I wondered if more of Scoobie's neighbors were as downtrodden as Reuben Harris.

I SAT IN THE PURPLE COW for an hour trying to write an ad that let people know that I had found some valuables and would be willing to return them to prior owners if an owner or descendant could offer a detailed description.

"Don't you think it's like saying come rob your house?" Ramona asked.

"You need to say items can be viewed someplace other than your home," Roland said. He had come out to see why I had been sitting at one of his showroom desks for half an hour.

I crossed out a line and wrote a few more words. "What do you think of this?"

Several valuable items found in a recently purchased Ocean Alley home. Possibly taken from local auctions many years ago. Will be returned to prior owners if they show proof of ownership, such as a photo. Items can be viewed at OA Police Station on the following two Saturday mornings.

"The police agreed to that?" Ramona asked.

"I'm thinking of asking forgiveness rather than permission."

Roland shook his head and made for the storage area. He called over his shoulder, "Have a lawyer look at it."

It was a good idea. When I met Scoobie in Java Jolt late in the afternoon I tried to get him to agree to go with me to see a lawyer friend of Lance's. "Then I'll be done with it once and for all," was my final point.

"You'll only be through with it if your house gets razed."

"I thought you liked that little place," Joe said.

I gave him what I hoped passed for a polite smile. "I wouldn't dream of giving Lester a listing."

Scoobie smiled, but he didn't look pleased. "Everyone will know it's you. Too many other articles."

"Do you know another way to reach people?"

"You know a lot of the auction clients. What about a letter?"

"A lot of them would end up at the dead letter office." I didn't crack a smile.

"Seriously," he said.

"I was serious. Many, maybe most of the clients are dead and I have no idea who their relatives would be."

"I guess George did buy you that security system." Scoobie took a final swallow of his large cup of tea and looked at me. "He told me what you said."

"I think he was okay about it."

Scoobie looked at Joe. "If you lean that far over the counter you might fall over."

"You must be channeling George." Joe turned to finish adding coffee beans to his large grinder.

"It would be nice to have a private life," I said.

"Move," said Joe and Scoobie.

BY THE FOLLOWING TUESDAY, AFTER THE AD RAN for two days, I thought about moving. I had decided to ask permission, and Lieutenant Tortino had surprised me by saying it was all right to view the items at the station. He thought it might help the police get a better sense of the scope of Fitzgerald's thefts. Since Fitzgerald was dead it seemed moot to some of the officers, but Tortino and Morehouse reasoned that more stolen stuff could pop up in other places around town.

No one who thought they had a claim could look at items unless they had a photo or described it well. So far, no one had come close. It looked as if I might have a cache of valuables to sell, or whatever.

The problem was that, as Scoobie and the attorney predicted, the people who crawled out of the woodwork or through a worm hole or wherever they came from knew that the jewelry had been found at my house. My phone was through an Internet company so it wasn't in the phone book, but that didn't stop folks from trying to find me.

Elmira knew where to look, which was a problem. Today she was on my front porch.

"Elmira, Mrs. Murphy said she gave you the folder from your mother's auction. You know there were only two things you weren't paid for, and I don't have either of them."

"There might have been something else," she said, in a stubborn tone. "Or maybe you want to keep the amethyst bracelet."

"Enough already!" I shouted. "Go away."

"Well I never," she said. "Jolie Gentil your manners…"

"Are almost as bad as yours." I shut the door and sat in my rocker and put my head in my hands. *I should have listened to Scoobie.*

SCOOBIE IS NEVER one to say I told you so, but he did invite me to go with him to an All-Anon meeting. "I'll go to NA, but we can drive over together. Since you're the one with the car and all." He grinned.

Scoobie and George had sort of tricked me into going to my first meeting, and I don't go to a twice-weekly meeting nearly as often as they do. However, I have grudgingly admitted that my All-Anon group has helped me take worrying off my regular to-do list.

I like the All-Anon group because anyone who is a friend or family member of someone with an issue, which is the most neutral word I can think of, can go. My mother was a control freak. My husband gambled our assets into the toilet, but since I didn't know that until just before we split up, I didn't find I had too much in common with the people who went to the family group associated with Gamblers' Anonymous.

What I have are trust issues. Big time. And finding a dead man on the porch of my house and then having a woman I barely know come at me with a gun only exacerbated them.

This night's All-Anon meeting started with a reading about "learning to identify illusions that make life unmanageable." After about ten seconds of thinking about it I started to giggle. I didn't have illusions. I had realities that made my life unmanageable.

I tried to pretend I was coughing, but that only worked for about five seconds. Though the meetings are fairly relaxed, there is a certain decorum. Laughing uncontrollably when someone else says something is not considered respectful. And I couldn't stop.

No one chided me, there was just companionable quiet (from everyone else) until I calmed down. When I had finally gotten to the point of wiping my eyes the woman who had done the reading said, "That might be the most open comment you've made in a meeting, Jolie."

I lost it again, but I did make it to the bathroom before I peed my pants.

Chapter Thirty-One

MONICA HAD BAKED a birthday cake for the Harvest for All meeting, and Jennifer and Ramona joined our usual group. All of the birthday people were invited, but Bill was seeing patients in Newark and Daphne had to work at the library.

"It's lovely, Monica," I said. "You must have been up half the night decorating it."

"I'm very quick with my icing gun." She pointed to a picture she had drawn on the cake. "Can you see that you're getting squirted?"

Scoobie ducked under the table, apparently pretending that he had dropped something.

Ramona looked at the cake more closely. "You're very artistic, Monica, but I do think Jolie got sprayed with every color of liquid string we had."

"I know." Monica was very serious. "But I didn't have time to mix all of them. They don't sell chartreuse and orange at Mr. Markle's store."

I smiled at her one more time, and turned to Lance. "Why don't you give us a quick update on what we took in?"

"It was far more than I anticipated, and our expenses were fairly low."

"No hot dogs to gorge on?" Sylvia sniped.

"I can cook you some," Scoobie offered.

"Ahem." That was all Dr. Welby needed to say. Scoobie wiggled his eyebrows at me and I tried not to laugh at him.

Lance acted as if no one had spoken. "We had generous donations in the form of a lot of people's labor, of course, and

Ramona's talented sketches gave us almost three hundred dollars. And of course we had the very nice gift from Stenner Appraisals."

Jennifer beamed, and I made a mental note to ask Harry if he wanted to do a late donation. Good publicity when we publish our annual list of donors.

"Thanks to the tennis club we had no facility fees, and I have already given the manager a bottle of his favorite scotch and I deducted that as an expense."

Aretha laughed. "If he tells people maybe it'll help us get space somewhere the next time we want it."

"And Mr. Markle always comes through for us," Lance continued. "We paid a fairly small amount for the oxymoronic liquid string."

Scoobie laughed aloud, unusual for him in these meetings.

"Markle donated all the paper goods that we used," Lance concluded.

"We really owe that man," I said, softly.

"Yes, we do. With what we earned that day and a few individual donations, including five hundred dollars from Jolie's friend Lester," Lance smiled at me, "we made just more than nine-thousand dollars."

There were murmurs of pleased surprise.

"Lester may think the way to Jolie's heart is through his wallet," Dr. Welby said, with a clear smirk.

"You're as bad as Harry," I said.

"Not even close," Scoobie said.

We didn't have a lot of new business, and Megan's report on volunteers was concise. For a change Scoobie did not hijack the meeting, so we were eating cake within twenty minutes and had cleared away the remnants of cake and paper plates within forty-five minutes.

"Sometime in the next month I'll have an open house, and you folks will be the guests of honor."

There were polite comments of "no need" and "happy to serve" as we left the church.

"Ride?" I asked Scoobie after we had said good-bye to Jennifer and Ramona.

"Of course."

"Thanks for everything, and I mean help with the house and all that."

"Including serving as protector in chief when you find bodies on the porch."

I winced but he didn't notice. "And helping empty Pebbles' litter box a time or two."

"That really is above the call…" He stopped talking as a fire engine pulled close to my car and I quickly veered right to get to the curb. Another truck, a police car, and two ambulances were immediately behind the truck.

Scoobie and I looked at each other. "Maybe follow those trucks," Scoobie said. "It's probably someone we know."

There was no need to attempt to match their speed in a town the size of Ocean Alley. We made a left on Conch and I was surprised to see the back of the second ambulance turn onto F Street. "God, you don't think…"

Scoobie's tone was grim as I pulled to the curb a half block from Scoobie's home. "The rooming house." He yanked open the car door and was twenty feet away before I could say anything.

Dark smoke billowed, but I could only see fire from one window in the front. Maybe the second floor. I realized I shouldn't park anywhere on F Street and backed up a few feet so I could turn left on Sea Shore.

As I ran toward the fire I saw Scoobie standing with two fire fighters. He was pointing to different rooms and yelling at the men. I realized he knew who occupied which rooms and was guiding them in a search for residents.

Two hoses streamed on the large Victorian House. I briefly noted that flames came out of three windows now, but the hoses had begun to have their intended effect. Still, there was enough smoke to kill anyone trapped inside.

Two additional police cars careened to a stop behind one of the ambulances and the officers talked to the firefighter I knew to be an assistant chief. Then they turned quickly, grabbed crime scene tape from one of the cars and began to cordon off the rooming house. It wasn't really necessary just yet, as onlookers stood far back to avoid the smoke.

George's voice came from behind me. "Anyone hurt?"

"I don't know. Scoobie ran up there, I think to tell them which rooms had people."

"Good thing it's mostly long-term residents." George said this more to himself than to me.

He walked closer to the yellow tape, but I hung back. There were maybe fifty people spread out on the streets and sidewalks, and they began to murmur as one. I looked at the house and saw that firefighters were carrying out a body. I hoped a living one. The shock of red hair made me think of Reuben Harris. They almost threw him on a gurney and left him to the paramedics as they went back inside.

They run in when we run out.

A knot of people stood to one side of the rooming house, and from their attire I thought they were the residents. Few had jackets, and it was only about fifty degrees. Almost magically people in Red Cross vests began passing out blankets and guiding the residents to a large van that had pulled into a driveway a few houses behind the rooming house.

It was dusk and I couldn't pick out Scoobie, but I wasn't worried about him. I hoped he was able to help the firefighters find everyone.

Just then the flashing lights lit up on one ambulance and it began backing up, very fast. That was good. It could mean the person they were transporting was alive.

"Yo, Jolie." Scoobie walked toward me. He had soot in his hair and a distressed look on his face, but otherwise looked okay.

"You could help them?"

"I think so. The owner ran up a couple of minutes ago, and he had a list of every unit and who lived in them."

He stood next to me and we stared at what was now a soggy scene with only wisps of smoke. I knew Scoobie's room was on the side of the building that had been on fire. I remembered which window was his and hadn't seen flames break through. But everything he owned had to reek of smoke and be soaking wet.

"At least you like the futon."

He grabbed me in a bear hug and we clung to each other.

FOR ONCE THE *OCEAN ALLEY PRESS* article was helpful. I had spread the Friday edition across the kitchen table so I could read it while I made bacon.

Rooming House Fire Follows Pattern

The fire at the F Street Rooming House appeared to have started in the residence of Reuben Harris, who has lived in the building for four years.

As with several other fires that damaged or destroyed cottages in Ocean Alley, there was no obvious use of accelerants. The Fire Marshal plans to have a tentative cause for the fire by late Friday.

Though he was not burned, Harris inhaled a great deal of smoke and was unconscious when fire fighters found him. He was lying near the door that led to the hallway, but it is not clear whether he was sleeping when the fire started, or if he started it.

The rooming house is often touted as a good example of single-room-occupancy living and there is little turnover in the eighteen rooms. However, it was built before today's fire codes, so there are no fire walls (which are of thicker construction) to prevent a blaze from spreading fairly quickly.

Chief Watterson of the Ocean Alley Fire Department said it was fortunate that the fire was spotted quickly. "It would likely have destroyed the structure if it had made it to the attic. Prompt resolution was possible because Ocean Alley's main station is only three blocks from the rooming house."

The Press was unable to learn more about the condition of Reuben Harris by its deadline. Harris is alleged to have been the Peeping Tom who troubled Ocean Alley for more than six months.

His public defender has been in discussions with the prosecuting attorney's office.

I went back to the turkey bacon I was frying. I'm not a big cook, but Harry was okay with me delaying an appraisal until mid-afternoon so Scoobie and I could have breakfast together. Scoobie is a big boy, but he would be mad or sad or both. Everything he owned was in his room.

The shower went off and I told myself not to be uncomfortable. When Scoobie stayed at the B&B we were far apart when performing what he called morning ablutions. When he stayed with me after Mr. Fitzgerald's death he'd gone home to shower.

We're both adults. *And good friends.*

I chalked up my nervousness to being queasy about last night's fire and reached down to pet Jazz, who was weaving around my ankles. Pebbles remained under my bed, though she had poked her head out a couple of times last night.

While I cracked eggs to scramble, the door to Scoobie's bedroom opened and shut, so I knew he'd be in the kitchen soon. I turned the electric kettle to high so he'd have his morning tea.

"Yo, Jolie." He surveyed the kitchen. "I'm not company, you know."

"Tis true. After this it's cold cereal. I thought we deserved a treat this morning."

He picked up the paper and scanned the article, then looked up. "I don't know Reuben well, heck, no one does. He's the classic loner."

"And feels really alone."

"How do you know that?"

"I talked to him the other day." Sensing that Scoobie was about to ask if I was nuts, I added, "We did it at First Prez. Anyway, he said he wasn't trying to spy on people. He just wanted to see what families were like."

"Damn." Scoobie sat in the chair next to my small kitchen table. "You believed him?"

"I think so, but I have no idea what a pathological liar or sociopath looks like."

"Just like anybody."

"Anyway, he said he'd been in several foster homes after his mom died, and he had no idea who his father was. And he just looked...sad."

Scoobie sighed. "So maybe it wasn't accidental. Maybe he was trying to commit suicide. But, damn, to try to take everybody else with him."

I had finished the eggs and slid them on two plates with bacon on each. I was about to take my first bite when I heard someone on the front porch. The doorbell received two pushes in quick succession.

"George," Scoobie said. "Eat your eggs fast."

I carried a piece of bacon with me and looked out the living room curtain. Lester's face stared back at me, his nose almost on the glass. "Jeez Louise! Lester!"

Scoobie's laugh drowned out whatever Lester said, and I opened the door to let him in.

"They got pictures on the paper's web page and I saw you and Scoobie watchin' the fire. What smells good?"

"Bacon and eggs. Come on in," came from the kitchen.

Lester started when he heard Scoobie's voice. "If I'm interruptin'..."

"Nope. You can have toast and bacon. I'm not sharing my eggs," I said.

Lester declined the toast and munched on bacon. We ate in awkward silence and then I saw the look Lester gets when he has what he considers to be a terrific idea. He looked at Scoobie. "You're gonna be needin' digs, right? Maybe do a rent with option to buy, and then when you graduate...you could..."

Apparently cold stares can silence even Lester.

"Too soon?" he asked.

"Too soon," Scoobie said.

"I drove over there this morning. Already electricians working to get the mostly undamaged parts of the place fit for people."

"That would not be my room," Scoobie said.

"You need a place to stay?" Lester asked.

"He's staying here."

"I meant if it's for a couple months. I got an extra bedroom."

"He's good for all the time he needs."

"Have you noticed she's kinda bossy?" Lester asked, looking at Scoobie.

It took me a few seconds to realize that Scoobie was working hard not to tear up. Lester and I both stared at spots on the wall.

"Thanks, Lester," he finally said. "George said the same thing."

"George ain't got room," Lester said. "I been trying to get him off the dime for years."

"Good luck with that." I stood up and picked up both plates. "You want that toast, Lester?"

"Nah. Had a muffin at Joe's place. He raised the damn prices this week."

"Higher insurance rates, I bet." I put the plates in the sink and looked at Scoobie. "I cooked, you clean."

"Ain't that cozy?"

I was pretty sure it was an accident when Scoobie spilled his tea on Lester's leg.

Chapter Thirty-Two

I HAD TO WAIT TWO days for an appointment with Annie Milner, so I made sure to arrive at the courthouse on time for our Monday meeting. She ushered me into her office and gestured to a chair in front of her desk.

"Thanks, Annie. I wanted to ask about Reuben Harris."

Her eyebrows arched. "I can't discuss a specific case, Jolie."

"It's not really about the Peeping Tom or fire stuff. It's about him."

"One and the same."

"I know. I'm not doing this well. What I'm trying to ask is will his mental health come into play when he gets to court? He seemed more troubled than dangerous to me."

She pulled a file toward her, clearly done with me. "That's because you didn't live in the rooming house."

I flushed. "I know. It was just something he said. He told me Harvest for All should have get togethers for people without family. If he thought he had anyone in his life, maybe he wouldn't have done…stuff."

Annie studied me. "It might be a good suggestion, Jolie, but he made his choices. And I really can't discuss him."

I left her going through a pile of work and thought about Reuben as I walked out of the courthouse. There was speculation about whether he had started the three fires the fire marshal (and George) were still investigating.

It was definite that the rooming house fire started in Reuben's apartment, but no one could say whether he set it deliberately. Aunt Madge, who knows half the staff at the hospital, had heard that he would physically recover. However, he was not talking to anyone, and it was apparently because of deep depression more than stubbornness.

I climbed into my car with the Beatles' song in my head. "All the lonely people, where do they all come from? All the lonely people, where do they all belong?"

MY NEXT STOP WAS Mrs. Murphy. I hadn't talked to her since the night Scoobie and I had told her about Peter's arrest. In part I'd been busy, but mostly I didn't know what to say. And maybe she was angry with me. *She has no reason to be angry with me. Or maybe she does. No. I've been trying to help her. Maybe she doesn't see it that way. Stop arguing with yourself.*

The assisted living place is open to all guests, assuming a resident wants them, and no one had ever stopped me as I came in. Today was different.

The woman at the front desk was in her mid-forties and tall, maybe five-eight. Her brown hair had a few streaks of white, and her very blue eyes bore into mine. "You should know that Mrs. Murphy has exhibited signs of decline the last two weeks. She hasn't said not to let you in, but please don't tire her."

"Of course. Is she, uh, sick?"

The woman hesitated and her eyes had more of a kind expression. "More like drained. You know what she's been going through."

I thanked her and walked down the carpeted hallway to Mrs. Murphy's small apartment. I hesitated, and then gave a light knock and said, "It's Jolie. May I come in?"

"Certainly." The usually brisk voice was light and tired.

The first thing I noticed was her hair. Usually it was neatly styled with a bit of curl. Today it was straight and flat, which went with her overall affect.

I sat across from her. "You've had a hard couple of weeks."

"Yes, but at my age, you expect to have down days."

"But you usually don't look it."

She looked amused. "You came here to comment on my appearance?"

I almost stammered. "No, of course not. I mostly wanted to see how you are, but I also wanted to talk about the things I found in the house."

"The things Arman was so intent on getting," she said, with bitterness. "He seemed like such a nice man."

I searched for words. "He was devoted to Patricia."

"He had a funny way of showing it."

I kind of grunted. "I wasn't too fond of it. But I do want to talk to you. You know there was a second bag, in the cedar closet."

"The paper said that Betty Fowler was looking for it," she said, dryly.

"That's a concise way of putting it. Anyway, if you put both little sacks together, I bet it's worth about twenty thousand dollars, maybe a lot more. No one has been able to identify any of it."

Her smile was genuine. "I'm happy for you."

"For us. I was thinking an eighty-twenty split, and…"

"Why would you do that? After everything you've gone through, you've earned any money that comes from that jewelry."

"Plus a bunch of really old silver dollars. And it kind of feels like blood money. I wouldn't keep any of it, but there are a couple of things I really need to do to the house."

She looked at me and I detected a bit of the usual Mrs. Murphy returning. "Going to buy a new porch swing?"

"Probably. The kitchen counters are really old, and I think I'd like to enlarge the closet where I keep Pebbles' litter box."

She laughed, and then became serious again. "I'd like to have something to contribute to Peter's legal fees. How much is twenty percent?"

I was confused for a moment. "I'm thinking eighty percent for you."

"Out of the question." She looked kind of angry.

"It should havve been half yours a long time ago."

"So, fifty-fifty," she said.

"Thirty-seventy," I was starting to feel amused that I was bargaining to give away money.

"Forty-sixty, and that's final."

"Jeez. You're as bad as Aunt Madge when you try to out-stubborn me."

"Thank you."

Chapter Thirty-Three

AN OPEN HOUSE is a lot of work. If I had known this I might have taken a bunch of people out for pizza.

"Yeah," Scoobie said, "but then they wouldn't see your house, which is kind of the point. Didn't you and Robby entertain?"

Nobody ever talks to me about my ex-husband. Scoobie's never met him, but he did see Robby with me on the boardwalk one night.

I flushed. "Yes, but it was always catered."

His eyes lit up. "Watercress sandwiches? Baby quiche? Paté?"

"Shut up. Chili, for football games, crab cakes for 4th of July."

He was cutting up a couple of pounds of carrots and I had made a double order of brownies. I'd forgotten the oil, and was trying to mix it into the two pans rather than pour the stuff back into the bowl.

"What's your sister bringing?"

"You just think she cooks better."

He nodded toward the brownies.

"She's bringing a crab dip that gets served from a crock pot, and a bunch of kinds of crackers."

"That sounds really good. I hope she brings enough for leftovers."

"I'll try to hide a bit in the back of the fridge."

I glanced at the clock. I had timed the brownies so that the smell would permeate the house as guests arrived.

The doorbell rang and I looked at the clock almost in a panic.

The door opened. Ramona called, "Jolie?"

George said, "Why in the hell did I buy you a security system?"

"You bought it?" Bill asked.

"Didn't you read those articles? He pretty much had to," Jennifer said.

They trooped into the kitchen and placed various goodies on the counters and table. I had told people not to bring anything, and had clearly been ignored. It was easily as much food as I was making. There would be lots of fun leftovers.

Jennifer looked at the room. "It's really cute. Now," her tone was all business, "those little quiches can only be in the oven for twenty minutes, so we'll have to time them carefully."

Scoobie had a coughing fit.

I met George's eyes and had a hard time reading his expression. I suppose if I'd been him and walked in on this scene of seeming domesticity it might be hard. I reminded myself that George and I usually brought in pizza, so seeing me in the kitchen would not be too familiar.

He grinned at me. "Looks homey."

Scoobie had stopped coughing, but more or less glared at George.

"I'm going to check out the skunk," George said.

"Fitting," I mumbled to myself.

Bill picked up one of Scoobie's carrots and took a bite. "I gotta admit, Jolie, when you said you'd gotten a skunk for your cat I thought you were kidding."

"No such luck."

"Come here, Bill," George called. "She's in her spot under the bed."

Within fifteen minutes we were all lounging in my small living room. I'd never been ready early for any kind of party.

Ramona demonstrated how to draw a hand and George and Bill seemed fascinated. Especially since she was doing it on a paper plate. Scoobie tried to convince Jennifer that it was possible that Pebbles still had some of her scent glands.

I looked around the room. Eighteen months ago I'd been torn from my life in Lakewood and felt bereft of friends. I was also almost broke. I'd learned that the large sums of money I'd earned as a commercial realtor hadn't bought any happiness, and that there could never be better friends than I had in Ocean Alley.

And maybe some friends would become even more special. Scoobie and I locked eyes. He grinned, and I knew he knew exactly what I'd been thinking.

It could be an interesting summer.

* * * *

About the Author

Elaine L. Orr writes four mystery series, including the thirteen-book Jolie Gentil cozy mystery series, set at the Jersey shore. Two of her books (including *Behind the Walls* in the Jolie series) have been finalists for the Chanticleer Mystery and Mayhem Awards.

Unscheduled Murder Trip, second in the Family History Mystery Series, received an Indie B.R.A.G Medallion. Other books are in the River's Edge Series (set in rural Iowa) and the Logland Series (set in small-town Illinois).

She also writes plays and novellas. A member of Sisters in Crime, Elaine grew up in Maryland and moved to the Midwest in 1994. She enjoys meeting readers at events throughout the country.

Authors always appreciate reviews. If you enjoyed *Behind the Walls* please post a review on your favorite web site or mention it on Instagram or Facebook, Let your local bookstore or library know that you liked a book. You can also contact Elaine to see if she would be available in person or via Zoom to talk to your community or book group.

elaineorr.com

elaineorr.blogspot.com

elaineorr55@yahoo.com

Books in the
Jolie Gentil Cozy Mystery Series

Appraisal for Murder
Rekindling Motives
When the Carny Comes to Town
Any Port in a Storm
Trouble on the Doorstep
Behind the Walls
Vague Images
Ground to a Halt
Holidays in Ocean Alley
The Unexpected Resolution
The Twain Does Meet (novella)
Underground in Ocean Alley
Aunt Madge in the Civil Election (an Aunt Madge story)
Sticky Fingered Books
New Lease on Death
Jolie and Scoobie High School Misadventures (prequel)

Family History Mystery Series
Least Trodden Ground
Unscheduled Murder Trip
Mountain Rails of Old
Gilded Path to Nowhere

River's Edge Series — *set in rural Iowa*
Logland Series — *set in small-town Illinois*

Books are at online retailers, or ask your library or bookstore to order them — in print, large print, ebook and audio. All books have Barnes and Noble editions, which makes them easy to order from those stores.

CAST OF MAJOR CHARACTERS
IN BEHIND THE WALLS

Alicia Ortiz – local high school student, daughter of Megan

Annie Milner – county attorney, went to Ocean Alley High

Aretha Brown – not the least bit shy Harvest for All committee member

Arman – boyfriend of Patricia Murphy, attended auction

Aunt Madge – best aunt ever, sister to Jolie's late grandmother

Betty Fowler – local real estate agent who competes with Lester

Bill Oliver – dentist in a nearby town, went to high school with Jolie

Cassie Stetson – co-owner of Ocean Alley Title Company

Charlotte Evans – Jolie's neighbor

Clive Dorner – nephew of Norman Fitzgerald, real estate investor

Dana Johnson – Ocean Alley police officers

Daphne – librarian and high school classmate of Jolie and Scoobie

Dr. Welby – retired doctor and Harvest for All committee member

Father Teehan – pastor of St. Anthony's

Fiona Henderson – adult daughter of Mrs. Murphy

George Winters – reporter at Ocean Alley Press

Glenn Stetson – co-owner of Ocean Alley Title Company

Gordon Richards – Aunt Madge's late husband and former rum runner

Lance Wilson – Jolie's favorite member of the Harvest for All Committee

Lester Argrow – annoying local real estate agent, and Ramona's uncle

Harry Steele – owner of Steele Appraisals, and Aunt Madge's husband

Jazz – Jolie's black cat

Jennifer Stenner – owns the other appraisal firm

Joe Regan – owner of Java Jolt Coffee House

Jolie Gentil – Ocean Alley real estate appraiser with a nose for trouble

Isaac Gibson – minister for the Unitarian Universalist Church
Harvest for All – food pantry for which Jolie chairs the governing committee
Lieutenant Tortino – member of the Ocean Alley Police Department
Mark Fisher – Ocean Alley jeweler
Max – friendly but brain-damaged Iraq War veteran who likes Jolie and Scoobie
Megan Ortiz – regular volunteer at Harvest for All Food Pantry
Mister Markle – owner of In-Town Grocery, who is good to Harvest for All
Mister Rogers and Miss Piggy – Aunt Madge's retrievers
Moira Peebles – the former (and late) owner of Jolie's bungalow
Monica Martin– very shy Harvest for All committee member
Mrs. Murphy – spry resident of local senior living home, mother of Fiona and Patricia
Norman Fitzgerald – local auctioneer
Patricia Franklin – adult daughter of Mrs. Murphy
Pebbles – Jolie's newest pet (!)
Peter – boyfriend of Fiona, local insurance agent
Quentin Wharton – CEO of Ocean Alley Hospital
Reuben Harris – sad man who lives in same rooming house as Scoobie
Roland – owner of Purple Cow Office Supply, Ramona's boss
Sam – Ocean Alley animal control officer
Sergeant Morehouse – member of the Ocean Alley Police Department
Ramona Argrow – clerk at the Purple Cow office supply store, and Jolie's friend
Reverend Douglas Jamison – clergyman for First Presbyterian
Scoobie – Jolie's best bud, studying to be a radiology tech
Sylvia Parrett – Harvest for All committee member who can be a tad grouchy
Tiffany – junior reporter at the Ocean Alley Press
Virginia Mulligan – Jolie's neighbor with precocious grandson, Nicholas

www.ingramcontent.com/pod-product-compliance
Lightning Source LLC
Chambersburg PA
CBHW071227210726

48293CB00002B/612